Charli Rae Warren is back home in Hazel Rock, Texas, spending her time reading, collecting, and selling books—at least, the ones that don't get eaten first by her father's pet armadillo. Running the family bookstore is a demanding job, but solving murders on the side can be flat out dangerous . . .

The Book Barn is more than just a shop, it's a part of the community—and Charli is keeping busy with a fundraising auction and the big rodeo event that's come to town. That includes dealing with the Texas-sized egos of some celebrity cowboys, including Dalton Hibbs, a blond, blue-eyed bull rider who gets overly rowdy one night with the local hairdresser . . . and soon afterward, disappears into thin air.

Dalton's brother also vanished seven years ago—and Charli is thrown about whether Dalton is a villain or a victim. After a close call with an assailant wielding a branding iron (that plays havoc with her hair), and some strange vandalism on her property, she's going to have to team up with the sheriff to untangle this mystery, before she gets gored . . .

The Book Barn Mystery Series
by Kym Roberts

Fatal Fiction

A Reference to Murder

Published by Kensington Publishing Corporation

A Reference to Murder

The Book Barn Mystery Series

Kym Roberts

LYRICAL UNDERGROUND
Kensington Publishing Corp.
www.kensingtonbooks.com

LYRICAL UNDERGROUND BOOKS are published by

Kensington Publishing Corp.
119 West 40th Street
New York, NY 10018

First Electronic Edition: May 2017
eISBN-13: 978-1-60183-733-2
eISBN-10: 1-60183-733-X

First Print Edition: May 2017
ISBN-13: 978-1-60183-734-9
ISBN-10: 1-60183-734-8

Printed in the United States of America

For JoAn

Acknowledgments

Thank you to the Chicks and the Sirens for constantly feeding my obsession and being the best support system a writer could have.

Thank you to my agent, Kim Lionetti, who supports my work unquestioningly with my best interest at heart. To Martin Biro, my editor, the most patient man to ever read a rough draft, thank you! And to the entire Kensington family who made this book possible.

But most of all thank you to my family, who analyzed video after video with me of a sport we knew nothing about. You're the backbone of my strength. Any mistakes are my own.

Chapter One

My time was up.

Literally. The clock over the bookshelf struck six and the class was over. Thank God.

Sure it had been fun, but it was the end of a long day and I was ready to call it quits. The students were in a good mood and the whispered tidbits of gossip had been friendly all evening, with no tinge of envy or meanness attached. It was the type of camaraderie a teacher dreams about with her students.

Not that it ever happened in my former kindergarten classes, but I'd given up teaching in an elementary setting a few months back when I'd chosen to follow my heart on an emotional journey home to work in the family bookstore. That decision had been the best one I'd made in over a decade.

Now my students ranged from eighteen to eighty-seven and gathered in the loft of the historic barn that my parents had converted into The Book Barn Princess when I was a little girl. And once a week my class gathered to create something new out of something old. Specifically, old and/or damaged books. This week we were repurposing books into wall clocks for a local charity auction.

"We need to wind things up, ladies and gentlemen." I smiled as they groaned at my clock-based humor.

Scarlet, the owner of the Beaus and Beauties hair salon across the street, developed our program and was the creative genius behind every project. She was also the sassiest woman in town, which was saying a lot. Her flaming red hair, worn curly and wild today, bounced as she sauntered across the room and joined the conversation. "Time flies when you're having fun."

"Big time," replied Betty, the local quilt shop owner, her blue hair bobbing up and down as if she wore a helmet two sizes too big.

"Maybe we could turn back the hands of time," added Jessie, my oldest student.

Jessie's wife eyed the other women in class who had the audacity to smile in his direction. It didn't matter that they'd all known each other for years, Daisy had a habit of establishing ownership of her man—repeatedly. "That's *my* husband," she warned.

My dad decided to chime in. "You can't beat the clock."

I stood, debating if my dad was referring to Jessie's fifty-plus-year marriage to Daisy, or if he was adding his own pun to the mix, when two incredibly good-looking men climbed up the stairway to the loft. One of them was a staple in our town, but the other was new to the circuit and had been turning heads for the past two days. He joined the conversation without missing a tick—or a tock.

"Darn, I was hoping to kill some time with y'all." Rodeo star Dalton Hibbs smiled. His blond hair glistened under the fluorescent lights, and his deep blue eyes made every woman in the room drown in their cool depths. He had what it took to melt the coldest of hearts, and I had to admit, even though he wasn't my type, he gave me warm fuzzies whenever he winked in my direction.

"Which will put you behind bars, *serving* time," said our handsome sheriff, Mateo Espinosa, who'd walked into the room with Dalton and wore a light brown uniform shirt with dark brown pants. The outfit looked downright terrible on most officers—on Mateo it was dreamy and steamy earth tones that complemented his dark complexion. His presence served as a reminder of how complicated my love life was without adding another guy to the mix.

"Time's up!" Joellen added with the blushing grin of a teenager as Dalton turned his pearly whites on her.

"I think I'm going to be ill," grumbled Jessie, holding his chest.

A laugh traveled through the room as Scarlet snorted.

Daisy looked over the top of her glasses at my best friend, who seemed to be enjoying Jessie's humor more than the rest of us. "That's *my* husband," she reminded Scarlet.

Scarlet blushed, while our newcomer, Dalton, appeared somewhat confused by Daisy's jealous outburst.

Betty patted him on the shoulder as she stood up from the long wooden table where she'd been working. "Daisy has been reminding every woman in town that Jessie is her man for the past fifty years. We're beginning to think those are the only words she knows in the entire English language."

A grin spread across Dalton's face. "Let me guess, Daisy's used to reminding women that Jessie's married because Jessie's a bull rider?"

Jessie stood up tall, all five foot seven inches of lean cowboy in boots almost as old as him and showed off the worn buckle on the belt that cinched his jeans up around his ribs. "You're looking at the nineteen forty-seven Champion Bull Rider. The best in North America."

"That's my husband," Daisy added, her tone full of sarcasm.

This time, everyone laughed at Jessie's wife, leaving the grumpy old codger at a loss for words, but his disparaging expression was still intact. I secretly believed Jessie was laughing at all of us despite the permanent frown creasing his face.

I addressed the class as a whole. "If you're going to donate your clocks to the auction, please leave them here to dry. Dad added the new shelves on the side wall this week so we'd have more room. Just make sure they're high enough to be out of the reach of the preschoolers who will be making book collages tomorrow morning."

I set my project on the highest shelf I could reach without the ladder we had yet to install. I'd made my piece of book art out of a first edition of Nancy Drew's *The Secret of the Old Clock*. Some readers might get their panties in a bunch and gasp at the destruction of such an iconic book, and believe I did something sacrilegious to a classic novel worth more in the world of literature than it was as a clock at auction. I would wholeheartedly agree, if my dad's pet armadillo, Princess, hadn't torn off the back cover and eaten a hole in the middle of the last thirty-seven pages of the book before I transformed it. As it turned out, my work was an improvement.

Princess, a nine-banded armadillo, was a freak of nature. Her pale pink coloring made it impossible for her to be let loose in the wild. She did, however, have her own pet door and roamed freely in the backyard behind our barn. She was also the reason we'd started the book art classes to begin with. She had a taste for books—too bad it had nothing to do with reading.

"You've got some mighty fine pieces of art downstairs for the auction." Dalton was talking to me, but his eyes roamed toward Scarlet, who turned as red as her name suggested.

"Thank you. We hope to make a little bit of money to add to all of the donations the rodeo stars are making to the cause." I was very aware of the members of the class watching our exchange. They couldn't help themselves. Dalton Hibbs was making small talk with a local girl and the town had dreams of him becoming one of our own. Except their eyes had gone to the wrong woman—they should have been watching Scarlet instead of me.

"Who made the incredible bull rider out of Zane Grey's *Light of the Western Stars*?" he asked.

I smiled, knowing I could direct Dalton's attention toward Scarlet, right where they both wanted it to be. "That would be Scarlet. She's the real artist. I'm just mildly crafty."

Dalton took advantage of the out I'd given him and gave Scarlet his full attention. "Is that so?"

All eyes pinged to my best friend, her skin now two shades closer to the color of her hair.

"I—I've always like sculpting," Scarlet stammered. Dang, if she didn't have it bad for the young rodeo star who was only in town for a couple weeks.

"You're good with your hands." Dalton's voice held all the innuendo a man of his looks and status could get away with, and the crowd was eating it up.

Including me. I couldn't help but envy all that charm directed at my friend. Not that I wanted Dalton flirting me up one side and down the other, but if those daring innuendos were thrown at me by someone else, it would be nice. I looked over at the sheriff, whose chocolate-brown eyes made me want to melt.

Dalton made his way across the room and stood in front of Scarlet. "I'd like to buy it."

Scarlet's disappointment was evident in the slight downward turn of her mouth as she shook her head, obviously saddened that she couldn't just give the piece of art to the sexy man in front of her. But the piece, like so many others in the store, was earmarked for auction.

"It's up for auction tomorrow," Scarlet said.

The annual Cowboy Ranch Auction ran in conjunction with the Cowboy Ranch Invitational, a rodeo that brought all the big names in the sport to our small town. Both events benefited injured and aging rodeo stars who'd given everything they had, and more, to the sport. It'd only been recently that the cowboys started making big money to put their lives, and health on the line. And even now, for every cowboy who made it rich, there were thousands working two and three jobs to make ends meet. The Cowboy Ranch stepped in to help those cowboys who'd suffered career, and life-altering injuries with no source of financial backing to get them through.

Dalton's charm, however, was a force to be reckoned with. His voice had a low register that made a woman's body stir. "Surely if I bid high enough now, I can bypass all the competition."

"There's no competition. Scarlet's single," interjected Jessie.

"That's right," added Betty, her bobblehead going so fast I thought for sure her wig was going to fly across the room. "If you plan on making a move, you better do it now. Otherwise, you never know who's going to be making a move in *your* direction."

Dalton laughed at the woman well past her prime. Betty had owned the quilt shop in town long before Dalton's momma was born. "I'd hate to turn down a woman with so much experience, but I'm afraid my heart has been roped," Dalton replied. He turned his eyes back toward Scarlet. "What's the opening bid?"

"Two hundred dollars," I replied before Scarlet sold it for less than half its worth. She'd worked on that particular sculpture for several months and had barely finished in time for the auction.

Dalton tipped his head in my direction. His eyes, however, never left Scarlet's face. He grabbed her hands and held them steadfast. "I'll give you two thousand for it."

"Dollars?"

"Unless you want Euros?" Dalton flashed his killer smile as he lifted her hands to his mouth and kissed the back of her knuckles. "Say yes."

Mateo cleared his throat and pulled at his collar. Betty sighed to my left.

"Yes," whispered Scarlet.

"What'd she say?" asked Jessie.

"Shhhh!" Daisy swiped at her husband's arm.

"How's a body supposed to keep up with these young 'uns if they whisper all the time?"

"Put your hearing aid in. Then maybe you'll find out what people are saying about you," Daisy replied.

"What?" Jessie looked over the top of his glasses, his stare landing on no one in particular.

"She said, put your hearing aid in!" Betty repeated.

Jessie turned his back on his wife and Betty, then winked at my dad. A look of pure devilry passed between them and I began to wonder if my dad would be torturing me in the same manner as he aged past his prime.

"Can I take you out for an early dinner?" Dalton asked Scarlet.

Jessie heard *that* proposition with no problem. He turned back toward the young couple and waited for Scarlet's response as if he had more riding on her answer than Dalton did.

"Well, I have to clean up—"

"It's my turn to pick up things around here," Dad interjected.

"I've got a roast in my Crock -pot—" Scarlet protested.

"She makes the best roast this side of the Red River," I added.

"Are you asking me to have dinner with you, Scarlet?" Dalton was still holding her hands and gazing down into her eyes like the rest of us weren't even in the same universe.

Before Scarlet could say a word, Jessie chimed in with his two cents worth. "Are you waiting for the red carpet, son? The woman just said she had a roast on. She didn't tell any of us she was cooking."

Actually, she had. That was my Tuesday night girl's night out roast dinner going up in the sparks between them.

Scarlet glanced in my direction, and I immediately let her off the hook.

"We still on for dinner, Dad?" I asked.

My dad didn't miss a beat. "I've got a mighty big hankerin' for a Rocker Burger from the diner, and the sheriff said he was going to join us."

Mateo's jaw quirked before he dipped his dark head in agreement. Both men read the situation faster than I expected. But it was the look on Scarlet's face that nearly brought tears to my eyes. Her very own fairy tale was unfolding in Hazel Rock, Texas.

"Give me thirty minutes and I'll treat you to a home-cooked meal you'll never forget." Scarlet beamed up at Dalton as everyone turned away, pleased with their matchmaking skills.

I was the only one who saw the promise of so much more pass between the couple as Dalton kissed her cheek. Then he headed for the register with my dad to ring up the purchase of his book art. Two thousand dollars was a mighty big start to a week of fundraising for The Cowboy Ranch.

And that small kiss was going to lead to so much more. Too bad it was surrounded by trouble.

Chapter Two

Scarlet's dinner had obviously gone well if the scene on the dance floor was any indication. Dressed in a black sheer mini dress with one bared shoulder, her two-stepping with Dalton had turned into pouty lips, swinging hips, and the full body contact dips of a country swing dance. It was sexier than all get out, and every woman at the Tool Shed Tavern wanted to be in Scarlet's black studded boots.

Except me. I currently had my hands full with the mayor, Cade Calloway. Cade was my high school sweetheart, who'd followed in his daddy's footsteps and run for political office after his professional football career fell through as a result of a serious back injury. The man lived to torture me with the possibilities of, "what if."

"Is that Dalton Hibbs dancing with Scarlet?" Cade asked, his hazel eyes narrowing in on the couple on the dance floor, instead of me. Not that it bothered me...much.

"If you can call it dancing." Joe Buck's heavy girth leaned over the bar, the towel draped over his shoulder skirting the wooden surface that had been smoothed out by use and age, not a polyurethane finish. He owned the Tool Shed Tavern and bartended while stirring up trouble with his contagious smile and friendly wink. I'd fallen for his angelic demeanor a time or two in the past. Since I'd returned to Hazel Rock, however, I'd been leery of his dares to do something stupid that no one else would try... or was stupid enough to do. I hoped I'd learned to refrain from making the same mistakes over and over, especially since those stunts had always come back to bite me on the backside in high school.

"Yes, and they seem rather smitten, don't you think?" I couldn't help the smile that spread across my face.

"That's more than smitten. Smitten is the way Princess follows you around the Barn," Cade said.

"Well, they've found something special. So leave Scarlet be," I warned.

Joe muttered something to Cade in reply, who stared him down as he took a swig of his beer. A silent communication passed between them and Joe laughed before he moved down the bar to a good-looking man in his early thirties who looked vaguely familiar.

Coming back to Texas after living in Colorado for a little over twelve years constantly played tricks on my memory. Placing names with faces was a chore. I constantly thought of a name from Denver, but the face never matched the person I was talking to. Bill was actually Ray, and Mistie was really Maureen. Or I'd remember the face from Hazel Rock High School, but the name never fell into place. It didn't help, that with time came age, and changes that I hadn't kept up with. I'd never friended anyone from my hometown on social media until the week I actually moved back to town. The years of growth and change were lost to me.

I stared at the man talking to Joe and I tried to picture what he would have looked like a dozen years ago. About my height with a solid tan and white teeth, his hair belonged on a television show with its expensive cut and perfect swoop across his tall forehead. His plaid shirt looked brand-new and straight from the dry cleaner with heavy starched creases running down the sleeves. His jeans also looked out of place for our local honky-tonk. The pressed lines down the middle of the legs were a shade lighter blue and started at his pockets and ended at his toes, accentuating his lean hips.

Joe pointed in our direction and the man looked toward us and nodded.

"Should I know that guy?" I asked Cade.

He turned and looked down the bar at the man, who was now walking toward us.

"If you watch the evening news, you should. That's Peter Kroft from CNCB News."

Recognition finally hit me about the time Mr. Kroft reached us. He held out his hand to shake Cade's much larger one, and I watched how Cade suddenly transformed into a politician. He wore a smile I didn't recognize. A little too polished; it was almost as if he put up a shield to protect the real Cade Calloway. His mannerisms were a tad stiff, and if I hadn't known the man since I was eight years old, I wouldn't have seen the differences between my mayor and my friend so readily. But they were most definitely there.

"Mayor Calloway, thank you for inviting me to your town." Mr. Kroft struggled not to let his voice get lost in the din of the music, clearing his throat and lowering the tone more than once.

"Thanks for coming to Hazel Rock. We appreciate you covering the auctions and the rodeo. Can I buy you a beer? The Shed serves the best Southern Ale this side of the Rio Grande."

"I'd love one."

Cade raised his bottle and indicated for Joe to grab a beer for Mr. Kroft. "I'd like to introduce you to Charli Rae Warren," he said as he turned toward me. "She owns The Book Barn Princess and is donating all of the proceeds from her book art auction to The Ranch." Cade leaned toward me. "Mr. Kroft is here to cover the Cowboy Ranch Invitational."

I held out my hand and Mr. Kroft grabbed it with both of his, then held on longer than necessary. His show of sincerity seemed anything but genuine. "It's nice to meet you, Ms. Warren. I understand you've got quite a collection you're donating."

I pulled my hand back and smiled to erase any unease my action might have caused. "Please call me Charli, Mr. Kroft. And to be honest, most of the art was created by the owner of Beaus and Beauties, the salon down the street. Scarlet is an incredibly gifted woman."

"Well, I'm looking forward to seeing it and meeting Scarlet. But I'll only call you Charli if you drop the formality and call me Peter."

I smile and nodded in agreement. Joe handed Peter his beer from behind the bar and winked. "I put it on the mayor's tab."

After thanking Cade, Peter asked, "So is this Scarlet here tonight?" He scanned the crowded bar as if he'd be able to identifier her on his own.

"She's on the floor dancing with Dalton Hibbs." I pointed them out just as Dalton swung Scarlet through his legs. The move was full of grace, with an undeniable sex appeal, and it put the biggest smile on Scarlet's face I'd ever seen.

"I heard Dalton wasn't coming to the Invitational because of too many bad memories about his brother." Peter took a draw of his beer.

"Dalton's brother? I didn't know he had a brother," I said.

"Wyatt Hibbs."

Apparently, my face looked as blank as an ex-teacher's blackboard, Cade explained. "Wyatt Hibbs was the best rider on the Championship Bull Circuit until he disappeared seven years ago."

A bad feeling started creeping up my spine and took hold of my neck. "What do you mean, 'disappeared'?"

A man who looked like he could have played football right alongside Joe Buck and Cade walked up to Peter with a large television camera sitting on his shoulder. The two began a conversation I couldn't hear over the music.

Cade leaned over and kept his voice low. "Wyatt was last seen seven years ago, right before The Cowboy Ranch Invitational. Scarlet used to follow him around like a lost puppy dog."

"She what?" That bad feeling grabbed hold of my larynx and made my voice squeak. I looked at the dance floor for Scarlet. She and Dalton had lost some of their swag and stumbled; whether it was from too much alcohol or exhaustion, I wasn't sure. But what had started out as a sight to see, was turning into a site of crashing and bumping into other couples. A few dirty looks were thrown in their direction as the lyrics to the latest country music hit about Southern girls wound down.

"When Wyatt disappeared, the sheriff actually questioned Scarlet." A frown marred Cade's strong jaw.

"Mateo actually thought Scarlet had something to do with his disappearance?" I asked.

"No, Jacob Sperry was still sheriff at the time, and Scarlet was the last person to see Wyatt before he disappeared."

I started doing the math. "But she was what, twenty? And you had to be gearing up for the NFL draft about that time." I realized I'd just given away entirely too much about my knowledge of his professional football career. Eight years ago, I'd been in Denver, having left Hazel Rock and Cade in my dust almost four years before that. He was the one person I'd kept up on while I was gone, even if it was only cyber-stalking.

I avoided the knowing twinkle in Cade's eyes. "How did you know about that?" I asked.

"My dad represented Scarlet," Cade replied.

I think my eyes must have been bigger than the star on the Texas flag hanging from the rafters of the bar. I had never heard anything about a missing cowboy, Scarlet being questioned, or J. C. Calloway Senior representing her in a criminal case.

The music came to a halt. A whoop and a giggle sounded from the dance floor as Dalton picked up Scarlet and twirled his way toward the bar. He stumbled and a collective gasp went through the onlookers. I cringed when Scarlet's boot struck the waitress's tray of drinks and Sugar scrambled to keep the glasses from crashing to the floor with absolutely no luck whatsoever.

"Hey!" Sugar yelled, her sultry good looks, blond hair, and short-shorts attracting the attention from every other man in the bar. But Dalton ignored her completely. He continued to push his way through the crowd and finally deposited Scarlet atop the bar.

"Dalton!" Scarlet's exclamation brought all eyes in her direction as she tried to scoot off to the floor. Dalton was having none of it. He pushed his chest between her legs and further embarrassed Scarlet with his hands on her rear end as she tried to pull her dress down to a respectable level.

I glanced toward Peter and his cameraman, hoping the action hadn't caught their attention. No such luck. The man with the expensive camera had the eyepiece glued to his face while he zoomed in the lens. Peter spoke in his ear and gave me an apologetic smile.

Fuzz buckets.

A beer bottle clanked on the bar next to me, and I jumped. "Let her go, Hibbs," Cade said from behind me.

Dalton never stopped leering at Scarlet's chest, his hands roaming as if he owned her body. "Mind your own business, buddy."

"I'm only going to tell you once more. Let. Scarlet. Go." The smooth sales pitch of the mayor disappeared in the edge of Cade's demand as he silently moved next to me.

Dalton's eyes lost their lusty sheen as he turned away from my best friend to square off with Cade, but his legs twisted as if he'd been a calf roped and wrestled in an arena. Dalton stumbled into Cade over his own two feet, too drunk to even walk.

The light on the camera behind me flashed on, illuminating Dalton's face in a deadly pale glow. He swung his arm up to block the light, but ended up punching me on my bicep instead.

"Ow!" I rubbed my arm and regretted opening my mouth when Cade's eyes narrowed and his chest puffed as he leaned over the man who was at his complete mercy. For a moment, I thought Dalton was dead meat. But the light of the camera kept Cade's anger in check and his career intact. That and the pushing and shoving that had begun around us. If anyone in the entire bar hadn't already been aware of what was going on, they were now. Numerous cell phones popped up above the heads of the people with the front row view. All of them recording the exchange as a surge of bodies pushed forward. The testosterone between Cade and Dalton was so thick, a chainsaw wouldn't cut through it. Scarlet took the opportunity to slide off the bar, just as Joe Buck was rounding the corner, ready to go to town on Dalton—fame wouldn't help turn a blind eye in Hazel Rock if one of our own was the object of disrespect.

But Scarlet was faster than Joe. She pushed her way in between the mayor and her not-so-prince-charming and placed a hand on their chests. "It's okay, Cade. He's just had a few too many drinks."

I'd only seen the man have two drinks, but Scarlet knew better than I. Still, a disrespectful drunk was not the fairy tale I'd hoped for Scarlet.

"Hey there, fellas! What seems to be the problem?" Erik Piper, the promoter for The Cowboy Ranch Invitational pushed his way through the crowd. His gray hair was slicked back and he angled his pointy nose at one man, and then the other. He held a cigarette in one hand and took a drag off it when Cade and Dalton looked right through him.

Erik was definitely out of his element. Frail and a bit taller than my five foot nine, he stretched up on his tiptoes and reached out his bony hands to pat the two men on the shoulder as if they would break on contact. Break him, was probably a more likely scenario.

He blew out a puff of smoke straight up between the two men and said, "I don't know if I introduced you to the *mayor* of Hazel Rock, Dalton, but since we're all gathered, what could be a better time?" Erik continued, his voice squeaking during the introduction. "This is Cade Calloway. *The* Cade Calloway. As in the *NFL quarterback* Cade Calloway."

Dalton snorted, a sloppy wet sound none of us expected to come from the neatly dressed rodeo star. "From what I hear..." He swayed as he poked Cade's chest over Scarlet's head. "...you went down after one hit."

If I had any question about Cade's ego ruling his actions, it was answered when Dalton took a swing and missed him altogether. It wasn't even close to making contact, but he stumbled into Scarlet, nearly knocking them both to the floor. Cade grabbed Dalton and Scarlet, his quick reflexes, the only thing that kept them from falling flat on the floor.

Erik didn't miss a beat. The seasoned promoter showed he had been around a bar fight, or two, as he stepped forward to take over. He stuck his cigarette in his mouth, draped Dalton's arm over his shoulder, and staggered to the left under the weight, but managed to stay standing. Scarlet wasn't taking any chances. She pulled Dalton's free arm over her shoulder and steadied the two of them.

"Can you pull my phone out of my pocket?" Erik asked. I reached over and pulled the smartphone from his shirt pocket. "Call Taylor!" Erik yelled toward the phone with his cigarette bobbing at the end of his bottom lip. He turned away as the ashes began to hang like a gray snake and tried to spit it out of his mouth. He succeeded in knocking the ashes off of the end and spitting the cigarette on Scarlet's bare shoulder.

"Owww!" Scarlet wiggled to get it off and Cade brushed it away with an irritated glare in Erik's direction.

Just then Erik's phone screen changed, and dialed a number that popped up with the picture of a pretty brunette.

"Taylor!" Eric yelled louder than was necessary. "I need you at the town tavern. Dalton has had too much to drink, again." Everyone in the bar was listening, but Erik didn't seem to care. Even Cade appeared disappointed in the man's lack of diplomacy.

The crowd began to separate as the four of us lead by Joe Buck, who cleared a path just as well as he'd cleared the football field for Cade in high school, headed toward the door. Cell phones recorded every step, and misstep, along the way.

"Baby, you need to take care of me. And don't tell me I gotta continue this small-town fiddle fartin' around courting business," Dalton whined to Scarlet, his deep voice holding anything but sex appeal. By the time we made it to the door, there wasn't a woman in the crowd who was envious of Scarlet's position. It didn't matter how cute her studded boots looked with her little black dress.

In fact, a few of them, like myself and the Shed's waitress, Sugar, were ready to take him to task, Southern belle style. We pushed through the front doors, Scarlet under one of Dalton's arms and Erik under the other, with Cade pulling up most of Dalton's weight from behind where Dalton couldn't see him. Or insult him. Or hit him.

Cade's face had that same look it had when we were in high school and he'd seen one of our classmates flip up my cheer skirt. At seventeen he didn't control his righteous indignation as well as he was doing now. But I wasn't sure how long it would last if Dalton kept spouting off like a toad marking its territory in a swamp that no self-respecting woman from Texas would want to enter. Hazel Rock had a lot riding on the rodeo coming to town and supporting the Cowboy Ranch, but our mayor wasn't going to tolerate the disrespect toward one of his female voters, either. Especially one he considered a friend.

By the time we made it out on the porch, Dalton was mumbling and Scarlet and Erik could no longer hold him. Cade and Joe took over and deposited Dalton on the split log bench on the wooden walkway outside the bar.

Tears glistened in Scarlet's eyes. "I don't understand... He only had two beers."

"Honey, it wasn't the beer that's got him acting crazy. Dalton has a habit of taking too many pain pills for a back injury that doesn't mix well with beer. He shouldn't have been drinking at all," Erik explained.

"O.M.W.! I had no idea! I would have never suggested we go to the bar." Scarlet's face nearly crumpled. Her brows knit as she chewed on her lower lip. Her polite language was still intact though, as she spilled out her favorite expletive for 'oh, my word.' She knelt next to Dalton who was currently sprawled out on the bench with slobber dribbling down his cheek. It was hard to see a prince charming hidden underneath all that over-indulgence.

Before any of us could say anything else, that dadgum camera light exited the bar and turned the dimly lit porch as bright as a sunrise. Cade shaded his eyes and Scarlet tried to block Dalton's face while using the corner of his shirt to wipe off his cheek. I did the only thing I could to help Scarlet and stood in front of her and Dalton, trying to block the view of the camera. I wasn't feeling too proud about protecting the man, but my best friend needed me.

Peter approached Erik. "It looks like Dalton is back to his old tricks. Would you care to make a statement on behalf of the Championship Bull Riders Association Mr. Piper?"

"I...ah..." Erik straightened his white shirt, which had looked neat before Dalton came along. He attempted to smooth back his hair, but a strand refused to be tamed and drooped over his brow. "Dalton is suffering from exhaustion and dehydration. Once we get him hydrated he'll be as good as new for his morning practice runs."

"So we'll see Dalton in the arena tomorrow?" Peter asked.

"Of course, of course. He wouldn't miss it for the world." A slick smile spread across Erik's lips, the salesman in him ready to lie his way through the interview for the sake of the rodeo and Dalton Hibbs. Only one deserved the support.

"And the world will be watching—is he ready for this round of bull riding?"

"Oh, yes. He's been cleared by his doctor. He's good to go."

We all looked at Dalton who was mumbling incoherently. He wasn't good for anything at the moment. I seriously doubted he'd be up for a ride on Joe's mechanical bull in the back of the bar by the next day, let alone a real life eighteen-hundred-pound angry bovine.

"I heard you say he was taking pain medication—"

Scarlet winced and I wanted to box Peter Kroft's ears. Did every reporter have supersonic hearing that allowed them to listen in on conversations through crowds, thunderstorms and earthquakes? How had he heard that particular bit of information?

"—is he really ready to go back on the circuit if he's taking that much pain medicine?" Peter asked again.

"This is about exhaustion and dehydration. Not pain meds. You wait and see, Dalton will be as good as new in the morning," Erik assured the reporter and all the fans behind the camera lens.

A black SUV with tinted windows drove up. A woman with long, flowing dark hair, who's image I'd seen on Eric's phone, rolled down the window. In her early thirties, she was an eye catcher. Cade's glance stuck to her like jam on rye bread and my irritation rose. Not that I had any right, but still. Manners are manners and it seemed none of the men around us had any.

"Load him up. I can take him back to his hotel. I've got the medics on standby," she told Erik as the camera turned and focused on her face.

Cade stepped up and pulled Dalton upright while the cowboy's head lolled back and forth. He slung Dalton's arm over his shoulder and stood him up straight, the taut strain in Cade's arms the only hint that Dalton wasn't helping in the least. For the camera, it appeared as if Dalton was just being assisted by Cade, not carried. I opened the back door and Scarlet and Joe loaded him into the back of the SUV. Before Erik hopped in the front seat, Joe grabbed his arm.

I was the only one close enough to hear the warning, but the message he delivered was loud and clear. "I'm not going to tell you again—no more smoking in my bar."

Erik dismissed the warning as if it was something frivolous, and closed the front passenger door. But I knew Joe. That man didn't get in anyone's face with a warning like that unless he meant business.

Before I could ask him what that was about, Scarlet asked, "Are you sure he's going to be okay?"

Erik smiled at her through the open window. "We're pretty adept at taking care of minor medical issues for the cowboys."

"Scar-let!" Dalton yelled. "Scar-let!" He sounded awful and desperate. A lot like Rocky Balboa calling to his wife, only Scarlet's name had two syllables, not three.

The camera zoomed in on my best friend, capturing a tear sliding down her cheek. I immediately grabbed her and turned her toward home as the SUV took off. It was time Scarlet and I had a heart-to-heart—chased with a half-gallon of Blue Bell ice cream.

Chapter Three

I barely got the kids out of The Barn and the glue and clippings cleaned up the next morning before I had to open the doors for the PR event we were sponsoring for the rodeo. The media began pouring in the front doors of The Book Barn Princess like flies to manure—elephant manure. My family's bookstore had been my mother's dream. After she died, my dad carried on for me, to give me a place to remember her. Plus, we lived in the apartment at the back of The Barn. My dad had since bought a house in town, and now I lived in the apartment with Princess.

"What is that?" Peter Kroft was staring down at the armadillo as if she'd be better off stuffed.

"That's Princess, our pet." I probably sounded a little angry; it might have had something to do with my hair still being in a kink from his intrusion last night. I could still see spots from that news camera.

"Pet? You have a pet armadillo?" Peter scooted around Princess, who sat with her front legs in the air and her nose twitching at the scent of fruit on the counter behind Peter. She loved strawberries.

"I do."

"Don't they carry diseases?" asked a female reporter I had yet to meet. I glanced at her press pass and read her name, Liza Twaine.

Sensing my short fuse, my daddy stepped up and put them all at ease with his slow talking Southern charm. "They are known to carry leprosy. But Princess has been cleared by the vet. She's disease free." It seemed he was always correcting people who thought armadillos carried the plague, Ebola, or the Black Death. Not that leprosy was any better, but he had her tested regularly since armadillos are more susceptible to the disease because of their low body temperature.

Liza turned and smiled at my dad. At fifty-seven Bobby Ray Warren was a littler grayer and a little leaner than what he used to be, but still quite the catch.

"What's that smell?" asked the squat male reporter next to Liza and her camerawoman, who turned out to be Aubrey Buchanan, a young teenager who'd just graduated from high school and had worked at our store a few months ago.

I wasn't about to tell them Princess probably needed a bath. I was pretty sure Dad was just acting like he didn't hear the reporter, who I finally recognized as Oscar Sanchez from a Dallas news station. Aubrey bent down, her blond curls dropping across the freckles on her nose as she scratched Princess behind the ears.

"It's nice to see our local talent getting an internship for the summer. Channel seven?" I asked.

Aubrey smiled, showing off her gleaming braces with fresh rubber bands in a shade of pink. "Yes, ma'am. Ms. Twaine has offered to take me on and show me the ropes."

"Congratulations, Aubrey." I put on my best host grin and addressed all the reporters. "You can set up your cameras in the loft in preparation for the news conference," I said. "There's plenty of room."

I'd prepared tables with name cards for all the bull riders coming to the event immediately after the kids left. I'd thought about conveniently leaving Dalton Hibbs' name off the table—make him stand with the reporters while the other bull riders sat. But my dad gave me that look of a father scolding his ten-year-old, and I'd placed Dalton in the middle of the table, where the top-seeded star should be seated. Right next to his rival, Travis Sinclair. Dalton was only 170 points ahead of Travis on the season's scoreboard, and the two were bound and determined to beat each other.

Peter had introduced his cameraman from the previous night as Aiden something or other, but the man had already gotten under my skin so I didn't pay much attention to him. He was currently set up in a prime location directly in front of the table. Liza Twaine, who was wearing a purple outfit with purple glasses and purple pumps, strutted up and took the place to Peter's left, crowding him as she turned her back and staked a spot for her crew. She was pretty in a studious, librarian sort of way, but would probably blend into the background if it wasn't for her boldly colored outfit. It screamed "pay attention to me!" The exact opposite of Aubrey's conservative white blouse and khaki pants. Oscar, who seemed completely taken with Liza, set up his own camera on her left even though he could have had a better camera angle elsewhere.

Other reporters filled the back of the room, while a couple of photographers lay down on the floor in front of Peter and Liza, neither of whom seemed to care for the intrusion. Why anyone would want footage looking up the noses of the cowboys was beyond my comprehension.

The chatter among the reporters died down at the roar of diesel engines coming from in front of the store. The cowboys had arrived in what sounded like a stampede of pickups. Everyone turned to look out the windows at the dust storm rising outside the barn. I cringed, knowing all the dust would get sucked inside when they headed in the front doors.

And sure as shootin', in came the dust and the cowboys with their swagger and swoon. Most were average height with long lean muscles except for the oversized biceps supporting their riding hand. A few, like Dalton and Travis, were over six foot, making their female fans sigh and the competition write them off before the cowboys were ready to ride into the sunset. This year they were both at the top of the leader board and enjoying every minute.

The bull riders sported every shade of brown, black, and white cowboy hats as they ascended the stairs to the loft. Their boots were scuffing, their big belt buckles were shining, and their moods were high spirited. Every single one of them looked ready to steal the show. However, every single camera was scanning for just one face, a face that didn't appear among them.

I couldn't help it; my smile grew. Dalton Hibbs was absent. Whether it was due to his embarrassment over his obnoxious behavior, or from his inability to drag his sorry butt out of bed, I didn't much care. He wasn't in my barn, and that's all that mattered.

Everyone took their marked seats, some choosing their own spot and tossing the name placards across the table. Travis sat in the middle. His blond hair was barely visible under the off-white silverbelly felt Stetson sitting low on his head. That hat cost more than The Barn made in a week, maybe two.

Peter was the first reporter to ask what everyone else was wondering. "Where's Dalton?"

A few cowboys shrugged. Dad acted like he didn't hear, leaving me to answer.

"I—I—" I looked around for Erik Piper, who apparently was also running late.

It was Travis who took the bull by the horns. "If you can't run with the big dogs, you need to stay on the porch. I guess Dalton's just starting to feel the pressure and can't hang."

The reporters laughed and a few cowboys snickered. A few others clearly didn't care much for the jab at all. I wasn't sure where I fit in.

"Why don't we go ahead and get started," I said. "Mr. Hibbs can join us when he gets here."

"Do you think you can pull ahead of Hibbs at The Cowboy Ranch Invitational, Travis?" Liza asked.

Travis leaned back in his chair and stretched out his long, muscular arms. "There's only one rooster in the coop at this invitational, and it ain't named Dalton."

Liza smiled, eating up the rivalry between the two lead competitors.

"No, it's Dusty," said the cowboy on the end, pointing to his paper name badge. His name fit his young age: Dusty Lamb.

"In your dreams young 'un. The hens will be celebrating my victory," Sly Alexander added from the other end of the table.

"Y'all are a bunch of hens."

I wasn't sure which cowboy said it, but it resulted in some brotherly pushing behind the table.

The reporters loved the banter between the twelve men seated in front of them. But all the cockiness you would expect from the top twelve bull riders in the nation, didn't squelch the effect of that one empty seat. I should have followed my instincts and left Dalton's card off the table.

Liza and Aubrey kept gazing at their watches and then down at the front door. When the door did open, it wasn't Dalton, but Cade and Mateo who strolled in. Our town's mayor and sheriff lead the way for the circuit's promoter, Erik Piper, and Taylor, the woman who'd driven off in the SUV last night with a drunken Dalton in the backseat.

"He's always been a bum." Erik's voice carried up through the rafters. But it was the disdain in Taylor's reply that affected the riders the most.

"Good riddance. After a stunt like last night, that snot-nosed punk is turning out to be no better than his brother. We should have known better."

The cowboys froze. Even Travis hesitated to take a drink, his bottle of water resting on his lips. Everyone turned toward the scene below. I was the only one to see the sly grin start and stop before it completely formed on Travis's face. His gaze met mine as he took a long, slow drink as if he could hide his glee. He winked and set his bottle back down on the table.

The reporters and cameras, however, missed his show of roguishness as they turned their focus toward the more interesting scene below. A few of the reporters sitting on the floor scooted toward the railing, capturing the thin line Cade's mouth had formed, his disgust evident to all. And as I looked down the steps toward the newcomers, it was only Mateo who seemed unfazed by Taylor's comment. He wore his ever-present sexy expression, which gave nothing away.

Erik looked up and began shushing his partner with the big mouth, who shrugged it off as if the public had a right to know the truth about their star bull rider. Maybe they did.

But then sometimes the truth was hidden beneath a pile of lies so deep, even the rats couldn't find it. If I was to wager, I'd bet there were a few in The Barn who wanted to make sure the truth was buried good and deep, even if they had to help dig the hole.

Chapter Four

"What do you mean he didn't make it to the press conference? He loves press conferences!" Scarlet's voice rose in what could only be described as near panic.

I grabbed her arm and ushered her behind the pink velvet curtain and into the backroom before any of the reporters turned their cameras away from our collection of book art and decided to make the lead artist's love life part of their story.

"Erik said that Dalton threw a fit last night and they ended up having to stop the car. Dalton was hell-bent on returning to your place to apologize, but Erik and his partner, Taylor—she's the woman out there with Cade right now—refused to take him because they thought it would end up on the news." I had no doubt that was a wise decision.

"But Dalton never showed up at my place."

"According to Mateo, a cab dropped him off at Beaus and Beauties around twelve-thirty."

"That's impossible. I was home!" Scarlet was a talker, but I'd never seen her so riled up before. The emotions flashing through her eyes scared me. She shouldn't have been this caught up over a man she barely knew. She'd mussed her perfectly coifed Grace Kelly up-do that she wore so well. As the owner of Beaus and Beauties Hair Salon, Scarlet was the most talented hairdresser I'd ever known. She'd rescued my curls on numerous occasions. But today, her normally perfect hair looked bedroom messy, like she'd just met Dalton for a rendezvous in the backroom of The Barn, instead of me.

I tried to deliver the blow gently. "The driver saw him head through the alley toward your trailer."

"He never knocked!"

"Are you sure you just didn't sleep through it?"

"I wasn't asleep, I..." She turned away without saying she'd been too upset.

But I knew she had been. I'd walked her home before heading toward The Barn. The entire walk she'd made excuse after excuse for the cowboy's behavior: *I didn't know he was taking painkillers. I bought him his drinks. He wouldn't have drunk anything but water if I hadn't pushed those beers on him. This is all my fault. Now the media will use this against him. He's never acted like this before.*

By the time we'd reached the refurbished Airstream trailer she lived in behind her beauty shop, I was ready to yank my hair out. Dalton should have been buying her drinks, not the other way around. The man made over six figures this year alone. But Scarlet had confided that she treated Dalton because he'd spent so much money on her artwork and she'd felt it was only appropriate.

Now she was going to blame herself for Dalton's disappearance as well.

"Last night was not your fault, and this morning isn't your fault. Dalton Hibbs is a grown man."

"I'm well aware of that, but—" Scarlet's eyes brimmed with unshed tears and I put my arm around her shoulder, knowing that a full-fledged hug would open the floodgates. And that was the last thing she needed.

"No buts. Dalton has brought all of this on himself. His mistakes, his cross to bear."

"But what if something's happened to him?" One tear spilled over and I grabbed a Kleenex from the shelf, refusing to allow it to become two.

"From what Erik and Taylor told me about his past, Dalton has a history of giving the media the slip before the preliminary rounds and then making an entrance at the last minute."

"What?"

"It's a media stunt," I explained.

"Dalton wouldn't do that."

"He's done it twice before. Once already this season."

"Once or twice does not make a history." Her fingers rose to emphasize "a history" with air quotes. "I'm telling you, Dalton wouldn't miss a media event. He loves them."

But I couldn't let her put her head in the sand. "Apparently, he loves it more when they speculate as to where he's been."

"I don't think Dalton would ever do that," she argued.

"Scarlet, you've only known the man a couple days."

I waited for her to agree, then tell me she'd known his brother years earlier. Had even been questioned about his disappearance and that's why she was freaking out now. Instead, she began to chew on her lower lip, and the woman who could chat my ear off 'til the sun didn't shine, said nothing. She dried her tears and after a long period of silence, she finally talked. "We need to go talk up our art so we can raise more money for The Cowboy Ranch."

My pride and my heart felt like they'd been poked with a cattle prod. Scarlet wasn't going to confide in me like I would have confided in her, and our solid friendship seemed a little less stable.

Instead, she headed for the curtain. She stopped in front of the mirror just inside the doorway, straightened her hair, smoothed out her sage green midi pencil skirt, and adjusted her white silk wrap-over halter. She had pearls at her neck and wrist that she twisted to make sure they were laying perfectly against her body. Which they were, as usual. But I knew beyond a shadow of a doubt that Scarlet had put extra time into her appearance this morning for Dalton—a two-time loser in my book. Except my book apparently didn't count.

"I'm sorry," I blurted out as she reached for the curtain.

Scarlet paused, looking over her shoulder. A sad smile slowly formed on her face. "Me too, Charli. Me too." Then she turned and walked through the curtain, shoulders pushed back with her head held high.

Chapter Five

It'd officially been twenty-four hours since Dalton Hibbs disappeared. Part of me felt good riddance when I thought of his treatment of Scarlet the night before. The other part was sad for my best friend, who was no doubt watching the news and scouring the Internet for any lead as to his whereabouts. And I confess, while setting up the artwork for the sale the next day, I'd listened to the national and local news broadcasts myself— only for news of Dalton. My gut was telling me he was up to no good in some dive hotel with a woman—who wasn't Scarlet.

Toenails clicked across the floor behind me and I looked down at the little creature who'd been following me around for the past hour. "Princess, I don't know about you, but I'm ready to call it a night."

Squeeeak. She twitched her nose and made some kind of grinding noise with her teeth.

"Girl, you could have used your pet door if you were that hungry."

Princess snorted and ran for the stairs.

"I'm just going to get all the lights. I'll be up in a minute."

This time, she didn't reply, but I heard her hopping up one step at a time at breakneck speed. Or at least her version of speed. I switched off the lights and made my way upstairs. Princess was looking at me from in front of the bookcase. A couple of months ago, I'd learned my dad had installed a hidden door to the apartment behind the bookcase. It was pretty cool not to have to go outside to use the exterior set of stairs to access the apartment. Not that it rained much in Hazel Rock, but when it did, it poured.

It was ten o'clock, well past closing time, but I was ready for the silent auction we were having for our book art the next day. Dad had gone home a couple hours earlier and Scarlet hadn't come back after the reporters departed. I had secretly hoped Scarlet would return after our falling-out that morning, but no such luck.

I flipped the latch for the bookcase and entered the dark space between it and the apartment when I remembered the coffeepot.

"Fuzz buckets. I forgot to turn off the coffeepot. I'll be right back."

Princess squeaked in protest.

"I've been smelling you since this afternoon. I'm not about to let you in that apartment until I'm there to get your bath ready," I argued.

She squeaked again but sat back on her haunches to wait.

It was our routine, especially since she liked to get on the couch or my bed when I wasn't looking. Armadillos have their own special odor. She wasn't getting on my furniture without a bath.

I made my way downstairs, not bothering to turn on the lights, since I knew the store better than any place on earth. I went behind the register and turned off the coffeepot and glanced out the front window. The front porch light was out when it should have automatically come on at dusk.

"Seriously? What else?" I said to no one in particular. The light would have to be fixed before The Tool Shed Tavern emptied for the night so the patrons could see the sign reminding them of the auction the next day. Otherwise, they just might sleep through it.

I went to the back room and grabbed a replacement bulb on the shelf. Then I removed the flashlight off the wall, before making my way back to the front of the store. Princess was descending the steps, apparently too impatient to wait for me upstairs.

I shut off the alarm, then flipped the lock open. Princess squeaked in protest.

"I know, but it will just take me a minute. Hold on to your shell!" I told her.

I turned back just as the two automatic barn doors swished open. I loved that my dad invested in the new doors to make them open at the same time like that. It caught everyone's attention.

Stepping out onto the porch, I nearly screamed when a cowboy suddenly stood up in front of me.

"Holy shcnikes, you nearly scared me half to death!" I laughed as I held the bulb to my chest.

But he didn't laugh in return. In fact, his back was to me as he fiddled with something in his hand. His dark plaid shirt looked like it could have belonged to anyone, but the colors were a little different. Not so Southern, or Western. But maybe a knock-off brand from a mall out west. Or back east. As he stood up, I knew this cowboy, wasn't a *real* cowboy. And suddenly it wasn't so funny. The hairs on the back of my neck started to tingle. Seriously, I wondered if I should whack him across the back of his head with the flashlight and run.

And then it was too late. He whipped around with something fire-red in his hand. My mind screamed danger while my heart felt like it shot right out of my chest as the cattle branding tool came in my direction. I lost focus on everything but that burning ember directed at my face. I swiped at him with the flashlight, while sending a silent thank you to my dad for buying the heavier metal light, instead of a plastic design. The flashlight came into contact with his forearm with a resounding thud, but I knew my strike was pathetic; I'd be lucky if he got a bruise. He rallied with a jab, the end of the branding iron glowing with an insignia I was too busy avoiding to identify.

The doors to the Barn swished open behind him as he came at me again. I tripped backward and my back struck the porch post. The flashlight and lightbulb both clattered to my feet as broken glass tinkled across the porch. I scrambled for my flashlight, knowing it was the only weapon I had. But before I could grab it, I found an arm wrapped around me from behind, while his other forearm came into view with the sizzling branding iron coming straight for my face.

I pushed against his arm with everything I had and tried to look up into his eyes, but his hat and the lack of light kept his face completely obscured. The doors swished closed behind him, closing off my escape route. The searing heat from the branding iron quickly became my only focus once again. It was like what they say about looking down the barrel of a gun. I could identify every nitch that didn't burn as bright as the rest. Every curve and curlicue in the design. I couldn't make out what that design was at the moment, but that wasn't because I didn't know it by heart. I knew every last detail. My brain just wouldn't process the information into a coherent thought. Its only function seemed focused on fighting and keeping my heart from exploding through the wall of my chest. I pushed against his arm with all my strength, and yet I knew, in the next fifteen seconds, I'd be wearing someone's brand across my face if I didn't do something else—fast. The smell of burnt hair reached my nose: it was only a matter of seconds before the brand marked me as part of someone's herd.

I swung my head back with all my force. I missed his nose and struck his jaw. Unfortunately, it wasn't made of glass, but rather stronger, sturdier stuff than me. My head felt like it was going to implode.

Then I remembered a bit of physics. If you can't beat the force, go with the force. I quit pushing *against* his grip, and instead directed his arm away from my face. He fell forward with his own momentum. The brand flew by my left ear, the heat much hotter than my curling iron. As he pulled back, I pushed, then released and aimed the branding iron at his nose but caught his forehead instead. He hissed and started backing away, but I wasn't done as The Barn doors swished open again. I kicked his knee and heard a crunching sound before either one of us could get away. He ran for the store as his leg buckled and he fell to the porch.

The doors swished closed and I fumbled with the lock. My fingers refused to do anything. The muscles and tendons tightened as if rigor mortis was prematurely setting in. I finally got the door locked and backed away. My breathing sounding like a donkey in heat as something slammed against the barn doors. The automatic motor tried to open the doors again as the motion detector was triggered. I ran back toward the switch and flipped it to the off position. Then I turned and ran for the steps. I didn't stop until I was in the apartment with my phone in my hand and Princess looking at me like I was an idiot.

Chapter Six

It was Mateo who knocked on my apartment door a few minutes later. He looked me up and down with his dark chocolate eyes, making sure I was in one piece. Then he looked at my hair. I'd forgotten about my hair.

"Is it bad?"

"I've seen worse."

"On me?"

"No, but you've had your moments."

"What's that supposed to mean?"

"The night you tackled Mike down by the river."

"So this isn't anything a good wash and comb can't fix?" I knew it was a pipe dream, but sometimes I liked having my head in the clouds. Besides, our banter was a welcome distraction from the harrowing experience I'd just had.

Mateo winced and pulled his notebook from his front uniform pocket. "I wouldn't go that far."

"How far would you go?" As soon as the question spewed from my mouth, my face heated. It got worse when Mateo's gaze left his notepad and those bedroom eyes met mine.

"Is that a proposition?" he asked.

"What? No…I…well…" My tongue was acting like it got burned, sputtering and oozing words that didn't come close to completing a sentence.

"Why don't you tell me what happened tonight."

"Come on in and have a seat." Mateo moved inside, his broad shoulders crowding me and I moved over to the other side of my leather sofa, indicating he should have a seat there while I sat in my mom's glider. The rock and sway gave me comfort after a stressful night followed by a too-hot-for-his-britches visitor.

I went through the events, answering a few questions supplied by a frowning Mateo. I described the cowboy as taller than me, but shorter than him, wearing a black felt hat, plaid shirt, and vest with jeans and cowboy boots. My description fit at least half of the men in Texas.

"Do you know if he was white, black, or Hispanic?" he asked.

"I think he was white, but he could have been Hispanic. All I saw were his hands and even then, I was focused on the branding iron. I couldn't even tell you much about his build. It just happened too fast and it was too dark."

"What happened to your porch light?"

"I don't know. That's why I went outside. I noticed the light was out and I was going to change the bulb."

Once I had given him all the details, I returned to an equally important subject. "Can I ask you one question?"

"Sure."

"Just how bad is my hair, really?"

"You might want to have Scarlet work her magic on it."

I sighed and closed my eyes. "Scarlet isn't talking to me."

When he didn't respond, I slowly opened my eyes, wondering if he didn't care what Scarlet and I did. Mateo had closed his notebook and sat there waiting for me to continue.

"I may have pushed our friendship further than she was ready to go."

He still didn't respond. He just sat there with his elbows on his knees and his pad and pen held in his hands, completely at ease as he waited for me to explain.

"I kind of told her that Dalton wasn't worth her time."

"From what I heard occurred at the Tool Shed, I would agree."

"But she wasn't ready to agree."

"And that's the problem. From my experience, you can tell a woman the right and the wrong way she should be treated, but the moment you say her man's no good, she clings to her idea of what he's meant to her." Mateo stood up and I followed. "She'll come around. Scarlet's a smart woman."

"The smartest one I know."

"So smart she gives me a headache." Mateo put his pen and pad in the pocket of his clean, crisp uniform shirt. "Let's go down and take a look at that light." It wasn't a question. It was one of Mateo's finely disguised orders that you didn't want to ignore. I had once. Never again.

I left Princess in the apartment despite her trying to scurry past our feet and we walked down the steps in silence. The frogs down by the river were singing to their future mates and the sign in the alleyway creaked on its antique iron bracket. My dad had hung the "Eve's Gate" sign when we first moved into the apartment when I was a kid. It marked the entrance to our private residence in the middle of town and was a tribute to my mom.

Mateo eyed the sign.

"Cade's been talking," I said.

"Everybody in town's been talking about that sign. Even Bobby Ray."

"Seriously?" I opened the latch to the gate that lead to the courtyard between our barn and the antique shop in the old hospital next door.

"Your dad says your mom is watching over you and makes sure anyone who passes through that alley has good intentions toward you."

"Well then, I guess you're safe."

"Cade wasn't. The sign has dropped on him twice."

"You don't seriously believe it was my mom who caused the sign to fall, do you?" When he didn't respond, I couldn't help but laugh. "You're a police officer. Next thing I know you'll be saying the chupacabra is real."

Mateo just looked at me. I really couldn't tell if he thought the legendary goat killing animal was real or not. I returned my attention back to the sign. "Cade and I were standing under the sign when it fell. It wasn't like it flew through the air and tagged him on the back of the head."

Mateo made that non-committal head nod I'd seen him make a hundred times since I'd met him.

"Don't tell me you believe my mom purposely knocked down that sign from heaven?" I asked.

We both looked up at the full strawberry moon that happened to fall today, the official first day of summer.

The fountain bubbling in the courtyard and the cool breeze slipping between the buildings made me remember one of the things I loved most about Hazel Rock—the nights were truly spectacular. We don't have a lot of street lights and when I stepped away from the porch lights, the stars were endless, the moon was dominant, and the sounds of nature made me feel like I was part of the earth—not just a person using all its resources for my own benefits.

The sky truly was amazing tonight. And it was weird to think that if I hadn't been attacked, I wouldn't have experienced this moment with Mateo.

"I missed this when I was in Denver," I confessed. It seemed I was always blurting out things to him that I wouldn't admit to anyone else.

"Dall—tonnnn! Dalllllltonnnn! Where are you?" The melodic voice carried down the street and I knew exactly who was yelling from the tallest point in town.

Mateo and I looked up at the Hazel Rock water tower and witnessed Scarlet, still in her classy pencil cut skirt and silk blouse, hanging onto the railing as her hair blew around her face.

Mateo cursed under his breath and stalked in the direction of his police car, muttering something about a crazy bleepity-bleep full moon. He told the officer at the front of The Barn to stay put and watch the crime scene. I took off toward the tower that was across the street and behind the strip of businesses that ran down Main Street. Surprisingly, by the time I got there, Mateo was on my heels with some kind of strap with hooks wrapped around his hand.

He shoved the strap in his cargo pocket and said, "Distract her while I head up the ladder."

"What are you going to do?"

"Get her drunk-a… Bring her down before she goes and kills herself."

"Scarlet wouldn't commit suicide over a guy she just met."

"Probably not, but I'm beginning to question her IQ if she's willing to risk her safety for a stunt like this."

Before I could argue further, Mateo ran toward the other side of the tower, ready to save Scarlet from herself.

"Dallllton!"

I looked up to see Scarlet fumbling with her iPhone.

"Scarlet!" I yelled.

She looked behind her, then down to her left and finally located me almost directly below.

"Hey, Princess! You should be up here!" She giggled, clearly showing she'd had way too much to drink. It was so out of character; it didn't faze me in the least that she'd used my high school nickname. Just as it didn't bother me anymore that my dad had renamed the family business or his pet armadillo after me. It was part of me. A part I'd like to keep as history, but a lot of people hadn't gotten used to calling me Charli yet, so it was understandable that Scarlet would slip in her drunken state.

"What are you doing?" I asked.

"Trying to find Dalton. What's it look like I'm doing?"

"It looks like you're drunk and need to come down."

"I don't think I can in this skirt."

"How'd you get up there in the first place?"

She looked around to see if anyone was listening, but she couldn't see the houses behind her. I decided it was best not to let her in on the fact that front lights were on and a few people were gathered in their PJs, peeking out from under their porch roofs.

Once she decided the coast was clear, she said, "I hiked my skirt up and climbed up the way you did."

She was referring to my junior year in high school when I climbed over the locked gate that covered the ladder and made my way to the top and began doing cheers to get the town to rally behind our football team. Mainly, my boyfriend the team quarterback. It had all been done on a dare and my stunt landed me in jail. I was afraid Scarlet had the same destiny.

"Dalton! Come back!" She yelled.

I cringed not sure if I was the right one to tell her to stop yelling his name. "Scarlet?"

She looked back in my direction.

"Do you really think he's going to hear you from his hotel in Abilene?"

"He's not there. I checked."

"You drove?" I looked around and saw her little white BMW Isetta parked next to her trailer. It appeared to be intact.

"No! I got a cab. I'm not stupid!"

I was beginning to wonder about that.

"Listen to this new song I downloaded."

"I won't be able to hear it. Why don't you come down and we'll listen to it together," I told her, wishing Mateo would get his butt up there and bring her down.

"Sure you will. I brought my speaker." Scarlet fumbled with a bag at her feet and pulled out a small square block. Then she began messing with her phone, concentrating on the screen so hard she didn't see Mateo approaching from her right. A moment later Charles Kelley's voice began serenading the town with "Lonely Girl (On Top of the Tower)". It was more than a little bit ironic and got pretty cheesy when she held the speaker above her head like a bad rendition of an 80s teenage love flick—minus the boom box and the cute guy. A sexy man, however, did approach her and wrap his strong arms around her middle before she even knew he was there.

She jumped—up, not down, thankfully. Mateo held firm, talking in her ear the whole time. I couldn't hear what he was saying but Scarlet nodded and they walked sideways with Mateo's back to the tower and Scarlet in front of him. I tracked them from down below, feeling helpless and more than a bit sad for Scarlet. They made it to the ladder about the time I heard sirens in the distance.

"Did you call the fire department?" I yelled up at Mateo, praying that he hadn't.

He ignored me and kept talking to Scarlet, his voice low and steady, but Scarlet saw the ladder and a little panic flashed across her face as she shook her head back and forth. She said something to Mateo and he released her for a moment with one hand as he reached into his pocket and pulled something out. He handed it to Scarlet and they did a one-eighty turn so that Scarlet was facing the tower. I heard the rip of material and instantly knew Scarlet was cutting her skirt.

The sirens continued to blare and a few people were making their way through the alley from Main Street—two of which I really didn't want to see.

"What's going on?" asked Peter Kroft, the reporter who'd been front and center to see Scarlet's humiliation the night before.

I tried to remain cordial but failed, big time. His report on the incident at the bar had not been kind. "Nothing worth reporting."

"Really? Cause it looks to me like a woman was going to commit suicide over how badly Dalton Hibbs treated her. What happened to your hair?"

Peter's cameraman, Aiden, was gearing up to get the shot of a lifetime, or at least Scarlet's lifetime, when I turned on him, completely ignoring Peter's question about my curls.

"Don't you even think about turning that camera on," I growled; it actually sounded pretty feral as I turned back to Peter. "If she was suicidal, Mateo wouldn't have given her his pocket knife." I knew Peter could see the knife as Scarlet handed it back to Mateo, who took the time to close it against his thigh and slip it back into his pocket.

But Peter's cameraman wasn't giving up. "We're here to cover the news."

"This isn't news," I insisted.

"Looks that way to me," Aiden replied and lifted the camera to his shoulder.

Surprisingly it was Peter who put his hand on the front of the camera lens and pointed it toward the ground as Mateo and Scarlet made their way down the ladder. Mateo had the strap he'd grabbed from his patrol car wrapped around his back. Scarlet had abandoned her speaker at the top of the ladder and had unfortunately left it on repeat as they made their descent. The process was extremely slow, each step requiring Mateo to release and then reattach the strap to the next rung.

As their feet touched the ground the crowd cheered and the fire department arrived. Peter stepped forward. The reporter slipped out of his suit jacket and held it in front of Mateo and Scarlet so she could cover the new slit in the front of her designer skirt.

The act of chivalry was not lost on the bystanders or me, and a little bit of my faith in the media was restored.

Chapter Seven

I listened to Scarlet babble on and on about Dalton for about thirty minutes and how, "He would never leave *it* behind." She continued saying, "Dalton loved his brother. He just wouldn't leave it." I had no idea what she was talking about and I wasn't sure she did either, considering she'd start to fall asleep and then repeat it for the tenth time before her head plopped back on her pillow. About the time I thought she was out for the night, her little sister, Joellen, arrived. Apparently, someone called somebody, who called someone else, who called Joellen. Joellen was ready and desperately wanting to step up to the plate and take care of Scarlet. I couldn't blame her; Scarlet took care of everyone else, so it was time the rest of us took care of her.

I left with a promise to check on them in the morning, which was only a few hours away, and I headed back to The Barn. Mateo was out front giving a statement to the media with cameras rolling. Ugh.

I tried to slip by, keeping my head down with my curls covering my face. No such luck. It was Peter's stupid cameraman, Aiden, who had eyes in the back of his thick skull that turned in my direction. The light on his camera acted like a beacon on my body for all the other reporters to follow. And they did.

Fuzz buckets.

I made a beeline for the gate that led to my apartment and raced right through, letting it slam closed behind me. Part of my brain registered a squeak, the other part was wondering if I had locked my apartment door. I erred on the side of caution and began fumbling in my pocket while taking the steps two at a time. I got the key out of my pocket and the door open just in time to hear the gate swing open, a clang, and my favorite cameraman yell, "Son-of-a-" as I slammed the door closed and pulled the shade.

Leaning against the door, I jumped when my phone buzzed on the counter where I'd left it plugged in to charge. I took a few deep breaths. I hadn't run far but my adrenaline was still pumping. I went and retrieved my phone and read the message that was, surprisingly, from Mateo.

Your mom struck again. Right on top of his head. ☺

He actually used a smiley face at the end. I wondered if that was his way of laughing.

Whose head?

I asked, hoping it wasn't a member of the media who would sue me for every dime I was worth. Which wouldn't amount to very many rolls of dimes, if I was honest.

Your favorite cameraman.

I smiled. I couldn't help it. Then I laughed as I half-scolded my mom up in heaven. Dag-nabbit, Mom. You're going to get me in more trouble. Then I texted him back.

You're lying.

Full moon, babe, he responded.

Babe. Mateo called me babe. Was that a proposition, or just a figure of speech like "catch ya later, babe" or "see ya tomorrow, babe"? I wasn't sure how to take it, or if I should even address it. I chose to ignore it.

Do I need to come down?

Please don't make me come down. Please don't make me come down.

No, the wind has really picked up in the past 30 minutes.

I wasn't sure if that was an excuse for the sign falling or if he was scared I'd blow away in the wind. Granted, I bordered on the thin side, but not *rail* thin. I sat there wondering how to respond when he sent another text.

Cade is here. When the media leaves, I think there's something you need to see. We'll be up in a few.

Well, that definitely put things into perspective. Mateo was texting in the friend zone. He had to be. Otherwise, he wouldn't be talking about coming up to my front door with his best friend and my ex-high school sweetheart who'd kissed me my first day back in town.

Cade, however, hadn't even come by to buy a book since that kiss and acted like I was just another voter in his reelection campaign for mayor in the fall. I knew he was extremely busy, but still. Would it kill him to follow through?

I put my phone back on the charger and made my way to the bathroom with Princess at my feet. I caught a whiff of her and my nose scrunched.

"Are you trying to tell me you need a bath, because I can smell you?"

She squeaked in response. I had yet to learn if one squeak meant yes, or if she was calling me an unpleasant name. One glance in the mirror, however, took my mind completely off her scent. I screamed.

Princess jumped. One of those straight up in the air, feet hanging with nowhere to go jumps, and her little beady eyes bugged out of their sockets.

My hands flew to my hair, only this time there were some expletives attached. I couldn't help it. When tragedy strikes, I cuss. It's ugly. I was probably going to lose my Southern belle card from not being more imaginative with my response. But I didn't care. The hair on the left side of my head was fried. Like curls gone, ends sticking out several inches shorter than it was supposed to and fried ends looking more like wire than natural locks.

In Texas, bad hair is a deadly sin, and what I saw in the mirror was beyond bad. If I was vain, I'd curl up in a ball on the floor and cry my eyes out. But I'm not that vain—I only let one tear escape. That's all I had time for because someone was at my front door knocking. More like pounding.

"Princess! Open up or I'm going to kick this door down!" Cade yelled from outside. When he used my nickname, I knew he meant business.

Fuzz buckets.

This is what happens when you act all girly and scream over stupid stuff. Men have to act all manly. They kick in your door and they see you with your hair looking worse than any man should have to see it.

"I'm fine! Don't kick my door! I'm coming!" I responded as I frantically looked for a hair tie. Finally, I found one under the sink and pulled my hair back in a ponytail. The left side stuck straight out from the side of my head. Afro gone bad. I whimpered and pulled out the ponytail and grabbed a towel and wrapped it around my head like I'd just washed it.

"Open up, Princess!" Cade yelled again.

I ran for the door and tripped over the little Princess, who was making her way to the door like Cade was there to see her, and not me.

I flipped the lock and opened the door.

Cade looked me up and down, his chest heaving as if he'd just run a marathon.

"Why are you out of breath?"

"Why are you screaming?"

"I didn't scream." I crossed my fingers behind my back.

"I heard you scream."

"It wasn't me."

"I heard it too," Mateo added as he stuck his head around the corner and saw my towel. A grin spread across his face. "Did you break a mirror?"

My eyes narrowed and the normally stoic officer of the law laughed. Cade looked at him like he was under the influence of an illegal substance.

"I thought maybe you cut your foot or something."

All three of us looked down at my feet. My combat boots were dusty and in need of a shine, but intact.

"I guess not," Mateo said.

"What am I missing?" Cade asked, his gaze traveling suspiciously between me and Mateo.

For some reason that look made me feel guilty for something that hadn't even happened. Which was utterly ridiculous since Cade was nothing but an old high school sweetheart.

"Nothing." I turned to Mateo. "Was there something you wanted to show me?"

"Well, first, I thought you might want this back." He handed me my mom's iron sign.

"Was he hurt badly?"

"A few staples and he'll be as good as new."

"Seriously?"

"His head isn't as hard as mine is," Cade said.

I couldn't help but laugh. It was either that or break down in front of these two, and that was the last thing I wanted to do.

"Tell Bobby Ray to figure out a way to hang it more securely next time. I'm not sure I can always blame it on the weather." Mateo's face turned serious. "I need to show you something on the front of the store."

"What is it?"

"Let's go down and take a look."

The three of us made our way downstairs, with me sandwiched in between them looking completely ridiculous with a towel on my head. I thought I should ask Cade about his campaign or something about The Cowboy Ranch Invitational, but I was beat and everything that came to mind sounded lame. We made our way to the front of the store and Mateo pulled his flashlight out of his pocket. The broken glass had been cleaned up and the crime scene tape was down, making me feel better about the sale that I'd be having in a few short hours.

The white-yellow beam of Matteo's flashlight hit the front barn doors. Off to the left, the pink paint had been blackened. Charred actually, with the branding iron that nearly fried my face. The barn now had a new symbol on the front door of a cowboy riding a bull and the number 611 prominently burned into the wood below it.

I knew that number. Not because I was a fan. But because I recognized it as the fiery image I'd almost been scarred with, and my best friend was more than a fan of the man who wore it on the back of his shirt. The number 611 was worn by one man every time he rode a bull.

Dalton Hibbs had branded my barn.

Chapter Eight

The next morning, after my shower and a frustrating attempt to fix my hair, I went over to check on Scarlet. Her head would be splitting when she woke up, but when I arrived, she was still wrapped like a burrito in her sheets. Joellen and I made the joint decision to leave her that way. I had no doubt she was going to have one heck of a hangover and helping with the auction this early in the morning would be a bad idea. I made my way back down to The Barn wearing my daddy's old straw Stetson and a pair of cowboy boots that belonged to my mom. I topped the outfit off with a pair of cutoff shorts and a pink bibliophile T-shirt from the store that read *Open the Doors to Heaven with a Book.*

Before I even started the sweet tea for the day, I called my back-up for the event. Joe Buck's waitress at the bar, Sugar, had started filling in for me on my days off when Aubrey decided she could no longer work at The Barn. Several months back we'd almost sold the family business, but our Realtor had been murdered and the sale fell through the cracks. From that day forward Aubrey was uncomfortable in the store. After the investigation was over, we'd run an ad for help and Sugar was our first and only applicant. I was so glad to have her; with her help, I didn't have to worry about dad trying to put in too many hours.

Sugar was also a good source of town gossip since she worked at The Shed. Of course, there were those rare occasions like last night when the gossip ventured outside the revelry of The Tool Shed Tavern.

Sugar arrived right before we were due to open and had to squeeze her way through the growing crowd of men, women, and children. If there was something people liked in small town, Texas, it was an auction. Even a silent auction would bring people out of the woodwork, and since the proceeds benefitted The Cowboy Ranch people were ready to come in and check out the new book art that I'd spent most of the previous day putting out on display, along with the bid sheets I'd placed in front of them.

Scarlet and I had worked for a several months to gather the rather large selection of different items. She'd created the more difficult pieces like the bull rider Dalton had purchased. She'd also sculpted several Disney princess themed items; my favorite was of Ariel from *The Little Mermaid* saving Prince Eric as he drifted to the bottom of the sea. Complete with a shipwreck and coral covering the bottom, the entire piece was backlit by a blue light. There was also a whimsical scene of The Lost Boys and Peter Pan flying through the air over Captain Hook in a rowboat paddled by his trusted first mate, Smead. The ocean waves were rough, with painstaking care taken into making the pages swirl and curl over the front tip of the boat as an alligator stalked them. Scarlet's pieces were over-the-top and I hated to see them go.

I'd spent my time making high-heeled shoes out of pages from a damaged edition of *Cinderella* and purses, which were actually functional, out of hard-backed books. With the pages removed, the covers became the purse and they were lined with material to complement the color and topic of the book. Each one had a different handle made out of chain, wooden rings, beads or anything else I could find.

Princess had a way of choosing my books for me. For instance, she'd shredded *One for the Money* by Janet Evanovich, and I'd almost cried. Yet despite the story being destroyed, the cover was still perfect and disposing of it seemed almost sacrilegious, so I turned it into my favorite purse with a money print lining and a shoulder strap made from a chain sporting coin charms. The clasp was made from a real quarter turned into a button and a loop of matching material added to the vintage flavor. I was pretty proud of how everything turned out.

My best piece, however, was a wagon I'd made out of Laura Ingalls Wilder's *Little House on the Prairie*. I'd made the wheels out of wire, but the rest was all from the book and I was amazed at the artist inside me dying to get out. For as long as I could remember, my art had not passed the kindergarten level, but apparently when I left my five and six-year-old students in Colorado, my skills grew up.

My dad had also gotten in the spirit and created a chest out of a couple sets of old encyclopedias bound in three different shades of burgundy with gold trim. He'd glued all the books together and then took his band saw to them and created four sides and a bottom. The lid was glued together to create a half moon with the middle carved out for the interior.

The latches were made from aged and weathered leather straps and gave it an antique appeal.

He'd also let the little kid in him come out and decoupaged a chest of drawers with the pages from *Calvin and Hobbs*. Princess had eaten the last half of the book so at least the spunky little kid and his tiger could still be enjoyed in a new way.

"I think it's about that time," my dad said as he brought out a box of last-minute additions our class had donated to the cause.

"I really need to sign up for one of your classes," Sugar said as she pulled out the clocks we'd made and laid them across the last bit of open space on the counter in the tearoom. "I love these!"

Sugar and I had started off on a bad note when I'd first come back to Hazel Rock, but now I considered her a friend. At the bar, she dressed sexy. At The Barn, her natural beauty shined with little to no make-up and her winning smile with one crooked tooth that made her real, captured the hearts of everyone. As long as no one brought up her wayward boyfriend, Dean MacAlister. He brought out Sugar's inner Annie Oakley and everything became a target for whatever she had in her hands at the time.

"Have you heard anything at the bar about Dalton Hibbs's disappearance?" I asked as I filled out the bid sheet for my Nancy Drew clock.

Sugar's ponytail bobbed as she spoke and for the first time, I noticed a scar on the back of her neck. It wasn't large, just about the size of a dime, but it puckered like it'd been from a burn and I wondered how she could have possibly burned herself there. "There's a wide range of speculation. Some of the cowboys are saying he buckled under the pressure. Others are saying that he's off with a few of the local women." Sugar rolled her eyes. "I had a mind to let them wear their beers when they suggested that, but I kept my itchy fingers on my serving tray."

A smile crossed my dad's face. He liked Sugar's spirit. I think she reminded him of my mom.

"What about the locals—what do they think?" I asked.

"They think he's off grieving over his brother."

"What's the story with his brother?"

"Wyatt disappeared seven years ago. But unlike Dalton, Wyatt was always in the thick of things, so when he went missing everyone suspected wrongdoing. Dalton was the first one to start hollering foul play."

"Did they ever find any evidence of anything?"

My dad hopped into the conversation. "Nope. One day he was here, and the next he was gone. There's still a reward out for his whereabouts, but no one has seen hide nor hair of the man since."

"Why was Scarlet brought in for questioning?"

Sugar looked at my dad for the answer. At the time she would have been too young to care much about anything but her own hormones and dating life.

"Scarlet had it bad for Wyatt. And when he disappeared, everyone expected her to know where to find him. But she didn't. No one did."

"Was Dalton in town when Wyatt disappeared?" I asked.

Both my father and Sugar nodded, then Sugar added, "Some said he was jealous of his brother's success, and that if there was any foul play, he was behind it."

A case of domestic violence sadly wouldn't be a rare thing, but despite my negative feelings toward Dalton, I suspected he was innocent of anything nefarious that may have happened to Wyatt. I may not like the way the man treated Scarlet, but I certainly didn't see him as the type to harm his brother just to rise above him in the rankings.

"You should know," Sugar added, "that several of the reporters were asking where Scarlet was when Dalton disappeared."

We didn't have any more time to discuss Dalton or Scarlet after that, as we were too busy opening the doors and starting the bidding for the various sections in the store. The media arrived, including Peter and his sidekick, Aiden, and Aubrey. She was tagging along absorbing everything Liza Twaine told her like a sponge in the middle of a Texas thunderstorm. Not a drop of media mentoring escaped her notice.

About noon Scarlet came in looking a little green around the edges to me. To everyone else she looked like a million bucks with her auburn curls pulled to one side by a jeweled comb at the nape of her neck and her hair hanging down over her shoulder. She had on a conservative navy suit that made her look like she belonged in a courthouse, not a barn. Liza spotted her immediately and sent an uncomfortable-looking Aubrey over to see if Scarlet would give an interview.

Scarlet politely declined and made her way over toward me. "You should have woken me up this morning."

"I didn't think you'd be in any shape to make it."

If it was possible, I think Scarlet turned a darker shade of green. "So it's true? Mateo had to help me down from the top of the water tower?" There was a hint of hope shining in her eyes.

I dashed it with a slow nod.

"Was I yelling for Dalton?" Again, I could see that silent prayer flashing behind her eyes.

It went unanswered with my second nod.

"Please don't tell me I held up my mini speaker and let *Lonely Girl* blare across the rooftops?"

I grimaced, knowing she didn't want the answer but gave it to her anyway with a nod.

For a moment, her shoulders slouched; then she held her head up high and took on all the speculative looks being thrown in her direction. "I'm really worried about Dalton. Has anyone heard from him yet?" she asked.

I thought that question deserved more than a shake of my head, but I certainly didn't want to tell her that Dalton had branded my front door and tried to apply permanent makeup on my face. Nor did I want to tell her that Mateo was looking for him right now. Instead, I went with a vague, noncommittal response. "I'm sorry. No one's seen or heard a peep from him." Technically I didn't see his face so I wasn't lying. I nodded toward my favorite cameraman standing with Peter, who was getting a close-up of the brand on my front door. I suspected the angle was purposely done to also get Scarlet and me in the background. "The media is looking at every angle."

"Every angle?"

I nodded again. I tried to let her know how sorry I was for everything I said, everything she'd already gone through, and everything she was about to face, with a squeeze of her hand.

Scarlet squeezed mine in return and then looked at the reporters and customers throughout The Barn. "They're asking about me, aren't they?"

Again, I nodded. The whole thing didn't make any sense, but it seemed the media had a burr on its butt with Scarlet's name on it, and they had a hankering to dispose of that burr anyway they could.

Chapter Nine

I woke up the next day to my phone ringing on the counter in the other room. I rolled out of bed and nearly killed myself on a hungry armadillo loitering around her food bowl in the kitchen as I made a mad dash to answer my phone.

Princess squeaked her irritation as her toenails clicked across the wood floors toward her food bowl.

"Hello?" I tried to hide my sleepy voice, but failed miserably.

"Why didn't you tell me about your hair?" Based on her tone, I could picture Scarlet with one hand on her hip and one finger in the air.

"You were having a rough day."

"And someone attacking you with a branding iron isn't 'a rough day?'"

"That was a rough *night*," I explained, rather calmly. My dad still didn't know about the close call with the iron. The vandalism to the door was enough to add more wrinkles on his forehead—I didn't want to be the cause of him needing a facelift.

"And yet you still came and put me to bed and let the whole town see your hair looking like that."

"It wasn't the whole town, more like a handful of the town."

"Hazel Rock has a population of 2,093 people. How many do you think live in that neighborhood?"

"Are you volunteering to take care of my hair?" I said a silent prayer that she was. Anything else would just be cruel.

"Be at Beaus and Beauties in five minutes."

We hung up and I was across the street and knocking on the front door of her business in three.

Scarlet took one look at my hair that I hadn't even bothered to touch, and tsk'd her way to the sink with me in tow.

"Can you do something with it?"

"You do know who you're talking to, right?"

"But this is a little challenging." I pulled at the singed hairs.

"Stop pulling before I get it trimmed and treated."

"Yes, ma'am."

I closed my eyes and let Scarlet weave her magic while the local country music station played on the radio. It had never been my first choice of music, but it was ingrained in my soul just as much as Hazel Rock.

"Do you know who did this?" Scarlet asked.

Technically, the answer was no. I couldn't positively identify my attacker because he was in the dark and his hat shadowed his face. But if I was a betting woman, I'd put down a buck on Dalton being guilty. That's a dollar bill, not a hundred dollars. I don't have that kind of money to gamble. I went with the safe bet.

"I didn't see his face."

"But you have your suspicions," she persisted.

"Everyone has their own opinions; it doesn't make them right." That was as noncommittal a response as I could come up with, because I did have some serious suspicions.

"Why would Dalton attack you?"

I opened my eyes as she finished the rinse. I met her gaze as she wrapped the towel around my head. "I don't know. Why would *anyone* attack me?"

"It wasn't Dalton," she insisted.

I let it go. Scarlet was my best friend and even though we didn't know each other that well, she'd been there for my dad when I was gone and she'd been there for me when I came home. It was time I returned the favor.

We moved to her chair in the front of the salon and she began trimming off the damaged section of my hair.

"How do you want to approach this? I can put in an extension, braid that side or all of it, or I can give you a new style with the left side a little shorter—almost like you were pulling it back with a comb."

I didn't want an extension, but the current style wasn't going to cut it either. Braids were nice every now and then, but it wasn't something I wanted to wear every day. "Let's go with the new style. But what about the lack of curl. Will it come back?"

"A little conditioning with the trim and it will grow back as good as new."

"Let's do it."

An hour later and I wanted to cry, this time out of joy. Scarlet had worked a miracle on my hair. It was stylish and fun and everything you'd never expect a bi-racial woman to get in small town, Texas.

"Scarlet, how can I thank you?" I got up and hugged her tight, wishing some of my happiness would rub off on her. It didn't. "If there's anything I can do, please just ask, you know I'll do it."

Hope glistened in her eyes. "Anything?"

Fuzz buckets. Nothing was ever free, including friendship, and I was the perfect example of how much that bond could cost a woman. It was my turn to fish or cut bait.

"Anything," I said it with the confidence of a friend willing to go through the swamp and back.

"I've got something I want to show you in my trailer."

We made our way back to her Airstream trailer she had parked behind the salon. It was her home away from home—home being the salon. Scarlet's trailer was done in retro 70s style in shades of orange and yellow and was absolutely adorable. It was too small for my taste, but Scarlet loved it.

Scarlet turned down the air conditioning as we entered, and the motor kicked up and left a quiet, dull buzz for background noise. We sat down at the table and Scarlet pulled out an iPad.

"You bought an iPad! How awesome! Do you like it?" I asked.

Scarlet shook her head.

"You didn't buy it?"

She shook her head again and I was beginning to think Bobblehead-itis was a real disease.

"You stole it?" That at least earned me an eye-roll.

"It's Dalton's."

"Dalton Hibbs? What are you doing with Dalton's iPad?" I asked.

"He left it the night we went to The Shed. We were planning on coming back here."

"What do you want me to do?"

"Help me get it open."

"Don't you think you should give it to his manager, or the promoter, or Mateo?"

Scarlet shook her head again. I was beginning to hate Bobbleheads.

"Why not?"

"Because then they might find him before I do."

"What's wrong with that?"

"Charli, you think he attacked you the other night. Everyone in this town believes he's done something wrong." Her back straightened with conviction. "He hasn't."

"How do you know?"

"The same way I knew you didn't commit murder when Mateo put you in jail for Marlene's murder."

There was no arguing from that point on. Even though Scarlet hadn't known me very well when I'd returned to Hazel Rock, she'd believed in my innocence when I was the prime suspect in our real estate woman's murder. And since then, I'd come to realize that she could read people and their motives better than most. I just hoped she didn't become illiterate when her heart was involved.

Chapter Ten

As it turned out, Scarlet had more than just Dalton's iPad. She also had his backpack full of toiletries, a change of clothes, and a well-worn reference book, *The Dangerous Eight*, that was all about bull riding. She also had his hotel room key that she'd used twice a day for the past couple days. She'd even gone there before she woke me up that morning. But his bed hadn't been touched, nor had his clothes been moved from the drawers in the dresser. She was worried, and if I looked at it from her angle, I'd be worried as well.

"If I get past his password, then I can use the locator app and find his cell phone."

"Are you sure he has an iPhone?" I asked.

"Yup. We took a couple selfies with it."

"What passwords have you tried?"

"What makes you think I've tried any?"

"Really? You want to go there?"

"Okay, okay. I've tried his birthday. His brother's birthday. Combinations of the two. I tried his mom's and dad's birthdays—

"You know his parents' birthdays?"

"I even tried his dog's birthday. But nothing. I've only got three more guesses before it permanently erases."

I was beginning to think there was more to their relationship than I, or anyone else in the town knew. Just as I was about to ask her how serious their relationship had become, I thought of the numbers burned into my barn door.

"Have you tried 611?"

"It takes four digits."

"Try a zero in front of it."

Scarlet tapped in the numbers. The screen paused and we both held our breaths. The display darkened momentarily and I thought we'd been locked out for good, that maybe in her desperation, Scarlet had miscounted the number of passwords she'd tried. Then the image of a bull and his rider in the middle of the arena popped up on the screen. The rider's right hand held high in the air as the black beast he was riding twisted in a completely unnatural position. The bull's back feet were kicked so high off the ground, I suspected a grown man could walk underneath and still have clearance. But the cowboy was in complete control with a wicked grin on his face and a time clock reading 8.03 in the background.

"That's Wyatt. He was the best I've ever seen." Soft and reverent, Scarlet's voice seemed as lost in the memory as she was.

And I saw my opportunity to get more information from her. My daddy always told me, *"When a door is open, you don't hesitate. You walk in and seize the opportunity in front of you."* I did just that. I asked the question the whole town believed they knew the answer to, yet I wasn't so sure they did.

"Did you care for him?"

"I did. But I didn't love him. I loved to photograph him. He was pure magic when he was in his element." She sighed and said, "I took this picture."

"You took that?" I pointed at the picture I would have sworn was taken by a professional.

"Yup. And I gave it to Dalton when Wyatt disappeared. That's how we met."

Still stunned, I stated the obvious. "But you were questioned in Wyatt's disappearance."

"And *you* were arrested for a murder you didn't commit."

It was true of course, but if I was willing to confess to anything, it was being able to see why Mateo arrested me in the first place. Dad was selling The Barn because of debt and was marrying our Realtor. I was against the sale, and would have been opposed to his engagement to the realtor if I'd known about it, which I hadn't. And then there were the facts that she'd been killed with my belt and it appeared as if her scarf fell out of my purse, thanks to Princess depositing it on top of my purse without any of us noticing. Plus, I was the one who found her body. So yes, I'd looked guilty as sin, despite my innocence.

Scarlet scrolled through the different icons and finally found the locator app. I reached across her and touched the symbol that allowed us to go to another screen…with another password.

We tried names and places and combinations but couldn't figure it out. Scarlet was growing more and more frustrated by the minute, and it was beginning to look like a lost cause when we got locked out of the app for the second time in a row. I grabbed a couple bottles of water from her fridge while we waited.

"Did you keep in touch with Dalton after you gave him the photograph?"

Scarlet looked up from the screen she'd been staring at. "Why do you ask?"

"I was just wondering if he'd ever told you what his relationship was like with his brother."

"They were best friends. Why?"

"They weren't rivals?"

Scarlet shook her head as if she couldn't believe I was headed in the direction I was going. "No more than Cade and Mateo."

"Cade and Mateo aren't brothers."

"No, but they were like brothers…at least before you came back."

I didn't like the way that sounded. At all.

"I think they're still like brothers," I insisted.

"Maybe. But there's a gap between them as big as the Rio Grande."

If her goal was to shut me up, it worked. We sat in silence, both of us deep in thought until the app reset.

"What was the name of the bull his brother rode in that picture?" I asked.

"Lucifer."

I choked on the cool drink of water that felt anything but smooth as it grabbed hold of my windpipe. "His last ride was on the devil?"

Scarlet ignored my question, went back to the app, and typed in the word *Lucifer*. The screen changed, allowing us to choose between three items to locate: Dalton's iPad, which we already had, his MacBook Pro, and his phone. Scarlet looked at me for approval and I immediately gave it to her. I needed to know where Dalton was almost as badly as she did, but for an entirely different reason. I wanted to make sure his branding iron was never used again.

Scarlet tapped the icon for his phone and we waited while the little circle went around and round, at the top of the page. The screen finally displayed a map of North America and quickly zoomed into the state of Texas. We held our breath as it narrowed the search to the woods surrounding Enchanted Rock, a state park about thirty minutes away.

Scarlet's eyes filled with tears. "Do you think he went for a hike and got hurt?"

"I think he's probably holed up in a cabin in the park. That's what my daddy likes to do when he wants to be alone." Or when he was hiding from the law. But unlike Dalton, my dad had been innocent at the time. Dalton was as guilty as the day was long.

"Should I call him?"

"Has he answered the phone any other time you called him?"

"No."

"Has he answered any of the messages you left him?"

"No. Should I play the sound so he knows I'm looking for him when his phone starts to buzz?"

"I wouldn't. He already knows from your messages that you're looking for him. How many have you left?"

Scarlet seemed embarrassed but answered the question. "Five."

If I doubted before how hard she'd fallen, my doubt was completely erased. Scarlet's heart was as soft as a one-minute egg for Dalton Hibbs.

"Then let's go find him—and the next message, you can deliver in person."

Chapter Eleven

I called my dad and asked him to man the store. I didn't expect it to be too busy because it was Betty Walker's turn to have the auction at her Bluebonnet Quilt Shop to benefit The Cowboy Ranch. She was serving breakfast with goodies that just happened to be made by her ever-present companion, Franz, the owner/baker of the town's only bakery. The quilts were gorgeous, and the food would leave her customers content with full stomachs.

There was just one hiccup in our plan, though. As we exited the trailer Scarlet and I were bombarded with reporters who seemed to be led by Erik Piper and Taylor, his promotion partner for the Championship Bull Riding circuit. We'd hadn't heard the commotion over the air conditioner blasting inside the tiny trailer. Taylor, whose big mouth had spoken poorly of Dalton the previous day during the book art auction, wasn't mincing any words. It was like she'd set up a press conference in front of Scarlet's trailer to call Dalton out as a spoiled child. I would probably agree, if Scarlet wouldn't be so hurt by it.

"Dalton is leading the circuit in points, and like his brother, he tends to play the pampered champ very well," said Taylor. "This isn't the first time he's failed to show up for the preliminary events." She swung her long brown hair behind her shoulders like it was a silk curtain, all sleek and smooth and muttered. "It won't be his last, either."

Peter was the first to spot us and spit out a question directed toward Scarlet, as his cameraman Aiden edged young Aubrey out of the best spot for the best shot. Aubrey glared at her older rival, and snuck up under his arm, capturing the same viewpoint from a lower angle.

"Where are you hiding Dalton, Scarlet?" Peter held his mic past me for Scarlet's response. I knocked his hand back and scowled, but he was undaunted. Aiden was even pushier and I wondered if Aubrey would end up on the ground. Other reporters began throwing questions in our direction from all sides.

"Are you going to meet him now?"

"When will he be here?"

"Will he be here for the qualifying rounds tomorrow?"

I pushed Scarlet back in the trailer and slammed the door closed, which made several of the reporters less than pleased. Too bad.

"We need a plan B," I told her.

Scarlet's eyes filled to the brim as she clutched the iPad to her chest. "I don't have a plan B."

I hugged her, then pushed back, holding her at arm's length by her shoulders, and tried to give her the confidence I didn't feel. "I've got a plan."

I didn't, but my mind was racing to find one as I filled in the dead air between us with meaningless words that were meant to make her believe in me. "We're going to go out there and make them work hard for a story that has nothing to tell. It'll be so boring it'll make them border on fits of narcolepsy."

That brought a smile to her face and I hugged her again as the plan began to develop.

"Here's what we're going to do…"

Fifteen minutes later we walked out of her trailer and the microphones stopped in mid-air. Scarlet and I were ready to play our parts, at least until we managed to escape their hounding questions.

"I absolutely love what you did with my hair, Scarlet. Why if I was any happier, I'd drop my harp right through the clouds!" I added a giggle to my deepest Southern twang and bobbed my head like there was absolutely nothing in it. "And the bounce!" I was the living, breathing example of the gross overgeneralization of a Southern belle that the general public seemed to eat up. Daisy Duke had nothing on me. Other than curves, that is. The bottom of my T-shirt was pulled through the neck showing off my midriff and my jean shorts were slung low on my hips. Scarlet's boots were on my feet—killing me a thousand times over with each step since they were two and a half sizes too small.

"Girl, no man will be able to resist you." Scarlet played her role to a tee. Her hand was on her shapely hip as she took the steps one at a time like she was a famous Madame at a brothel and I was one of her girls. Her form-fitting red dress hugged her curves, which she flaunted like the most experienced seductress I'd ever seen wearing five-inch stilettos. "If y'all have girlfriends or special women who want to add a little spice to their lives, y'all send them my way, ya hear? Beaus and Beauties is a full-service salon."

Mouths dropped open. Reporters backed away as we walked into the back, and then out the front door of the salon without anyone following us.

Except Aubrey. She knew the drill. Her mom worked at Beaus and Beauties, and she came running through the alley completely out of breath as we were getting in my truck. Luckily for us, she'd had to push and shove her way through much bigger reporters only to get a glimpse of us closing the doors on my daddy's pick-up truck, which luckily was parked and waiting for us on Main Street.

"I don't know what you're up to, but I'm betting Scarlet will need a pair of shoes that are a little more versatile." Aubrey pulled a pair of tennis shoes out of her shoulder bag and passed them through the open window to Scarlet, who looked like a proud auntie.

"Thank you. Your momma will be very proud."

"And Liza's gonna be pretty P.O.'d," I added.

Aubrey cocked her head, a pout crossing her mouth. "Y'all know I'm just all sweetness and light."

I bumped fists with the young girl and we all laughed. Then Scarlet and I drove off into the rising morning sun.

We hit the freeway and I pushed the speed limit, knowing if Mateo stopped me, I could honestly blame it on the lack of feeling in my feet. Scarlet whooped out the passenger window like a teenager on a joy ride, her hands in the air, as her hair lost its perfection and her grin got bigger than all get-out. It was the happiest I'd seen her since she'd danced with Dalton.

We stopped in the next biggest town, Oak Grove, and I made a quick trip into Country Mart, the local department store, after I undid the knot in my T-shirt and put on a pair of my combat boots that were behind the driver's seat. I left Scarlet in the truck while I bought her a Rangers T-shirt and a pair of jean shorts. I didn't think I'd ever seen her wear something so plain, but it was meant to make her blend in a little bit. She was one of those women that commanded attention when she walked into a room. With her alabaster complexion and deep auburn hair, her big blue eyes drew you in and you couldn't look away.

Once we were on the road again Scarlet changed her clothes during the short spurts of open freeway between passing cars. We headed north on Highway 16 and then turned East on 965. If we'd been going to the park, we would have kept heading southeast, but the locator app had us turning off on a dirt road that led us to another one and then another. The last one lead to a dead end.

"Are there any cabins up here?" Scarlet asked, her tone hopeful.

"There must be." Although I was fairly certain there hadn't been any in this area when I was a kid. Hopefully, someone had built one.

I parked the truck and it chugged and clanked before the engine finally gave out what sounded like its last breath. We looked around before getting out, and I locked the doors.

Scarlet gasped. "O.M.W. It just went off-line."

"What went off-line?"

"His phone! It went off-line!" Panic laced her voice with an unnatural shrill.

"We can still trace his last position, though, can't we?" I asked.

"I don't know." Scarlet played with the iPad and let out a heavy sigh. "Yes. We just need to follow this path."

It wasn't exactly a path meant for humans, although I saw several pieces of very human trash like a milk jug, candy wrappers, a tire, a couple of rusty cans, and even a red high heel sticking out from under a bunch of leaves.

Well-worn, but extremely narrow, the path had probably been created by deer or coyotes. Despite it being broad daylight, I was starting to get a little spooked. The temperature had already reached the nineties at ten-thirty in the morning and sweat had immediately begun to drip down the middle of my back when we headed for the trail.

"Okay, I'll lead. Keep your hand on my shoulder and watch your screen so you can direct me which way to go."

"Deal."

The woods were made up of Live Oak trees that had stunted growth because of the lack of rain in the area. The ground was rocky, but the scraggly underbrush was still able to thrive and scratch our bare legs. Branches pulled at my hair and scraped across our arms as we turned this way and that.

"Are we close?" I asked. We'd walked for over ten minutes and I was beginning to worry that we wouldn't be able to find our way back out of the woods. A squirrel chattered to my left as if scolding me for being that stupid. Or worried, I'm not sure which.

"Just around the bend. That's where the cabin should be."

"You're sure? Cause you said that the last two bends." I could tell she was squinting at the screen from the grip on my shoulder getting tighter. She did that every time she concentrated.

We turned the corner and I stopped. Scarlet ran into my back. The iPad jabbing my eighth vertebrae.

"Ow!" Scarlet exclaimed. "Is it there? Do you see the cabin?"

I tried to answer, but all I could do was back away slowly. My stomach bottomed out, and my brained stopped working beyond my desire to protect Scarlet. I did everything I could to block her view as she struggled to get past me. It was an ugly dance of desperation on both sides. But this was the last thing I wanted Scarlet to see. It was the last thing anyone should see.

Because Dalton was there in front of me—buried much less than six feet under the dirt, with his arms outstretched, as if he'd been reaching through the earth in a mangled attempt to escape death. I recognized the tattered sleeves of his shirt; the same shirt he'd worn when he'd tried to brand my face…and his prized belt buckle, was the only headstone he'd been given.

Chapter Twelve

A couple hours ago, Scarlet and I had been celebrating our show for the media, now we were surrounded by them and we couldn't have cared less. There were more important things to worry about. Like the crime scene tape that not only circled the grave site, but also the path and area where I'd parked my daddy's truck. We couldn't see the truck from our current location, neither could the reporters gathering around the crime scene tape fifty feet behind Mateo's car, but they had helicopters flying overhead. And they knew who was sitting inside the police vehicle. We weren't about to slip through their fingers again.

Mateo had gone to some serious lengths to block off the dirt road at the last intersection before leading us to his car. Now I was sitting in the back seat, which was made smaller by a Plexiglas shield that the sheriff could fold up any time he wanted to. Then I'd be stuck in a cage, unable to open the door, unable to crawl over the seat. It made me somewhat claustrophobic. I would rather have been scrunched in the front seat between Mateo and Scarlet with his car computer under my backside and the barrel of his rifle pushed against my nose.

Instead I was sitting in back trying to control my breathing before I started to hyperventilate while the media waited to pounce on us as soon as we exited the car. Scarlet was shedding a bucket load of tears and the more she tried to stop, the more they flowed. Which softened Mateo's just-the-facts-ma'am attitude and allowed me to do most of the talking for the time being.

"Tell me again why you thought it would be a bright idea to use his iPad to locate his phone without telling me about it?"

"Because no one believed there was foul play involved. Everyone thought he went rogue. Off wilding with women or playing games to catch the attention of the media. You heard the other cowboys. Even the promoter said not to worry about him. It was all a joke to them." I shook my head; I'd been one of those people—not worried a bit about the man buried in the middle of the woods. But this was about as far from a joke as it got.

Mateo sighed, a long drawn out breath of capitulation that was completely out of character. He didn't give up information—not to me, anyway. "His manager reported him missing."

"What?" Scarlet and I asked in unison.

"His manager couldn't make this trip. His wife had surgery and he wasn't too concerned about the news reports until Dalton didn't return any of his messages. He started checking up on Dalton, but couldn't find him. He said it wasn't like Dalton at all and he reported him missing last night."

"O.M.W." Scarlet sobbed.

I reached for Scarlet's shoulder in the front seat and squeezed, but it didn't help. "He left his backpack at Scarlet's the night they went dancing. He was supposed to go back to her place afterward."

Mateo handed her a small packet of tissues. "Is that right, Scarlet?"

Scarlet blew her nose and sniffed. "Yes."

"Do you still have his backpack?"

She nodded, tears silently falling down her blotchy-colored cheeks.

Mateo jotted down something in his notebook and as hard as I tried to read it from the backseat, I couldn't.

"Before you work yourself up in a tizzy, Charli," Mateo's voice took that tone I didn't like, "I'm going to need both of you to come to the station and give statements. Okay?"

I started to argue. "Mateo, you know darned well—"

"I want to help. If there's anything I can do to help, please, please let me." Scarlet grabbed Mateo's forearm, her desperation obvious in the marks her fingernails were leaving. He didn't bat an eye, but rather patted her hand. His voice soothed and comforted. "I know you will Scarlet. There was never any doubt in my mind."

Scarlet's head bobbed up and down as if she was glad he understood her need to do everything she could to find justice for Dalton. Mateo's right eyebrow rose as he looked at me over the front seat and nodded in Scarlet's direction.

I got the hint loud and clear. Cooperation would take me far in my dealings with law enforcement.

"Can you tell me about the belt buckles you found in the woods?" he asked.

"I didn't see them; Charli wouldn't let me."

If she had, she'd have been haunted for the rest of her days. I didn't want that for her. It was hard enough for me.

"I saw it lying in the dirt like it was a marker...or a headstone at the end of the grave."

"What about the second one?"

"The second one?"

"There's another buckle."

Scarlet's eyes searched his. "O.M.W. Is it another grave?"

"We won't know for sure until the crime scene guys start excavating the site. But it looks like it's been there a while. I'm surprised the buckle was still there."

That brought more tears from Scarlet, the sting of sorrow burning in my own eyes as well. This really couldn't be happening. The blame, for the torment Scarlet was going through, rested solidly on my shoulders. I should have worked harder at convincing her to turn the iPad over to Mateo. But I'd failed her, and in the process, I'd failed Dalton as well.

I barely heard Scarlet's next question, but we were definitely on the same wavelength. "Do you think it's Wyatt?"

"Could be. Again, we won't know until the scene is processed and the lab runs some tests."

But we were all thinking the same thing—two brothers missing, two graves found.

"If I showed you photos of the belt buckles, could you tell me if they belonged to Dalton or Wyatt?"

"Dalton's, for sure. Wyatt, I don't know if I can or not."

I saw where that belt buckle was and there was no way I wanted Scarlet to get a look at it as well.

"I don't think that's a good idea," I said, shaking my head.

"It's up to you, Scarlet. It's only a couple close-ups of the buckles." Mateo looked at me like I was really doing him a disservice thinking he'd show Scarlet the gruesome images I couldn't wipe from my brain. I guess I was.

Scarlet took a deep breath and exhaled loudly. "I'll help, if I can."

He pulled out his phone and held it for Scarlet to view, but her eyes were closed. Scrunched so tight, it had to hurt.

"If you're uncomfortable—"

"No." Her eyes flew open. "I want to do this." She stared at the image and her head began to nod. "I'm pretty sure that's Dalton's."

Mateo pulled his hand back and swiped to the next picture. This buckle was older and dirtier; the rope design along the edge was crusted and the color had tarnished. The bull in the middle was still visible, though, along with the words, *"World Champion,"* with the year before Wyatt disappeared imprinted below.

"I—I'm not sure."

"It's okay." Mateo put his hand on her shoulder and looked her in the eyes. "It's okay. You've helped tremendously."

Scarlet's chin quivered. "I've got a picture of his buckle…and Dalton's."

"Can I see them?"

Scarlet pulled the iPad away from her chest for the first time since we'd found the graves and started to tap in the password.

"Wait. Is that Dalton's iPad?"

"Yes, sir. Why?"

"Don't open it. I'll need to get a warrant. Why don't you just give it to me and I'll put it in evidence."

Scarlet hesitated. "But the pictures are right here."

"I don't want to taint this case. Just give me the tablet and I'll get a warrant to access all of the content."

"Oh for heaven's sake, this is ridiculous." I grabbed the iPad before either one could argue and tapped in the password.

"Charli, dam—" Mateo reached for the tablet but the braces for the protective shield between the driver and the rear seat occupants blocked his path as I slunk back in the corner of the seat.

I held up the picture of Wyatt riding the bull. In plain view was the belt buckle he'd won the previous year. The same belt buckle that marked grave number two.

Chapter Thirteen

It'd been almost two hours since Mateo had said two words in my direction. After I'd shown him Wyatt's buckle his jaw had clamped shut and he'd snatched the iPad out of my hand.

Somehow Scarlet was oblivious to the tension, which was the only good thing I could say about the whole day.

Mateo talked to his two detectives on the scene, Youngblood and Wilson, whom I'd met on a previous investigation. Detective Youngblood had shared some of his wife's cookies with me and later brought his kids into The Barn to check out our new kid's section. He wasn't quite a friend, but I suspected he and his wife would become friends as long as I stayed on the good side of the law.

Which seemed to be a problem for me only when I was in Hazel Rock.

Mateo came back to the car and wiped the sweat off his brow with his arm. I had no doubt his deep brown uniform was scorching almost as much as his anger was toward me.

"Scarlet, you said you had a backpack of clothing that belongs to Dalton at your trailer. If it's all right with you, I'd like to search it."

"Her trailer or the backpack?"

Mateo's nostrils flared. He really didn't like me much when he was investigating a case. "Both, if that's okay." He held his palm up in my face in the universal signal of stop, but was probably telling me to talk to his hand. "I'm not looking for evidence against you. I'm looking for clues as to how Dalton could have ended up out here."

"Could have? You don't think that's him?" Hope glistened in her eyes, but Mateo dashed it immediately.

"He's been missing for a couple days... It's a fresh grave and it has his belt buckle on it and even though we don't have his phone yet, you followed the signal straight to the grave. We won't, however, be able to officially identify who's buried out there until the ME gets the dental records. Will you give me permission to search your trailer and take the backpack?"

"No," I answered.

"Yes." Scarlet overrode my response.

"Scarlet—"

"I've made my decision, Charli. This is the best I can do to help Dalton. And I'm going to help him."

"But—"

"No buts, Charli. Let's go, Mateo."

He nodded and met my eyes in the rearview mirror. "You better buckle up, Charli. That's the law."

I did as I was told, but stuck my tongue out at the back of Mateo's head. I felt like one of my belligerent five-year-old students, but I couldn't help it. Scarlet needed a lawyer. There were two bodies sitting over there in the woods and she'd already been questioned in regard to the disappearance of one of the men possibly buried there. On top of that, we'd led the police to the other grave—and that victim had last been seen outside the front of her salon. The cards were stacking up against her.

We made it to Hazel Rock in almost complete silence. The town was fairly quiet, except for the quilt shop, which had quite a few cars parked out front. Through the front window, we could see a crowd of people squeezed into every nook and cranny. Mateo parked by the salon and I had to wait for him to open the back door for me. The look he gave me as he bent down and peered through the window said if I didn't behave, he was going to put me right back inside. But then his gaze traveled down the street from where we'd just been.

"Grab that roll of crime scene tape," he ordered.

I heard the traffic before I saw it. A slew of media trucks had followed us from the crime scene. Those vehicles were the only reason I didn't ask questions about what Mateo was going to do with that tape.

"Fuzz buckets."

Mateo's left brow rose in question to my cuss word that was anything but scandalous. He turned toward Scarlet and began sheltering her from the camera lenses that were undoubtedly already recording as the reporters raced down Main Street, creating a fog of dust behind them. I was pretty sure the last car in the string couldn't see squat but the brake lights in front of it.

"Let's hurry up and get in the trailer before they figure out where we're going."

We dashed into the salon. Mateo locked the door behind us and turned the *Open* sign to *Closed*.

"The salon is closed for the time being," he said to the handful of women who were getting their nails done and their hair highlighted. Scarlet's sister looked up from the job she was doing on Sugar's nails.

"What's going on?" Joellen asked.

Those three words opened the floodgates. Scarlet's face crumbled and everyone was out of their chairs faster than Mateo could roll his eyes. I shrugged. It's what women did in Hazel Rock. If one cried, a huddle formed.

It took about thirty seconds for everyone to get the gist of the story and more tears to start flowing. Even I was having a hard time controlling the waterworks. So much misery deserved company.

"Ladies, I have to take Scarlet to her trailer," Mateo said when he returned from a brief trip out back. He put his arm around Scarlet's shoulder to guide her to that back room.

A knock on the glass made us turn around. Aubrey's face was pressed against the tinted window, her hand cupping her eyes so she could see in. Her mom made a move to open the door.

"Don't you let her in!" I yelled. "She's gone to the dark side!"

"Charli Rae Warren, you best not be bad-mouthing my baby," Mary growled.

"Mateo you better take Scarlet out the back," I said, but Mateo and Scarlet had already gone. The curtain to the back room was flapping like a set of saloon doors.

I tried to reason with Mary to give them more time to escape. "Aubrey's trying pretty darn hard to be like them." I pointed to the reporters who were ready to take the place of Mary's teenage daughter at the first moment of weakness Aubrey showed. All for the chance at the story. My pointing out the overzealous shoving turned out to be a mistake. Mary didn't take too kindly to her baby being pushed, and before I could do anything about it, her protective momma gene went into offensive mode. She opened the door to a pack of dogs after that proverbial bone, Aubrey leading the charge.

Aubrey, however, was the only one who made it past her momma. Mary started threatening to break every living bone in the bodies of the rest of the reporters. Her anger was burning hotter than the hinges of hell.

Recognizing her advantage, Aubrey scooted through the salon to the back door with me hot on her heels. She pulled up abruptly at the back door and asked, "Sheriff Espinoza, is this a crime scene?"

Mateo didn't answer. Instead, he gave her that commanding tone I hated when he used it on me. "Ms. Aubrey I need you to step back inside, and close the door."

"I know my rights, Sheriff, and the public has a right to know what's going on in Hazel Rock. Is this related to the two graves found earlier today at Enchanted Rock?"

"Ms. Aubrey, unless you'd like to find yourself in jail for criminal trespass, I suggest you back up, and close the door."

I heard the warning in his voice, but Aubrey shrugged her shoulders and bolstered her confidence just a bit too much. I would have been proud of her, if she wasn't being such a pain in my backside.

"I know my rights, Sheriff. I'm behind your crime scene tape—"

"And you're on private property. I have a request from the owner of that property to arrest anyone who refuses to leave," Mateo warned. It was his very last warning.

I knew it. I just hoped Aubrey knew it.

She looked at me and I shook my head, trying to get her to listen to that little voice of common sense. But on her other shoulder was the voice of her mentor, Liza Twaine, demanding she get the story, no matter what.

"I'll close the door, Sheriff," Aubrey said. Which showed she had more sense than me. I slipped past her before she could close the door and ducked under the tape. When the door clicked, it was my signal to lose it. And lose it big.

"What do you think you're doing putting bright yellow tape across the door that says *Crime Scene Do No Cross*?" My chin waivered with my anger. My frustration with the whole scene becoming a huge knot in my gut. "Are you trying to get them to nail Scarlet to the wall in the headlines?"

"Charli—"

"Oh, I can see the caption now." My hands raised to put the title in quotes. "*Black Widow of Hazel Rock Buries Rodeo Champs*."

"Charli—"

"Or better yet, *Brothers plagued with Scarlet Fever and Die*."

"Charli—" His voice was getting louder, sterner, but I was on a roll and there was no stopping my ire.

"What about, *For Whom the Southern Belle Tolls?* You've made her the number one suspect in a double homicide without saying a word!"

I stomped my boot on a paving stone leading to Scarlet's trailer; the whimsical flip flop shape seeming to mock my anger.

"That's enough, Princess!" Mateo took several steps forward and stopped within inches of my face. He was so close I could see the fire burning in his black eyes. The sweat beading on his forehead and upper lip in the sweltering afternoon heat. His irritation ticked in his jaw. And despite it all, he was still one of the best-looking men I'd ever seen in my life.

Drat the man.

"Someone broke into Scarlet's trailer."

"What?"

"Don't you find it a bit odd that the day you and Scarlet find two graves in the ground at Enchanted Rock her trailer gets broken into?"

"I—I—"

"So, yes, *ma'am*." His emphasis on ma'am was a little offensive. "This"—he waved around at the area behind the building he'd already taped off—"is a crime scene. And you're standing in the *middle* of my crime scene."

I wouldn't have been worried if my mind wasn't completely focused on my best friend. "Where's Scarlet?"

He sighed and stepped past me, wiping his forehead with his sleeve before pulling out a pair of rubber gloves from his back pocket. "Bobby Ray came and got her and drove her to his house."

"Daddy was here? How'd he get here so fast?"

"He saw us arrive with the media on our tails. He said you had a propensity to run out the back door without saying good-bye, so he figured he'd get in his car and be your getaway. I told him I wouldn't let you escape."

"Oh." My daddy was right of course. At seventeen I'd run out the back door of The Barn and packed my bags while my dad worked in the store. By the time he closed for the night, I was long gone. I teepeed several houses, then came back and teepeed The Barn before hightailing it out of town to the bus station. It was my aunt Violet who'd told him where I was when I arrived on her doorstep in Denver. Despite his attempts to get me to come back, it was decided I would stay with her. We hadn't spoken in over a dozen years until I came home a few months ago and we began to mend the tears in our hearts. But obviously, some of the damage was still there. From daddy's response, I supposed the fear of me up and leaving still resounded in his heart.

"Is there something I should be doing?" I asked.

"A tall glass of iced tea would be a welcome sight. I've got no one to process this scene so I'll be doing it myself. Then the two of us will get Scarlet and head for the station for your statements."

I couldn't tell if he was irritated with me, or if his tone was due to his day going to hell in a handbasket. Mateo gently opened the trailer and disappeared inside. And I made myself useful without running away.

Chapter Fourteen

A long night at the police department meant a long day at The Barn the next day. Scarlet and I had given our statements and Joellen had cleaned Scarlet's trailer after Mateo was done processing it. Only one thing had been taken by the thief: Dalton's backpack.

The media, however, was lead in a different direction, since they didn't have the full story. The morning, noon, and evening news pointed the finger at Scarlet. They focused on Scarlet's descent down the steps like she was Miss Kitty on that old Western series my dad watched on cable reruns. They were able to make Scarlet's three steps look like an entire staircase while the sound bite focused on her comment about Beaus and Beauties being a full-service salon. It was horrible—unless of course, Scarlet was planning to rent rooms by the hour. Which I seriously doubted.

Guilt racked my brain and tugged at my heart all day. Scarlet hadn't been able to show her face at the salon with the media parked outside and that's exactly the support system she needed. Yet we'd had to hide her, even from her employees to ensure Mary didn't let anything slip to her daughter, Aubrey. To keep Scarlet occupied, my dad had taken the day off and he and Scarlet were at his house creating book art in his garage. It was the only way to make sure the media didn't hound her while keeping Scarlet busy at the same time.

Her wardrobe was limited to the plaid shirts of a man pushing sixty, her shorts, and tennis shoes from one of the reporters currently searching for her since none of my clothes came close to fitting her curves.

Princess squeaked at my feet and I looked at my watch. Fifteen minutes until closing time.

"Are you hungry?" I asked.

Squeak, snuff, snuff.

"I take it that's a 'Yes'?"

Princess turned and walked to the side door next to the tearoom, where she stopped and looked at me. Then her head bobbed up toward the door handle. If I believed an armadillo could communicate, then I'd know she was telling me to close up shop.

The view out the front of the store showed no movement on Main Street. If anything, it looked like a ghost town. Even the media had abandoned their perches outside the salon. They'd completed their evening broadcasts and left to cover the candlelight vigil at The Ranch for the presumed loss of two of the best professional bull riders in history.

Dalton hadn't made it quite as far as his older brother, but everyone had expected him to surpass Wyatt. And the assumption was that both had been killed way before their prime and buried right next to each other.

Princess scratched at the door, demanding we leave for the day.

"Okay, let's go," I said. I'd already done the pre-closing rituals; locking the doors was last on the list. Princess and I went out the side door and up the exterior steps to the apartment and I looked up at the vacant iron bracket that should have been holding my mom's sign. "Eve's Gate" still needed to be rehung. Princess made her way to the top of the steps, hopping one at a time, her arched back making her look like a cat bouncing from one step to the next.

We walked into the apartment, I dropped my keys on a shelf next to the door, and looked around my childhood home. My bedroom was in the back overlooking the river, while my parent's old bedroom was toward the front with a secret panel in the bookcase that lead to The Barn's loft. The apartment was decorated the same as when I'd left at seventeen, which was left over from before my mom died when I was ten. Dad hadn't had the heart to change it, and so far, neither had I.

Princess took three steps toward her bowl before I stopped her. "You have to have a bath first."

She looked up at me and snorted.

I shrugged. "That's the rule, babe." Armadillos have an odor that is very distinctive. Luckily, they also like water, so Princess's daily baths didn't put her out too much. I filled her tubs, one scented with lilac soap and the other to rinse. Then, while she rolled on her back and slopped water over the rug, I prepared her can of cat food with a few vegetables added to the mix.

I toweled her off and put her bedazzled dog bowl down on the floor. I'd learned not to put the food down first; otherwise, she'd make a beeline for her dish while leaving a stream of water from the front door to the kitchen. And whether either of us wanted to admit it, we both enjoyed the process of me toweling her off. Princess enjoyed having her belly tickled and I liked having a pet for the first time in my life. I dumped her tubs of water over the railing of the steps and then went to clean myself up for the candlelight vigil.

When I arrived at The Cowboy Ranch thirty minutes later, the parking lot and the adjoining field were packed full of cars. The last glow of the sunset was abandoning the horizon and media trucks with tall satellite masts polluted the view from their perch on the street. Lack of space forced me to park right behind Liza Twaine's media van, and of course, it was Aubrey who pointed my daddy's truck out to her mentor.

"Ms. Warren, can you tell us if Scarlet Jenkins will be at the vigil?" Liza asked.

"I have no idea," I answered and stepped around Aubrey, who was trying to focus her camera lens on my face.

"Could we get an interview with you?" Liza persisted, jogging up the gravel drive after me in her trademark purple stilettos, which appeared to be made out of alligator. Her flouncy skirt lifted in the wind and she shoved it down. She should have watched the weather report. The wind gusts were going to make her the next generation's Marilyn Monroe.

"No, I'm here for the service. Not for an interview."

"What about tomorrow?"

I ignored her and gave her sidekick, Aubrey, a scowl before I escaped into the crowd. Catching a glimpse of Joe and Leila Buck on the other side of a mini stage, I made my way through tons of people I'd never seen before, to stand next to the owners of The Tool Shed Tavern. Leila hugged me and Joe engulfed us both in a bear hug that was over the top, but very comforting.

"How are you doing, Princess?" Joe asked. The man was never going to call me Charli.

"I'm okay, but I'm worried about Scarlet." I pulled back and looked at my friends.

"We're worried about you. Did you get a look at the man who tried to burn you?" Leila fingered my new hairdo as she searched my face for any signs of fear. If she kept that up, my emotions might get the better of me.

I shook my head. "No, it was too dark."

"Funny thing, that," Joe said.

"What do you mean?" I asked.

Leila shook her head. "Don't start that again, Joe. What happened to Charli has nothing in common with Sugar's accident."

"What accident?"

Leila glanced over her shoulder, her exasperation with her husband evident. "Last year during the rodeo we had a big thunderstorm blow through. We had power outage at the bar during a really busy night—"

"It wasn't that busy," Joe argued.

"Anyway," Leila continued. "The crowd got a little spooked and Sugar got burned on the back of her neck by someone's cigarette."

"That's what that scar is from?" I'd noticed the puckered scar at the base of her neck for the first time while she was working in The Barn just the other day.

Joe nodded with a deep, "Um-hmmm," that conveyed what he thought about the injury being accidental.

Leila elbowed him. "We banned smoking from that point on. It wasn't a big deal, since none of the locals smoked in The Shed, anyway. It just became an inconvenience for the out of town visitors. How's Scarlet taking all of this?"

"Not well, I'm afraid. I've never seen her like this. I had no idea she cared about him that much," I confessed.

Leila's eyes moistened as she handed me an extra candle she'd been holding. "She's not coming, is she? The reporters have been asking all kinds of questions about her relationship with Wyatt and Dalton."

"No. My dad and Mateo convinced her to stay away."

"That's a shame. I know she wanted to be here. She doesn't deserve any of this."

As the only other black woman living in town, I felt comfortable around Leila in a way I didn't with my other friends. Not that Leila and I were best friends; our bond was like an American meeting another American in a foreign country. A sense of belonging when you were a little out of your element, even though there was absolutely nothing wrong with that environment in the first place. Commonality brought us closer.

I wiped the corner of my eyes before they began to fill. "No, first Dalton, then the graves. And now this. At least Mateo doesn't think she's a suspect," I told her.

"Is there something we can do?"

"The media keeps looking for Scarlet...if you could point them in any direction but hers, that would be great."

Joe smiled that big grin. It was scary how easily it suckered people in; he should have it registered as a weapon. "I'm pretty good at leading people astray...."

Leila elbowed him in the gut. Her short stature concealed her strength. Joe grabbed his stomach and doubled over in feigned injury. Some people gawked and wondered how to react to his antics; his close friends knew it was an act. Even Cade, who was up on the stage preparing to start the vigil, recognized the part Joe was playing. If it hadn't been a solemn occasion, Cade would have been calling Joe out for the stunt he was pulling. Instead, he shook his head.

"I should have warned you about him before I left town," I told Leila.

"You were too busy trying to get out of the trouble he led you into."

"Hey, you can lead a horse to water—" Joe started.

"But you can't make it drink." Leila and I finished and turned away as Cade took the stage with Taylor on his arm. The promoter was few years older than Cade, but the way her body was plastered to his side suggested she didn't mind their age difference in the least. I couldn't help the frown forming on my face as Cade started introducing the riders who wanted to say something on behalf of the Hibbs brothers.

Joe leaned over, his oversized hand resting on my head and ruffling my curls. "Girl, you are too cute when you're jealous."

"I'm not jealous," I hissed. At least I didn't want to be.

Leila elbowed him again. "Stop snapping her garters, Joe. You know he's her weak spot."

"What? The only garters I snap are the ones you wear, darling." Joe pulled his wife up to him as he nuzzled her neck.

Joe's teasing didn't bother me. What bothered me was that Leila thought Cade was my weakness. Fuzz buckets.

Cade said a few words, then rejoined Taylor in the row of chairs lined up on the stage that were occupied by town leaders. Dusty Lamb was the next person to take the microphone. He'd been on the same team as Dalton and felt like Dalton was the big brother he never had. The two had become close in the past three years. He told stories of Dalton encouraging him, being there for him when his mother died, and the friendly competition between them. Sniffles started and spread throughout the crowd when his voice broke while delivering a promise to be there for Dalton and Wyatt's parents.

Sly Alexander jumped up on the stage next. He was the oldest rider on the circuit and knew Wyatt better than he'd known Dalton. To him, Dalton was just like his older brother and women loved them both. Most of the men in the crowd thought that was funny, but it was entirely different for the women, including Taylor. She immediately got out of her chair and shooed Sly straight off the edge of the platform to the righteous nods of at least half of the crowd, including myself.

A local pastor, seated next to Cade, stood and asked everyone to light their candles. Those who didn't have candles held up their cell phones, illuminating the night. The pastor said a short prayer for the two souls buried near Enchanted Rock and for Wyatt and Dalton, wherever they may be, assuring the crowd that their spirits would live forever in the community of Hazel Rock, and The Cowboy Ranch. He prayed for a speedy investigation that would hopefully give the Hibbs family some peace and ended his prayer with an, "Amen," that was heartily repeated by the crowd.

Cade was about to disperse everyone who had gathered when Travis Sinclair, Dalton's main rival, got up on stage and whispered something in his ear. Cade nodded his approval and handed the mic to Travis.

We all watched as Travis took off his cowboy hat to address the crowd. "Dalton and I have had a very spirited rivalry for several years. Because of that, I'd like to say a short prayer from the hearts of all the bull riders."

Everyone bowed their head.

"Dear God, I wish you would bring Dalton back so I could compete against him this weekend." Several "here, here's" were heard from the other riders as Travis paused.

"I gotta tell you"—he looked around the crowd—"only Dalton would leave the fans hanging like this."

I opened one eye and peeked at the handsome cowboy with his head still bent at a respectful angle. Unsure where Travis was taking his prayer, I noticed I wasn't the only one in the crowd who eyed the stage suspiciously.

Travis didn't seem bothered as he went on. "Just when I was going to prove to the world that he couldn't carry my spurs, much less wear them, he goes and messes with the wrong woman. Again."

Some cowboys in the front row, lifted their heads. Straightened their shoulders. And began to frown at the tone of Travis's petition to God. It wasn't prayerful at all, and hats were returning to heads as several jaws tightened.

Travis was undaunted. He finished his prayer with a misplaced passionate plea as Cade stood up. "I hope he burns with the devil. Amen." He held the microphone straight out at a ninety degree and dropped it to the stage with a loud thud. The crowd gasped. The clunk and clattered, however, was drowned out by the rumble of the crowd as a rush of masculinity headed in Travis's direction. Some in support, some ready to take his head off, as fists started flying. Cade began corralling Travis and Taylor back away from the angry mob.

Joe pushed Leila behind him even though she was ready to join the melee and help break up the fights erupting all around us. That's when I saw Jessie and Daisy Mahan attempting to get out of the ruckus near the stage. The elderly man was attempting to shield his wife with his body but was having difficulty getting through the crowd.

I pushed forward, ducked a wild punch that came out of nowhere, and heard it land on someone else's face with an "ooff." I bumped shoulders with a cowboy rearing back to hit another, then bounced off a belly that had more spring than muscle. I was having a hard time staying on my feet and wasn't sure anyone would listen if I tried to interfere, so I just kept my head down and did the only thing I could do to get Jessie and Daisy the heck out of Dodge—I began stomping on feet. One boot here. Another there. There was a yelp, a stomp, and then another stomp before an elbow hit me on the temple.

"Oowww!" It hurt like the dickens and I staggered. When I saw a tennis shoe in the midst, I lashed out and stomped hard, the soft leather shoe getting the full brunt of my anger.

"Aye! Dios Mio!"

Recognition of his voice made me cringe.

I looked up as Mateo grabbed my arm and numerous uniformed officers started rounding up the crowd. It was surprisingly more under control than when I first started ducking punches.

"Mateo? Sorry, I didn't know that was you. I've never seen you wearing tennis shoes." I know it sounded stupid, but it was true. I'd also never seen him wearing basketball shorts and a T-shirt with the sleeves cut-off. On his days off, he always wore cargo shorts, hiking boots, and a T-shirt with the sleeves intact.

"When you're coaching basketball, you wear tennis shoes," he growled.

"You coach?"

"Yes, at the YMCA in Oak Grove."

"Oh."

"So if you're done stomping on my feet, can we let my officers handle this mess and get you out of here?"

"Wait, Jessie and Daisy Mahan need help!"

Mateo pointed toward the stage. Somehow the elderly couple had reached the platform and were standing there shaking their heads at all the other cowboys in the crowd. From the looks on their faces, I suspected Jessie had partaken in similar events back in the day.

"Oh. I guess they don't need my help."

The look on Mateo's face said he didn't think they ever needed my help, but he wisely kept his mouth shut.

The initial noise that had been deafening, lowered to a disgruntled grumble. The crowd was calmer, but a few fights continued among some guys who were too stupid to know when to say when.

"Now, can we get out of here?" Mateo asked.

I wasn't that stupid. "Sure."

Mateo and I walked toward the ranch, away from the media. Through it all, I couldn't help but notice that Travis was smiling from ear-to-ear, embracing his image of the bad boy in the circuit, while Cade looked like he was ready to tear his head off. Yet, I also wondered if Travis didn't have the biggest motive in the world for wanting Dalton dead—fame and a whole lot of money.

Chapter Fifteen

"At the rate you're going, you need self-defense classes," Mateo said as we drove through the center of town.

"Should I get a gun?" I asked.

"No! Not unless you plan on training with it eight hours a week for the rest of your life."

I scrunched my nose in distaste. "I can't see myself doing that."

"I can't either. But you do need to learn how to get yourself out of the jams you keep putting yourself in."

"It was a candlelight memorial! How am I supposed to prepare for that?"

He was completely unfazed by my defensiveness. "It started going bad, and you ran into the thick of it, instead of the opposite direction."

"Jessie and Daisy were standing up front when all heck broke loose. I was going to help them."

"If you wanted to help them, you should have gone around the crowd, not through it."

That warm feeling started spreading through my chest. I looked at Mateo through the corner of my eye. "Were you spying on me?"

"You mean, was I watching out for you? Yes."

"Why?"

"Does the other night at The Barn or a branding iron ring a bell?"

Somehow finding a dead body had wiped that memory from my head. "I wanted to talk to you about that. I don't know why I didn't say this when I gave my statement, but I recognized Dalton's shirt…at the grave site."

Mateo shook his head. "Dalton didn't attack you."

"Are you sure? Cause I could have sworn the shirt looked the same."

"I'm sure."

"Well if it wasn't Dalton, then it was just a random crime."

"I don't have any other reports of someone nearly getting their face tattooed with a branding iron." He held his hand up when I started to protest. "A branding iron that had a dead guy's rodeo number on it."

I hadn't even thought about that. This whole time I'd thought Dalton had been the one leaving his mark on the barn and my hair, but it couldn't have been Dalton. When I was attacked, Dalton was in a shallow grave. I shivered. The grotesque view lived in my dreams. Not to mention my thoughts throughout the day.

No, unless Dalton had been a zombie stepping out of his grave the night I was assaulted, he wasn't the one who left his mark on The Barn.

Mateo parked in front of my family's store and turned to look at me. "Since you returned to Hazel Rock, you've been the victim of several aggravated assaults."

"Are you telling me that's my fault?"

"I'm telling you that your decisions need to improve. You have to listen to the instincts in your head."

"I am. There was a man outside The Barn whom I caught in the middle of an act of vandalism. I startled him, and he lashed out. Had I seen him first, I would have called 911. Then tonight an elderly couple I consider friends, were in danger. Anyone would go to their aid."

"I saw a lot of people who didn't care one whit what happened to Jessie and Daisy."

Before I could argue further, Mateo got out of his patrol car and came around to the passenger side to open my door. When I got out of the car, I couldn't help but notice how he didn't step back. In fact, he closed the door and stood so close, looking down at me, that I could feel the heat emanating from his body. The breeze was light, the stars were bright, and the blinking yellow traffic signal at the end of the street was the only witness to a perfect scene for a first kiss.

My heart pittered, and skipped the patter altogether. Mateo wasn't as tall as Cade, yet he was still several inches beyond my five feet nine. As I looked into his chocolate brown eyes, I wanted to melt.

"You are a magnet for trouble."

"Are you trouble?" I asked, my voice sounding breathy even to my own ears.

The corner of his mouth quirked before a full-blown smile spread across his face. I'd only seen it a few times, and if he used it all the time, women would be falling like flies at his feet. It was that powerful.

"Yeah, I'm trouble."

His gaze dropped to my mouth and I knew this was it. The moment I'd wanted, and dreaded at the same time.

"I'm trouble because you still have some unfinished business with our mayor."

"Cade? What about him?"

"You have a past together."

"Keyword—'past.'"

Mateo grabbed my hand and kissed it. His lips were warm against my skin and in that single act, I knew I wanted more. No one had ever kissed my hand before. It was romantic, disappointing, encouraging, distracting, not enough and too much all at the same time.

"The look on your face says it's not that far in the past."

"He hasn't called me once in the past two months."

"Yet you've been hoping he would."

Okay, he had me there. Drat the man. Everything always came back to Cade. It was frustrating. Maddening. I hadn't had a date in…I didn't know how long, and Cade was keeping me from having one now. Fuzz buckets.

"Come on, I'll walk you to your door." Mateo laced his fingers through mine and we walked across the courtyard and through the gate to the steps leading to my apartment.

"I'm glad to see your dad hasn't rehung the sign yet. I'd hate for your mom to give me stitches."

"You don't honestly believe my mom's spirit rules that sign, do you?"

Mateo raised his left brow, his eyes dancing with mischief. My mom would have loved him.

"Let's just say I'm not a gambling man."

"Some would say you're taking a gamble just being with me."

"Risking life and limb is different. I do that for a living. But I aim to make nice with the mommas of the women I pursue."

"Does that mean you're pursuing me?" I asked as we climbed the steps to my apartment.

Mateo waited for me to dig my keys out of my purse and I opened the door. "That means I'm interested, but I'm also a patient man." He turned and kissed my forehead. "Good night, Charli."

"You're the only one who doesn't slip and call me Princess. Why?" I asked.

"That's because I'm interested in the woman in front of me. Not the girl who grew up in Hazel Rock."

"Oh."

Mateo bent down and kissed my forehead again. "Good night, Charli." Before I could say a word, he headed down the steps.

"Be ready at 7 AM," he called over his shoulder.

"For what?"

"You've got self-defense classes in The Barn."

"I didn't hire anyone. Besides I told you, I can't afford lessons."

"For you, they're free."

"Who's teaching me?" I asked.

He turned and grinned at me right before he disappeared around the corner of the bookstore. "Me," he said, and was gone.

I sighed. One of those soft, pleasant sounds women make when a man does something that turns their brain to mush and their heart to Jell-O. A squeak at the bottom of the steps drew me out of my haze.

I looked down to see Princess. "Good evening, Princess. I hope you were a good girl while I was gone."

Princess twitched. And when I say "twitched," I mean she smiled, just like a dog or a cat smiled at its owner. Her nose wiggled. Her eyes glistened, and the corners of her mouth turned upward right before her entire body waggled and started hopping in my direction. I waited and scratched her ears as she did figure eights around my ankles.

"Come on girl. You need another bath."

We went inside together and after her bath, we headed for the bedroom. I opened the balcony doors and let the breeze blow in while I watched the stars twinkle from my bed. It was the same thing I'd done as a kid, listening to the sounds of frogs looking for a mate on the river's edge as crickets serenaded theirs. The water lapped softly against the rocks as I drifted off to sleep.

Luckily no zombies visited my dreams or disturbed my slumber until the alarm clocked buzzed at six-thirty.

I may have been a kindergarten teacher, but mornings were never my thing. I dragged myself out of bed and headed for the shower. After a quick rinse, I dressed in a pair of gym shorts and a tank top. Then I brushed my teeth and put my hair in a ponytail before slipping into my tennis shoes.

Princess was still in her bed, fast asleep. I'd say she was sawing logs, but it was more like fingernails scratching against a chalkboard. I didn't bother going outside; instead, I made my way through the secret door in the front bedroom. I used it on my lazy days or days when someone wanted me to wake up with the rising sun.

I went downstairs to find Mateo waiting for me at the front door.

"You're early," I said.

"You're late," he replied.

His dark, almost onyx, hair was damp at the edges and his jaw was unshaven. I think it was the first time I'd seen him with heavy stubble. He was once again wearing basketball shorts, but today he had on a white T-shirt with sleeves that read *Los Bravos Muertos* on the front with a scary-looking skull.

"It's a band if you're wondering. I don't have a death wish."

"Good to know. Can you tell me what that is in your hand?"

Mateo held up a Styrofoam bat. "This?" He smirked. "This is my weapon."

"And just exactly what do you plan to do with that weapon?"

"Beat you."

"You really think so?"

Mateo chucked me under the chin like I was a little girl and walked past me.

"Before we get started, I need some caffeine. Would you like a glass of tea?"

He shook his head. "Water. A wedge of lemon would be nice."

"Do you ever indulge in anything else?"

"Overtime makes me turn to black coffee." He said it like he was admitting he hoarded chocolate in his closet.

"Ooooh! The horrors!"

I got our drinks and put them in to-go cups. We ascended into the loft and Mateo asked me to help rearrange the furniture to give us a large open area to work. For the next hour and a half, I learned high blocks and low blocks and middle range blocks. From the left, the right and straight on. It was an exercise in reaction time, and my reactions were pretty dadgum slow. By the time we finished, my arms felt like they had road rash from that stupid Styrofoam bat.

As we made our way back downstairs, I was pretty sure I was the only one who'd worked up a sweat. We went into the tearoom and I made us another round of drinks and then got out the leftover muffins from the media panel we'd hosted for The Cowboy Ranch. Mateo settled for a bran muffin that looked as good as cardboard and I chose a cranberry strudel with vanilla icing drizzled over the top. It was heaven.

We sat down at the table and began talking about nothing of importance. Then out of the clear blue Mateo asked, "When were you going to tell me about the pictures?"

I stopped, mouth full of muffin. "Pictures?" I mumbled over the crumbs tickling my throat that made it almost impossible not to choke.

Mateo sighed. "Did you really think we wouldn't be able to see that you had e-mailed some photos from Dalton's iPad to your email account?"

I chewed the bite in my mouth, the heavenly taste gone, replaced by dry, gritty sawdust. It went down just about as easily, scraping and tearing at my throat. "No. I just didn't expect you to find out so soon." I gulped some sweet tea to get through the next few moments.

"Really? Why?"

"I don't know, I just didn't."

"So tell me what you planned on doing with them?" He leaned back and folded his arms across his chest. His legs stretched out in front of him and brushed mine.

"If you'll remember, I didn't have the iPad long enough to do anything with it when I was with you and Scarlet."

Mateo's gaze was unwavering as he waited for me to continue.

"I did it before we found his body, while Scarlet was in the bathroom and getting her shoes."

"So Scarlet doesn't know you did this?"

I shook my head, a guilty smile forming on my face.

"What were you going to do with them?" he pressed.

"I was going to find out who he was cheating on Scarlet with and catch him in the act."

His leg brushed my own. I was pretty sure he did it on purpose. But not entirely.

"Did you really think she'd listen to you when you delivered the news that Dalton was seeing other women?"

"I don't know. I just couldn't stand by and let her get her heart trampled on."

His leg brushed mine again. *That* was definitely on purpose. I returned the favor—loving the way his leg hair tickled my calf.

"In my experience, only the owner of a heart can protect it from getting broken."

"You've had experience with a broken heart?" I suddenly realized there was a whole lot I didn't know about Mateo. But his eyes gave nothing away and he certainly wasn't going to divulge any more personal information. He was waiting for me to capitulate. "You're right. I just couldn't stand idly by, and watch her get hurt."

"I need you to promise you won't try to interview the riders about Dalton," he said over the top of his water glass.

"But—"

Mateo put his glass down, his mood serious, giving me no options but to listen. Especially since his leg was now applying steady pressure to mine. "No buts, Charli."

I blew out an exasperated breath. "Fine."

"I need you to promise."

I blinked. "You don't trust me?"

"I don't think you trust yourself."

"That's ridiculous."

"Is it? Then promise me and put my mind at ease so I don't have to worry about you being a victim."

"Okay, I won't interview them," I promised.

"Thank you. Now, that wasn't so bad, was it?"

The sound of my teeth grinding told him otherwise. What Mateo didn't realize, was that I hadn't promised I wouldn't interview any paramours, promoters, or stock contractors. I knew I was pushing the envelope on trustworthiness, but I didn't care. First, and foremost, was Scarlet—even though I knew it would damage any chance of Mateo rubbing against more than just my calf.

I was prepared to do whatever it took to clear Scarlet's good name.

Chapter Sixteen

Mateo taught me several methods of strikes that wouldn't leave me with a broken hand, but would stun an attacker long enough for me to escape. Pressure points turned out to be a very effective way to release some of my frustration while not really hurting Mateo. Much.

He left and came back forty-five minutes later in uniform. He gave me a ride to the rodeo and we found my dad's truck still parked on the street where I'd left it. I decided to leave it parked in the same location so I could make a quick getaway after I did my volunteer shift at the ticket window that afternoon. Mateo left with a warning for me to keep my promise.

I planned to—I would not question any of the riders. Today, at least.

As he drove away, I waved and headed toward the stables behind the ranch. I still had several hours before I had to work, and I figured the best place to get information was from the cattle hands and stock contractors who owned the bulls. They traveled with these riders on tour and knew exactly who was doing what.

The Cowboy Ranch itself was about a four thousand square foot house that had been converted into a nursing home for old, and/or injured cowboys from the circuit. They were a staple in our community and kind of a treasured mascot for Hazel Rock and Oak Grove, since the ranch was located in-between the two towns. The house had been converted from an old dude ranch to the nursing home back in the mid-nineties when bull riders didn't have the potential to make as much money as they did today. And although the pay could reach into the millions now, only the select few riders at the top of the leader board ever attained it. Everyone one else struggled to make ends meet and worked multiple jobs. Teams had started to form in the past few years and sponsorships were starting to come into play.

Behind the ranch, an indoor arena had been built by none other than the Calloway family. Cade's family was the source of most of the money in the community. It always had been, and I suspected it always would be. They'd gone all out on the arena, making it handicap accessible and handicap friendly for those who had suffered life-altering injuries. It seated up to a thousand people, but most of those seats were only filled once a year at The Cowboy Ranch Invitational.

As a volunteer for the ticket booth, I had a pass to access the arena and the barn. The residence, was off-limits to everyone except those with special invitations. I made my way around the outside of the arena and watched some of the clowns entertaining the early birds. I nodded to a few of the riders I recognized from the press conference and ducked out of the way behind some rodeo tack when I saw Taylor walking by with a heavy-set man in a western suit too small for his belly. He had a cigar hanging out of his mouth and the cloying scent nearly made my breakfast muffin rise from the deep recesses of my stomach.

I pretended to be working on a saddle as they passed, and listened to what I could.

"There's too much money at stake to risk it." The man's words sounded wet as he spoke through lips that were way too big for his face. Taylor's mouth pulled back in a grimace, and I had no doubt the man had just given Taylor a nasty shower of spit.

"Everything will be fine. Erik's in Austin handling it now. There's nothing to worry about," she replied.

The last thing I heard as they exited the arena was the man telling Taylor she had better hope everything went well.

I let go of the strap on the saddle, hoping I hadn't messed anything up for the owner and walked down to the bull pens. The bull riding event wasn't scheduled to start until noon, so the stalls were pretty quiet. The sixty-some animals had already received the required ten to fifteen pounds of protein-heavy grain and were quietly milling around their stalls. Quiet, for that many eighteen hundred-pound bulls that wanted sex when no cows could be found however, wasn't exactly like visiting a library. Especially since they were housed next to a bunch of other males in the same situation.

I headed down the aisle, toward the back of the barn where the cowhands were known to congregate, but as I turned the corner a bull kicked the stall. He huffed and snorted and then bellowed. I jumped back and the pen door was flung open as two men emerged from the stall. To say I was alarmed would be an understatement. I knew exactly how mean those bulls could be and I expected an angry animal to come racing out after them.

But instead of a beast chasing us down the middle of the barn, I faced a cowboy I didn't know, along with a skinny young man who had to be the traveling vet tech by the look of his white lab coat and name tag that'd been washed too many times to read. The cowboy cussed as he slammed the pen closed and latched the door.

"He'll never make the buzzer."

They stopped when they saw me and there was a moment of silence. Kind of like we were all saying, "Oh, shoot." Yet I wasn't sure why I'd be saying it, except from the looks on their faces.

"Ah, hi. Is everything okay?" I asked, not sure if that was the right thing to say or not.

"Who are you? This is a restricted area," the cowboy demanded.

I never take well to demands. Especially the rude kind. I picked up the ID pass hanging on my neck and waved it in his direction. "Authorized," I said, with probably too much sass.

"Then mind your own business." He grabbed the skinny vet, who was clutching a medical briefcase and a red plastic trash bag that reminded me of biohazard bags in a doctor's office—it was so thick, I couldn't make out the contents. The tech looked over his shoulder as they walked off. His eyes were wide, his demeanor far from comfortable around the bulls…and me. A peek into the stall they'd exited yielded nothing. It was completely empty. The bull next to it, however, seemed agitated. I looked at his name plate on the stall.

Twister Mister
The Starlight Corral
Pierce Brown

Unsure of what I had just interrupted, I headed toward the back of the barn as I'd originally intended.

Forty-five minutes later, I emerged with the knowledge that the ranch hands had respected Dalton and didn't have one bad word to say about him. I chalked that up to a strong male bond, I wasn't about to crack. That, and their unwillingness to speak poorly of the dead. I did notice, that a few of them sported black eyes, busted lips, and one actually had a crooked nose. It looked like it hurt like the devil and when he talked he sounded like he was trying to communicate through layers of cotton.

On my way back down the rows of bulls, I heard a squeal and a groan of distress from the stall belonging to Twister Mister. I peered inside, but couldn't see the animal. I heard another pathetic, guttural moan and felt the agony it was going through. It was one of those sounds that tugged at every thread of humanity in your body. To move on would be the mark of a cold, heartless person. Unable to just leave and mind my own business, I called out to see if anyone else was around.

"Hello?"

No answer.

"Hello? There seems to be something wrong with this bull."

The only sound that met me was the distressed groan of the eighteen hundred-pound animal that had a reputation of challenging the devil.

"Fuzz buckets." I looked around for a stool but didn't see any. Not willing to open the stall and meet the bull face to face, I climbed up the front of the door and hung on for dear life. I peered over the top and was surprised to find the bull lying down on its side.

"I'll bring help. I promise," I told the beast.

I was about to jump down when I felt hands against my ankles. I started to look back, expecting to see Mateo or some equally irritated male, who thought I was butting in where I didn't belong. Except I didn't have time for anything, but a gasp. My feet were suddenly lifted airborne; away from the railing, and shoved up over my head. I grabbed at the top board of the stall as my body leaned over the top rail in the balancing act of my life.

"Stop!" I yelled. "This isn't funny!"

The bull's eyes shot wide open below me. If I'd thought the animal was dying, I'd been mistaken. Lethargic, or lying on its death bed, obviously wasn't in the animal's vocabulary—especially when he made eye contact. It was the scariest look any creature had ever given me. I felt like I was viewing my death through his vantage point—possibly quick, but extremely painful. A second shove caused my body to teeter at the top of the gate, and then go completely over the edge, sending my feet over faster than my head.

"Ahhh!" I yelled as my head nearly slammed into the steel and wood fencing. Grasping at life with all my strength, I somehow hung on to the top of the stall. Shoulders straining, I faced the bull as my feet flung toward the ground. Pain radiated through my hands as something struck my fingers from the other side and caused my grip to fail. I tried to maintain my balance, land on my feet as the bull struggled to get up, but I couldn't. The momentum was too powerful and I slammed to the pen floor on my hands and knees. I'd literally flipped into the stall; flying eight feet over to the floor with so much force, I wasn't sure I hadn't damaged my hands or my knees. The scent of manure and urine broke through my panic about the same time the bull snorted—hot, putrid air filled with spittle and foam blasted across my body. I didn't have time to think, or worry, or do anything but look up into the bloodshot eyes of Twisted Mister, a white bovine with black speckles that made him look like chocolate chip ice cream. The look on his face, however, told me I was the one who looked like dessert, not him.

I scrambled to my feet at the same time he gained his balance, and he caught me as I ran toward the side wall. The blow from his head somehow didn't involve his massive horns, but I flew into the wall with so much force I could have sworn my body smashed through the enclosure.

No such luck.

Avoiding those stout and sturdy horns with blunt ends that could still pierce my chest, I began climbing and clawing toward the top just as he came at me a second time. Only this time, he wasn't intent on just ramming me into the side of the stall. No, this time, he put his head down, bellowed at me, and lifted me up and over the wall. I landed on my back in the middle of a pile of hay.

I hadn't done a flip in ten years. I certainly hadn't been prepared to do one today, let alone two.

Once more I scrambled to my feet, expecting to confront whoever had knocked me into the bullpen. But the stall was just full of hay. No bovine. No scumbag willing to feed me to the animals. Just me and hay...until the door suddenly slid open.

Chapter Seventeen

I yelped. Remembering Mateo's training, I prepared to block an oncoming assault.

"Ms. Warren, what are you doing here?" Travis Sinclair looked me up and down and then looked around the stall.

I'm afraid my next question was full of expletives for the man who'd thrown me over the top of the stall. By the time I was done, he'd tipped his hat back and crossed his arms.

"Hold on now, Ms. Warren. I was just walking through the barn when I heard you screaming."

"I don't scream," I ground out.

"What would you call it?" He genuinely sounded perplexed.

"I'd call it yelling for help after some no-good piece of trash sent me to my death over the top of the stall where I got to meet Twisted Mister, face to face!"

Now that I was thinking about it, my butt hurt, my ribs were sore, and I was feeling a little woozy. I bent over and grabbed my ribs. Travis advanced and I reared back like a cornered animal: fists up, teeth bared, mouth sneering, with a possible growl to go along with it. I was a cornered animal and no one, I mean no one, was going to throw me in with that bull or any other bull ever again.

"Whoa." Travis put his hands up in the air in the traditional signal of surrender. "I didn't mean to frighten you. I just want to help."

I still wasn't taking any chances. "Then back away from the door and let me out."

He did as I requested, and I limped out of the stall, but still didn't feel any safer, since this was exactly where I'd started out.

"Now can I help?" he asked. His voice was soft and respectful, everything it wasn't the previous night when he'd bad-mouthed Dalton and started a brawl at the memorial. The change made me trust him even less, but I really needed to sit down and inventory my injuries.

"Go get someone else. That's how you can help."

When he started to turn, I added one more qualifier on my request. "Make sure it's someone from Hazel Rock."

"Yes, ma'am." His hand went to the brim of his hat in another gesture of respect right before he left, rounding the corner and disappearing from my sight. It was only then that I slumped against the wall and bumped my head against a paper towel dispenser

"Ow." I was too tired and hurt too much to lift my arm and rub the back of my head. It was the least of my worries.

I slid down to sit on the concrete floor and winced. My backside hurt and as I looked down at the floor for a softer place to sit, I couldn't help noticing that the floor *looked* clean. I knew it wasn't. It must be covered with bacteria from animal excrement, and yet somehow I didn't care. I leaned to one side so my tailbone didn't feel any part of the concrete.

A grunt behind me told me that Twisted Mister wasn't happy he'd missed out on the opportunity for dessert.

"Dessert is bad for your health," I told the irritated bull.

He responded by slamming into the wall of the stall and scaring the bejeezus out of me. I decided to scoot down the aisle, thinking it was a good idea to keep him from smelling my fear any longer. It worked... sort of. The next bull bellowed and kicked the door. I looked up at the name plaque and recognized the championship name the cowboys had been whispering about. Anger Management kicked a second time, which Twisted Mister answered in kind. Only Twisted's response was twice as angry as he began kicking the stall repeatedly. I guess that's why the champ had the name he did; Anger Management could control his irritation better than most. I certainly hoped it didn't focus on me.

Feeling somewhat safer sitting next to the champ, I started cataloging where I *didn't* hurt. I had a headache, but I thought that was from my heart hammering my brain cells up against my skull. Otherwise, there were no bumps or bruises to my head or face. Hay, however, was sticking out of every inch of my hair.

Whatever.

I moved to my shoulders. My left shoulder was sore; I tweaked it when I tried to hang on to the wall of the stall. My right arm had a pretty good scrape going across the skin from the elbow to the shoulder.

I knew I should have worn sleeves.

It hurt like the dickens, but it really was the least of my worries. My chest was filthy with more abrasions decorating my skin. My ribs were beyond sore. Each breath felt like an exercise in pain endurance. My tailbone hurt, and I really, really wanted a donut to sit on.

The last straw, so to speak, was when I looked at my legs and saw fresh cow patty smeared across my knees. And once I saw it that triggered my ability to smell it.

My chin quivered.

"She's right around the corner," I heard Travis say, and I looked up as he rounded the corner with Cade. The Mayor of Hazel Rock. Attorney. *GQ* gorgeous and the man who ruined my love life. Cade Calloway took one look at me, ran to my side, and crouched down to put his hand on my cheek.

"Princess, are you okay?" His eyes searched my face. His brows arched in concern and wrinkles appeared on his forehead. That was the first flaw I'd ever seen mar his good looks. If you'd call worrying about a friend an imperfection. He reached up and plucked some hay out of my hair, which didn't help me get that quiver under control.

In all my life, I have never worn dung. Yes, I was "born in a barn" but it was a house and a store. We'd never housed cattle. Even as a kindergarten teacher when my students had accidents in my classroom, I had gloves to protect me. But this, this was just too gross. And as I tried to speak, I began to worry about it being other places on my body.

"I have cow poop on my legs."

Cade looked down at my knees. "Yes, you do."

"I have hay sticking out of my hair."

"Yeah, I can see that."

"My arm hurts."

He looked at my arm. "Is that the only place that hurts?"

I sniffed, refusing to cry as a crowd started to grow around us. "My ribs and… my…my backside."

"Can you tell me what happened?" he asked.

"He tossed me over the side of the pen with Twisted Mister." I pointed a shaky hand in Travis's direction.

Cade's eyes narrowed and his jaw clenched as he turned toward Travis. Travis was once again taking that innocent stance with his hands in the air.

"Whoa, Cade. Buddy, you know I wouldn't do that to your girl."

Cade turned back to me. "Are you sure he's the one who did it?"

When I nodded, he asked, "You saw him before you were tossed over the side?"

"Well, no but he was here when I got out of the pen."

"That's because I heard you screaming—"

"I wasn't screaming!" Even if I currently sounded a little screechy.

"I heard you *yelling*," Travis said. "And came to find out what was going on. Before that, I was using the facilities."

"Facilities?" I asked.

"The bathroom," he clarified.

"I was with Travis before he came in to use the restroom. Are you sure there wasn't someone else present?" Cade asked.

I wasn't sure of anything, but I certainly didn't want to admit that in front of the riders and cowhands staring down at me. I shook my head.

"Do you think you can stand?"

When I nodded, Cade grabbed my good elbow and helped me to my feet. The pain in my side stabbed me with an intensity I wasn't prepared for, and I made an animal sound I've never heard escape my lips before.

"Why don't we take you over to the medical office and get you checked out?"

"Maybe I should just go home." But holy crap, I wasn't sure how I was going to sit in the truck let alone drive it.

"The doc's at the urgent care in The Ranch. She's scheduled to be there all day just for this type of emergency. Do you want me to carry you?"

"Good God, no."

Cade's brow smoothed a bit with my reaction, so I figured he wasn't insulted. I wasn't sure if that should bother me, or not.

"I'll just help. How's that?" he asked as he put his arm gently around my waist.

"As long as you don't touch my ribs, that's good."

"I promise. Scout's honor."

That's one thing I could always rely on when it came to Cade: his honor.

After having my scrapes cleaned and bandaged, and having several X-rays taken, the doctor announced, "It's a case of bruised ribs and a bruised tailbone. I'll give you some Naproxen for the pain and swelling. You're going to be sore for a while, though. I recommend getting a donut to sit on. They have them at Country Mart."

"Country Mart will be my first stop. How much do I owe you?" I really didn't want to see that bill. Medical insurance for the self-employed ate a chunk out of my salary that made me thankful I didn't have to pay rent.

"The mayor is handling my fees during the rodeo."

"All of them?"

"Every last one." The doctor smiled and began writing out a prescription.

It seemed I was always owing Cade money and it did nothing for my self-esteem. Granted, he was rich. The old money kind of rich that seemed in endless supply, but Cade had also played in the NFL and he owned half the town. Literally. There were only a couple shops he didn't collect rent on.

She helped me off the table and I hobbled out the door on my own two feet. The lobby for the doctor's office was at the front of the house but it had a secondary entrance from the residence to allow cowboys who didn't live at the Ranch to seek medical assistance without disturbing the residents. It had a very rustic charm with tile that looked like hand-scraped wood and beige walls. One wall, was textured heavily with a burnt umber paint, and then antiqued. Photos of the great rodeo stars who had graced The Cowboy Ranch with their presence were hung neatly on the walls. The chairs looked like soft, worn leather and the tables were definitely antiques. A large picture window overlooked the packed parking lot and equally crowded field. On a normal day, the view of the field would be typical of North Texas, with wild grasses and native flowers in shades of purple, blue, orange, yellow, and white that some people called weeds. Wild Oak trees grew sporadically, their gnarled trunks twisting as their branches grew out, instead of up. After living in Colorado, I suspected some Northerners would consider them the size of bushes, but they held the charm of Texas—tough and willing to work hard to make something beautiful out of nothing. The entire room, and its view, gave the impression of the cozy Old West lifestyle.

Cade was waiting for me with a woman I didn't recognize. When they heard the door open, they stood in unison; signaling that they were waiting for me…as a couple.

Drat the man. It shouldn't bother me, but it did.

The woman's long brown hair fell over one shoulder and glistened, but it was her only outstanding feature. Everything else about her was unremarkable. As if she was self-conscious about her appearance, she wore her cowboy hat low on her forehead, hiding her features completely.

"O.M.W. What happened to you?" The woman tilted her hat back and if the acronym didn't tell me who she was, the facial features certainly did. Scarlet had changed her hair color, and for the first time since I knew her in high school, she wore shapeless clothes. Her T-shirt was a man's box-cut style, which completely hid her curves. I could still tell she was well-endowed, but I couldn't tell she had an hourglass figure. Her shorts looked more like mom shorts. She'd cut off a pair of her jeans and rolled up the hem to just above the knees. To top the outfit off, she had on nursing-style tennis shoes with bobby socks. She looked nothing like my stylish best friend.

She ran over and hugged me. I would have returned it, except it hurt too badly. Instead, I moaned.

"Sorry, did I hurt you?" She stood back and took inventory of my injuries, from the rat's nest in my hair, to the wrap on my arm and smaller Band-Aids on my chest. She took in my wobble and the way I held my uninjured arm close to my side.

I smiled, because having her there meant the world to me. "I had a date with a bull," I replied.

"That's not funny, Charli. You could have been killed!"

It felt kind of like a dramatic thing to say, considering we were in a nursing home for bull riders who risked life and limb in the name of the sport time and time again. And all I'd done was spend a few moments in the company of just one bull.

"It wasn't that bad," I said, but Scarlet was having none of it.

"Wasn't that bad? One look at your hair and the way you're walking and I can tell you're talking as if you and the truth aren't related."

Cade cut in. "Mateo's sending a deputy over to get a report from you. He didn't sound very happy."

That was probably because he thought I'd broken my word to not get involved. But I honestly hadn't. In fact, I hadn't even had the chance to break the spirit of the agreement, unless of course, he counted me accusing Travis Sinclair of attacking me.

Scarlet started messing with my hair, pulling pieces of hay out and dropping them in Cade's hands. I let her. Who was I to push away the help of a born perfectionist who'd worked miracles with my hair in the past?

"I'm supposed to work the ticket booth when the bull riding starts, but look at me." The cow patty was no longer present on my legs, but I could still smell it. My shirt and shorts were dirty, and my boots looked like they'd been worn to the dust bowl.

"Cade called and asked me to bring you a change of clothes. We both knew you'd insist on staying, but looking at you...Girlfriend, you're not staying."

"I have to buy a donut."

"A donut? Why don't I just get you a funnel cake here?" Cade asked.

"I need a donut to *sit* on," I explained.

Cade's eyebrows shot up but he didn't say a word.

"I'll take you to buy a donut and then take you home," Scarlet offered.

"I have the truck here."

"Cade and I will bring it by the bookstore this afternoon."

"What about my shift?"

"I'll work your shift." She had an answer for everything.

"Scarlet—"

"No one recognized me. Not even you."

"I did when you tilted your hat. How do you expect everyone in town not to recognize you?"

Scarlet tilted her hat back down and spoke in a Boston accent. I had to admit that it worked; I would have thought she was a transplant looking for milder winters, not a seventh-generation Texan who'd never left the state for more than a couple weeks at a time.

"O.M.W. Girlfriend, even you would look right past me with this accent." She grinned that sly smile that was all Scarlet. It was truly nice to see, after everything she'd been through.

"Not if you say O.M.W. I seriously doubt there are a lot of other women in the state of Texas, let alone Boston, that use that acronym.'"

"Noted." Her face turned serious. "I need to be around people. Even if they have no clue who I am. I *need* this."

Despite her pleading, I still wasn't convinced. "What are you going to do if someone does recognize you?"

Cade put his arm around Scarlet's shoulder and drew her close. It seemed he did that with everyone woman he ever met—except me.

"She's going to call me and I will get her out of here."

Cade released Scarlet with a final squeeze. "Then it's settled. Scarlet will take you to get your donut, and then take you home. We'll drive the truck over later this afternoon."

I had no doubt that donut was going to be the butt of many jokes to come, once he felt safe enough to let the first one fly.

"What's that noise?" Scarlet asked.

We turned toward the growing noise out front. Through the big picture window in the front lobby, we observed one of the riders heading toward The Ranch. Reporters were running from every direction trying to get his picture.

The cowboy opened the door to the medical office. "It's going to be a show you'll never forget," he promised the assembled crowd of reporters.

Scarlet began shaking. Cade's jaw dropped. And I was beginning to believe the zombie apocalypse was real. Because Dalton Hibbs was back from the dead.

Chapter Eighteen

Scarlet didn't hesitate. She ran to Dalton, threw her arms around his neck, and began kissing him in front of God and all the cameras aimed in their direction. It was a like a scene from a romance movie. The kind I never went to.

Dalton laughed mid-kiss but didn't seem quite as enthused as my best friend. His hands were on her waist, but I suspected that was a natural reaction to a woman ambushing him. Especially a woman he didn't recognize.

He gently pushed her away with a grin on his face and looked down at Scarlet. Something I couldn't identify passed through his eyes. Pain mixed with disbelief, possibly a little anger before he stepped back even farther.

"That was good for the cameras, but one notch in your lipstick case is enough for this rodeo, don't you think, darling?" Dalton turned his back on Scarlet, dismissing her like she was yesterday's news.

Cade was the first to state the obvious. "You're alive."

Dalton chuckled as all three of us gaped at him. "Just because a man takes a few days off, doesn't mean he died and went to heaven."

Scarlet's face grew red as the media continued to record the entire meeting. She clearly didn't expect the brush-off, but that's exactly what Dalton was giving her. He was ready to walk through the lobby of The Ranch and straight through to the staging room for the riders on the backside of the residence without a second look in her direction. If Scarlet didn't care so much, she would have run and hid. But she did care. She wanted to know how he was alive. Why he hadn't called her. How we'd tracked his phone to a dead body—that wasn't his.

"Where were you?" I asked, putting my back between Scarlet and the media. Cade moved over to stand next to me, and I was happy that at least one man had a clue when it came to Scarlet's emotions.

"I do have a private life, Princess." Dalton reached for the back door, but my anger stopped him dead in his tracks.

"My name is Charli. Why didn't you call Scarlet?" I demanded.

He let out a little puff of air as if he was thinking, *this chick is unbelievable,* before he said, "I didn't realize I said I would."

"Dalton, stop this. This isn't like you." Tears filled Scarlet's eyes as she stepped forward and placed her hand on top of his. Dalton, however, wanted no part of it. He pulled his hand back so fast you'd think she'd scalded him.

And once again I wanted to slug the cowboy. Scarlet was better off with this man in the ground.

Dalton watched her brush away her tears, and again it was like witnessing two people struggling in one body. The part of him that was melting, stepped forward. The other part, which I had no use for, checked himself. Stiffened his spine as if he knew better than to be human.

"We had a good time. Let's not make this messy," Dalton said. Again, he made a move toward the exit.

To my surprise, Cade stepped forward, hands clenched at his sides.

"She thought you were dead you son-of-a—"

Scarlet was the rational one. Although some may say it was irrational to defend Dalton Hibbs after he discarded her in such a crass manner. "Cade, it's all right. He's okay; that's all that matters."

Dalton's happy-go-lucky attitude faltered. "Why in the world are you people acting like I'm the living dead? I was gone for a couple days. Erik knew where I was."

"Erik went back to Austin the day after you disappeared, and I've been calling your phone...." Scarlet's lower lip quivered. "We tracked it with your iPad, which you left at my place."

"You hacked my iPad?"

"Because I was worried half to death about you!"

"I'm sorry. I can see you were upset, but I just took a couple days off to rest before the rodeo." The man was determined to run out the back door. Scarlet's next sentence changed that.

"We found two graves."

His eyes shot back and forth among the three of us, trying to see if Scarlet was telling the truth. Cade gave him a grim nod. I wasn't that calm. Maybe it's because I was one of the few who had witnessed what I thought was his mangled body. Only now I didn't know who those graves belonged to, so my response was a tad bit angrier. "Yes, we did. And your phone was in one of those graves."

"My phone was… My phone was where?"

"Buried six feet under," Scarlet replied.

I wanted to say it wasn't that deep, but I held my tongue.

"So that's why all the media is hounding me, because they thought I was dead? That's why they kept asking me if I was the real Dalton Hibbs?" He scrubbed his face with his hands and then looked up at us with all kinds of worry written across his face. "My parents? Do they think I'm dead?"

It was Cade's turn to add what he knew. "They provided the DNA samples for the ME to test. We've been waiting to hear."

"Holy crap." He looked around the lobby frantically. "I need a phone."

Scarlet was the first to offer her cell phone. Their fingers touched and I could see the hope on Scarlet's face, but all Dalton gave her was a sheepish, "Thank you," before turning his back and dialing his parents.

"I think Mateo might want an update on his case," I told Cade.

Cade pointed out the window. Mateo was pushing his way through the growing crowd of spectators and reporters who were jockeying for a glimpse of Dalton. Microphones were being shoved in his face, but he just shook his head and if I was reading his lips correctly, he told each one, "No comment."

Mateo made it in the front door with Peter and his cameraman, Aiden, close on his heels. They didn't make it inside despite their every attempt to attach themselves to the sheriff.

"Unless you'd like to be introduced to the deputy in my jail, I suggest you wait outside for Mr. Hibbs to release a statement," Mateo said and closed the door with a solid thud.

Mateo looked at Dalton and shook his head. Then he took in Scarlet's smeared mascara and his jaw softened. Finally, he looked in my direction. His expression completely void of any emotion as he cataloged my injuries.

"Are you okay, Charli?" he asked.

"A couple days, and I'll be like new." As long as "new" didn't involve sitting without a donut or reaching for anything above my waist. I probably wouldn't be wearing a tank top dress and heels anytime soon. Of course, a woman without a date didn't have to worry about that.

Dalton hung up the phone and turned back to us.

Mateo reached out and shook his hand. "I'm glad to see you're okay, Dalton. You gave us quite the scare if you haven't figured that out already."

"Yeah, I'm really sorry, Sheriff. If I'd known, I would have come and talked to you immediately."

"Where were you?"

"Up at a cabin near Enchanted Rock."

Mateo pulled that ever-present little pad of paper out of his shirt pocket. Sometimes I liked that pad; most of the time I really hated it. At the moment, it was my best friend.

"Can you tell me what cabin?" Mateo asked.

"Crabapple Cabins off 965."

"Are you still renting it?"

"Erik rented it for me , and I haven't checked out yet."

"So you haven't been back to your hotel room?"

"No. I planned on going this afternoon..." Dalton cussed under his breath. "I don't have a room anymore, do I?"

"Sorry, no you don't. Your items were collected as evidence a couple days ago."

"So...to the entire world, I'm really dead."

"For all intents and purposes, yes. But you have not been officially declared dead by anyone. You've been listed as a missing person."

The entire reality was starting to sink in for Dalton. I wanted to feel sorry for him. I wanted to help, but I just couldn't shake how he'd treated Scarlet.

"How did you get here?"

"Erik rented a car for me. I had it at the cabin." Dalton removed his felt hat and ran his hand through his hair as if the mounting problems were becoming too much. "You said there were two graves..."

Mateo nodded but didn't say a word. Scarlet's eyes filled again, and Cade looked like he wanted to say something but wasn't sure what. Silence filled the room and you could see a sense of dread seeping through Dalton's body. He wanted to know...but didn't. Because if our suspicions were correct, there was no hope of ever finding his brother.

"Have a seat, Dalton." Mateo held his out toward the chairs that were out of the view of the windows and Dalton complied.

"We found two graves, one with your phone buried in it, and the other with evidence that would lead us to believe it was Wyatt."

"Was it?"

"We're still investigating."

Mateo talked to Dalton for a few more minutes, but their voices became hushed and the rest of the conversation transpired without us hearing the details. Dalton took the news better than I expected. Maybe the fact that he had been missing and presumed dead, when he obviously wasn't, gave him hope. Or maybe it was because his brother had been missing for so many years, having any answer was better than none. I wasn't sure. Mateo took more information from Dalton, including his cabin number at Crabapple Cabins, and asked him to come in to give a statement to detectives after his qualifying round. Dalton was happy to oblige.

His next actions caught everyone off guard, except Scarlet. He stood up and reached for her hand. She went willingly, and Dalton pulled her back into the corner for a semi-private conversation. With the cameras outside trying to capture the angle, Mateo, Cade, and I talked quietly, but were ready to pounce on the man if he so much as said one wrong word.

Okay, one of us was ready to pounce. I wasn't sure what the other two were thinking. Cade's brow was furrowed and Mateo's face lacked all expression. Cade, however, was the first to leave when the doctor came out of her office and seemed a little shocked that we were still there.

"Are you going to be okay, Princess?" he asked.

"I'll be fine."

Cade's hand rose to my cheek and for some stupid reason, I leaned into it. Enjoyed his touch as I gazed into his eyes.

"Take care of yourself," he said like he would to his sister. The lack of heat in his eyes was even more evident by the heat rising on the other side of the room between Dalton and Scarlet. His hand fell and Cade headed toward the staging area for the riders, the attractive doctor at his side.

"How are you…really?" Mateo's voice was soft.

I gave him my undivided attention. "Me? I'm fine."

"You broke your promise," he scolded.

"No, no…" I shook my finger back and forth. "I did not go back on my word. I was walking through the barn when this bull was making funny noises. I looked inside the stall, but all I could see was him lying on his side. I climbed up to get a better look… And someone pushed me over the edge."

My mind suddenly started working in a direction Scarlet wouldn't like. Whoever pushed me over the top of the stable wall had a knack for disappearing. Just like Dalton. Could he be the one who wanted to see me gored?

I looked over as he kissed Scarlet's cheek. That happiness she felt a few days ago was returning to her face—and it scared me, way more than the thought of Dalton being the one who tried to kill me.

"Don't." Mateo interrupted my thoughts.

"Don't what?"

"Don't say what you're thinking. I know he looks guilty, and I promise you no one wants to find the person who attacked you more than I do, but I need you to promise me to stay out of it completely. You'll just cause more trouble."

"I can only hobble like a newborn filly and I can't raise my arms. How much trouble can I get into?"

"You don't seriously expect me to answer that, do you?"

"Funny. Why did you become sheriff when you had such a promising career ahead of you in comedy?"

He smirked and it was way too cute for my comfort.

"How are you getting home?"

"Well, Scarlet was going to take me to Country Mart to get a donut—" When his expression turned blank, I thought I'd better explain. "It's to sit on, not to eat."

His brow furrowed. "That bad?"

"Unfortunately, and my ribs feel even worse."

"Meet me out back by the barn and I'll pick you up in my patrol car so you don't have to go through that mess." I looked out the window, expecting the crowd to have dissipated. But if anything, it was worse.

"Deal. I can't imagine pushing my way through that."

Mateo walked to the front door with swagger, while I went down the hall and out the back at a pace that could be compared to a sloth's. The doctor had also given me a script for extra-strength Naproxen, which I planned on filling at Country Mart; otherwise, I wasn't sure I'd be walking the next day.

I made it out the back door and down the steps just as a volunteer was emptying the trash outside the barn. He lifted the barrel up, not expecting it to be that heavy, but lost his balance as the weight of the barrel threw him backward. Most of the trash made it into the large bin, except for a few items.

A red plastic bag caught my attention and before I knew it, I was trying to run and stop him from throwing it into his trash container.

"Excuse me!" I yelled, but he didn't hear me over his earbuds. "Excuse me!" My second attempt stopped him long enough for me to get to his side. I was completely out of breath and hunched with pain.

"I'm sorry. That bag is mine. I've been looking for it. It has my meds in it."

He pulled one bud out of his ear. "Your meds?" he asked.

"Yes, the doc gave me some meds for my injuries. I had no idea where I left it but apparently someone thought it was trash."

"Oh, you mean this?" He started to pick it up, but I warned him.

"Careful, I've got a used syringe in there from my insulin."

He scanned my appearance suspiciously, so I built up my lie just a tad. "I had a diabetic seizure and fell out of the stands."

"Wow, you're lucky to be alive."

He had no idea how lucky, as he bent down, picked the bag up by the top corners, and handed it to me. It was sticky from a soda that had spilled on the outside of it but was otherwise fairly clean.

I smiled, more grateful by the moment. "Thank you."

"No problem, lady, but you might want to be more careful with that stuff. There are kids everywhere."

I nodded and said I was sorry, duly chastised for my carelessness. Then I looked inside the bag. Just as I suspected: two large needles and two empty vials, both wrapped in paper towels. The same thick, blue towels found in dispensers outside the stalls where they kept the bulls. The kind of dispenser I bumped my head on. I was pretty sure I'd been right about Twisted Mister being sick. In fact, if I was a betting woman, the bull had been drugged for a better performance. More vicious. More out-of-control. And definitely a ride one of the cowboys would never forget.

Scarlet came running up to me, panting heavily and fanning her bright red face. "O.M.W. Princess, I nearly forgot I said I'd take you to Country Mart!" Despite feeling bad about forgetting me, Scarlet couldn't have been happier. Her eyes were sparkling and she didn't give a fig about how much she was sweating or the smear of mascara under her eyes. She was less than her perfect self, yet all the more beautiful because of it. Then again, maybe it was because she was in love.

"It's okay. Mateo is going to take me. He wanted to talk to me about what happened with the bull, anyway."

She blew out a sigh of relief and wiped her shiny brow. "I'm so glad. I called Joellen to work the gate, and now I can watch Dalton do his qualifiers. Will you forgive me for getting caught up in the moment?"

"There's nothing to forgive, Scarlet. Go enjoy the rodeo."

Scarlet's hug came faster than I expected and knocked the wind right out of me. I moved the bag out of the way so neither one of us got poked with a bull-sized needle.

"I'll call you later."

I watched her run back toward the arena. Only then did I think of the one question I forgot to ask:

"Scarlet, who's he riding?"

She beamed with pride. "Twisted Mister! It's going to be a ride for the history books! See you later!"

Chapter Nineteen

Mateo pulled up and got out of his patrol car to help me into the passenger side. I held out the bag, being careful neither one of us got stuck.

"What is this?"

"I suspect it's the reason I was tossed over the side of the stall."

"What are you talking about?" He reached for the bag.

"Careful, there are needles inside it."

He hesitated and then pulled a pair of plastic gloves out of his rear pocket. "What kind of needles?"

"Based on the size, I suspect they're what a vet would use on a bull."

Mateo's face relaxed a bit. "It's not unusual for the bulls to get checked by the vet before a big event, Charli." But he reached into the bag and pulled out a needle and one small glass bottle. He read the label on the bottle. "Well, would you look at that."

"What is it?" I asked.

"It's a concoction of drugs—steroids, hormones, and stimulants. If given to a bull, it would make his behavior highly erratic."

"Wouldn't it be highly suspicious if I heard someone say, 'He'll never make the buzzer,' and then exit a stall next to a bull whose behavior became highly erratic?" I asked.

"You saw someone with these needles in the barn?"

"No, I saw someone with a red bag coming out of the stall next to the bull that was acting sick."

"And?"

"And the cowboy with him said, 'He'll never make the buzzer.'"

"Has anyone checked on the bull?"

"He's the bull that attacked me."

"Did Cade report it to the commission?"

"I don't know; I was getting checked out by the doctor. But Scarlet just told me that Dalton is about to ride him."

"I better get over there. There's a reason the CBR has over sixty bulls at this event. If one doesn't pass its medical exam or is disqualified for any reason, the riders can draw one of the other bulls. Are you okay if I leave you here for a minute? You can sit in my car," he offered.

"I'm coming with you. I want to make sure Scarlet's okay."

Mateo pulled his cell phone out as he started jogging toward the arena, while I made my way at sloth's pace. I caught a glimpse of him slipping through the crowd but then lost him somewhere around the entrance. The media seemed to have multiplied since our press conference, and the crowd lining up for the event looked to be record size. There was well over the expected number of fans milling around the gates trying to find a faster way into the arena.

I made my way through handfuls of people all asking if the rumors were true—was Dalton Hibbs really alive? Trying to ignore the crush and avoid being crushed myself, I suddenly found myself next to Aubrey and Liza Twaine.

Perfect.

"Charli! Why didn't you tell me Dalton was alive?" Aubrey's young, upturned face held an expression of betrayal. I wanted to tell her that was exactly how I felt about the way she was hounding me. Instead, I let her down easily.

"We just found out."

She began adjusting the camera on her shoulder and fiddling with her mic. "Scarlet knows?" she asked.

"Yeah, she's inside watching Dalton now."

"So he's been approved to ride?"

Her question caught me off guard. "Why would he need approval?"

"Because they took him off the roster. It's almost like being disqualified."

"All I know is that Scarlet said he was going to ride Twisted Mister."

Aubrey turned toward Liza, who was on her cell phone and repeating everything I said.

"Where's he been?" Liza asked Aubrey even though she could have asked me herself. I was her unwilling source; the least she could do was give me the time of day.

Aubrey parroted the question. "Where's he been?"

"Oh for Pete's sake! If you want to know where Dalton was, ask him yourself." I would have stomped off, but I'd reached the security checkpoint and there was no turning back. Plus, at my speed, I wouldn't have made it ten feet before Aubrey was in my face with a camera lens. Instead, I paid attention to everything around me, except the incessant questions Aubrey threw my way. None of them were worth my time.

Aubrey and Liza got to slip through with their press passes and didn't bother to wait for me to catch up. Which was totally fine by me. I made it through security fairly quickly thanks to my volunteer pass and suffered relatively few jolts to my ribs despite the desperate tension of the crowd to get inside and see for themselves that Dalton Hibbs was very much alive. I kept walking, or rather slothing, after I got inside and made my way down toward the arena's underbelly, where most of the bulls and riders awaited their turn. I kept going and didn't stop to do anything else. I even passed the restroom calling my name.

Because I still had my pass, I made it through to the waiting area for the cowboys and looked around for Mateo, with little luck.

Travis entered the room and stopped in front of me. He'd added his riding gear to his black shirt covered with sponsor patches. The left sleeve was cut and rolled up to show off his bicep, but the true purpose was to keep it clear of the bull rope he'd use during his ride. A black leather protective vest lined with high-impact foam matched his black chaps trimmed in gold and a prominent car manufacturer's logo was displayed across his chest. Both his chaps and his vest had intricate designs and had to have cost a fortune. His black felt hat was back on his forehead but still covered most of his chocolate-brown hair. He looked good, but even with Cade clearing him from any wrongdoing with my earlier encounter with the bull, the man made me uncomfortable.

"I'm glad you're okay, Princess."

"Charli," I corrected him quickly. Only a few were allowed to call me Princess, and Travis wasn't one of them.

"Sorry, Charli." He wore a sheepish grin, which seemed totally out of character. "I'm glad I ran into you, because I wanted you to know that the whole prayer vigil scene was just an act."

"An act? You mean you really didn't wish Dalton was burning downstairs in another dimension, or are you just saying that now because he's alive. Your behavior certainly didn't look like part of an act last night."

His laugh sounded a little self-deprecating. "Well it's true, Dalton and I have always had a healthy rivalry, but—"

"This is the Bible Belt, Travis. You said the man could, 'burn with the devil.' I hardly see that type of hatred as healthy competition."

Travis scrubbed his jaw, the whiskers of his week-old growth scratching across his one leather glove. He looked over his shoulder toward the room full of people. "If you knew Dalton, you would know that he often says he's going to burn with the devil for doing this, or doing that. It's what he says. He would get a kick out of me saying that at a eulogy for him...at least in private he would. In public, we put on a show."

"A show? That's a sick show." My voice carried to the people at the edge of the room and earned the attention of Sly Alexander along with a few other cowboys waiting for their call.

Travis looked around and when he saw a few autograph seekers lurking a few feet away with headshots in their hands, he grabbed my arm and pulled me down the hall.

I hissed with pain and he dropped my arm faster than a dead skunk.

His grimace was apologetic. "Sorry. Are you okay? I didn't mean to hurt you."

I nodded but kept my mouth shut, lest I really say what I was thinking. Once out of earshot of anyone else, I turned back toward Travis but suddenly felt like that caged animal...again with this man cornering me.

Get a grip, Charli. This is your chance to get inside information from the ring of riders.

I didn't wait any longer to ask the question that had been eating at me. "Did you know Dalton was alive?"

Travis winced. "Not exactly."

"What does that mean?"

He looked around before answering. "I overheard Erik talking to Taylor about the lack of media attention in Hazel Rock. He suggested if one of us *disappeared* before the show, the media would come in droves. So even when the graves were found, I just couldn't believe it was Dalton."

"Did anyone else hear that conversation?"

"Nope."

"Did you tell the sheriff?"

"Nope."

"Why not?"

"I figured that was up to the promoters. And it wasn't like the sheriff was telling the press that one of the bodies actually was Dalton."

I had to check myself and not blurt out that Dalton's phone and belt buckle were found at the scene. It wasn't my place to disclose that to anyone. Mateo would share that when he was ready. But it definitely drove me and Scarlet to the belief that Dalton was dead. Mateo too.

I changed the subject. "Why would someone drug one of the bulls?"

"Excuse me?"

"Why would one of the cowboys drug a bull?"

Travis thought about it for a minute, and it took everything I had not to fill in the silence with more questions. But this question was extremely important to me personally, since I'd unwittingly gotten caught in the middle of it.

He finally answered. "I suppose you could improve your score by having a bull that was juiced up, but that's taking a chance with your ability to stay on as well."

"Don't most riders have healthy egos?"

Travis's smile was stunning. "You could say that, but we also know our limitations and the last thing we want is to get caught in the chute with a juiced bull."

"What if a rider was wanting to make sure someone didn't stay on?"

Travis frowned and I could tell he didn't like that idea one bit. "Again, it's a crap-shoot. If he stays on, his score could blow away the competition. The worst part, is what it could do to the bull."

"So one of the stock contractors wouldn't do it to his own bull?"

Travis was shaking his head before I even finished my sentence. "No way. CBR-quality bucking bulls are worth a minimum of ten thousand dollars and can go up to five hundred thousand. They breed the line, and when they're done doing shows, the bulls go off to stud. I can't see any of the stock contractors at this level doping their bulls to increase the animal's score. The risk is too great."

I'd learned more about the business end of riding in the last ten minutes, than I had in my entire life in Hazel Rock. Like the state fair, the rodeo was an annual event I'd gone to every year as a teenager. But just because I went to a carnival, didn't mean I knew the life of a carny. The same was true about the rodeo…until now.

"Listen," Travis said, steering the conversation back to our earlier topic. "My stunt at the prayer vigil was just that. A stunt. Taylor asked me to stir things up. She said without Dalton, the media and the crowds would leave before the rodeo started. I kinda figured Dalton would show up sometime before the show, and the bodies would turn out to be animal bones."

God, I wish they were animal bones. But I'd seen the tattered and blood-stained plaid shirt sleeve, the one I'd wrongly thought belonged to Dalton and I didn't know any animal that wore a Western-style shirt. Even Princess, who apparently had been known to dress up for Halloween, didn't do that.

A few riders walked by on their way out for their ride, and greeted Travis. The exchange was friendly; Travis wished them luck and then waited for them to pass through the doors to the arena before continuing.

"A few years ago when I finally made it up in the CBR, Erik Piper decided that if he had a little drama in the circuit and a little animosity between the riders, ticket sales would increase. He learned it through a true hatred between Wyatt Hibbs and Sly Alexander. Ever since then he's picked rivals and made us sign gag orders that prohibit any talk about our real relationships."

"Yet here you are, telling me the truth? Why?"

"Because I don't want you to think poorly of me."

"Everyone thinks poorly of you. Why would you care what I think?"

"I would think that would be obvious. You really don't think our chance meetings have anything to do with luck, good or bad, do you?"

"Excuse me?"

"You define your nickname, Princess. You're tall, elegant, and have eyes that make me want to throw in the towel. I'd love for you to go out with me." For the first time, I saw a bit of sincerity in Travis. He wasn't saying he loved me, thought I had a great personality, or felt a connection between us that couldn't be denied. He was saying he found me attractive, in a very nice way, and I found myself wanting to experience a first date with an attractive bad boy from the circuit.

It had been months since anyone had asked me out; even well before I moved back home. The last date I had was with a new fifth-grade band teacher back in Denver. Our dinner and a movie turned out to be a fast food deli and a nap for him during a foreign film with subtitles. I would have cut the poor guy some slack, since he'd been working long, hard hours for months due to a band competition, but the truth was, he tipped his cards by snoring louder than a chainsaw. That and subtitles were a bad combination and there was no way I was signing up for that for the rest of my life. It was our first and last date.

"You're asking me out." I stated the obvious and looked down at my bandages and the dirt smeared on my shirt and shorts.

He laughed; a hearty, attractive sound that showed a part of him I'd yet to see. I didn't think he was laughing at me, or my situation, but rather his timing. It was charming.

"What cowboy wouldn't want to go out with a beautiful western princess who wears hay in her hair, has a pet armadillo. and lives in a barn?"

With a declaration like that, I felt I should come clean. "She's my daddy's pet. He took her in when she was abandoned as a baby. I was pretty reluctant to adopt her until I was told she'd die in the wild because of her coloring."

"All the more reason I'd like to take you to dinner. A good woman, who won't kick an orphan out of its home, is definitely my kind of woman."

I blushed at that. Literally blushed. But the whole time he'd been laying on the charm, I couldn't help but think that having an inside track to what was going on would be a very good thing.

"I'm going to have a constant companion for the next couple weeks. If it's all right with you, can I bring a third wheel?"

I could tell he was a little disappointed, but he didn't bat an eye before agreeing to have someone join us for dinner.

"Good, because I will be picking it up in a little bit."

"It?" He seemed a little confused and leery. I guess a woman with an armadillo would do that to you.

"The doctor ordered me to use a donut to sit on for the next couple weeks due to a bruised tailbone."

Travis laughed and that mischievous look in his eyes that he wore so well, returned. "As a man who's had a companion donut or two in his career, I would be honored to have a third wheel join us for dinner. Seven o'clock okay with you?"

I told him seven would be great. He tipped his hat with a wink before he disappeared through the doors to the arena. I couldn't help but smile. I finally had a date—even if it was to find out more information about Dalton Hibbs.

Chapter Twenty

I couldn't find Mateo anywhere, so I slowly made my way back toward the bleachers to see if Dalton had already ridden Twisted Mister. I thought about easing myself down onto the bleachers but then decided against it. The arena was full and I'd have to ask several people to move down to make some room. Then I wasn't sure I could ease myself down, without grabbing a hold of someone. Standing, had more appeal.

Over to my left Sly was straddling a bull in a chute, as the bull kicked the wooden pen. I couldn't help but notice his choice to wear a black cowboy hat instead of the protective helmets that so many of the younger riders had donned for safety purposes. Sly was busily messing with his bull rope, making sure his grip was good and the rope was wrapped tight around his hand. He pounded on the rope around his riding hand as three cowboys stood by to keep him safe, if the bull acted up in the pen. One held his hand straight out to protect Sly's face and head, while two others were ready to pull him out. If things went south.

Two more cowboys stood inside the arena, one to unlatch the gate, another to pull it open with a rope. Two clowns positioned themselves on each side of the field, and another one stood in the middle, ready to distract the bull away from the rider if he fell off.

The scoreboard said Sly was riding a bull named Missile Tow. It also listed the next four riders. Dalton was in line after Sly and was scheduled to ride Twisted Mister.

I looked around the crowd for the cowboy and vet tech I'd seen down in the pens before I'd gone for a rough ride, but didn't see anyone who came close to the pair. With the number of plaid shirts scattered through the seats, there was no way I'd recognize the cowboy at a distance. And that bright white lab coat was nowhere to be found. Nor did I see one familiar face sitting in the bleachers in my section; this was the one time of year that outsiders completely outnumbered the residents of Hazel Rock. Gazing down toward the other end of the chutes, I finally spotted Scarlet and Cade on the opposite side.

A clank of metal followed by a cheer from the crowd signaled the gate opening and I turned back to see the bull charge from the gate. The bull immediately dipped his head low, and Sly lost his grip with his feet. He leaned so far over the bull's head that he appeared to be lying across his back. His feet rose toward the rump and his left hand, which was supposed to be high in the air, was dangerously close to touching the bull's neck.

Missile Tow bucked, twisting his hips to the left, as his head went to the right; the change of direction cartwheeling Sly off the bull's front right shoulder. Sly's legs were sprawled wide from the force, and his brown leather chaps flew through the air like wings—until they landed on the ground and buckled as Missile Tow turned toward him.

The crowd gasped. Despite the throw, Sly wasn't free from the bull's force. His riding hand was stuck in the bull rope as the bull continued to thrash and shake Sly like a rag doll. His shoulder strained in an unnatural position as he tried to grab for the rope, as he got caught under the bull's front legs. Clowns dressed in bright pink and high impact vests ran in front of the bull's vision yelling, "Hey, hey, hey, hey!" to distract the beast as another tried to help Sly release his hand from the bull.

Sly curled his body into a ball under the bull, still trying to loosen his hand as hooves attacked his ribs, hips, and legs. His hand finally slipped loose and he fell to the dirt floor.

Another gasp traveled through the onlookers as Missile Tow turned on Sly again, his head and horns slammed into Sly's upper torso as the bull rolled the cowboy's limp body across the ground. A rodeo clown risked everything to distract the bull by running directly in front of it and then turning away from Sly. Missile Tow took the bait and ran as a roper on a horse moved in and two gatemen opened the exit chute for the bull to escape. Missile Tow took the path of least resistance, and the gate closed behind him.

But Sly remained in the dirt. A clown stood over him and waved for medical staff to come into the arena as a hush fell over the crowd.

Mateo walked up next to me. "You should be resting. Come on. I'll take you to get your donut."

"Wait. Don't you want to know if he's going to be okay?"

"He's got a good medical team looking at him with an ambulance on standby. They'll take care of him. Let's go take care of you."

"I'm walking; he's not moving." Even though I didn't know Sly personally, he'd sat in The Barn and he'd even bought a piece of book art for his mom. His mom. A guy who does that, will win a woman's heart every time. I couldn't leave.

"There's a reason why they call bull riding the most dangerous eight seconds in sports."

Sly raised his arm and gave a thumbs-up to the crowd. It was returned by thunderous applause that grew louder a few moments later when he sat up.

"Why would anyone want to do this sport?" I asked.

Mateo laughed. "Because it's the most dangerous sport in the world."

I could tell I was missing something very important in that statement, especially when his eyes sparkled with amusement. "Are you telling me you've done bull riding?"

"I grew up on a ranch in Texas. What do you think?"

I wasn't sure what to think of him. He didn't wear cowboy boots or a hat, which had been standard uniform for the sheriff when I left Texas. Yet he was a true cowboy.

Sly stood up on his own two feet and looked fairly stable. He was holding his left arm close to his body, and his smile looked forced as he waved his cowboy hat at the crowd before disappearing into the exit chute.

The announcer introduced the next rider. "You can never keep a good cowboy down and when we say never die, we're talking about the one, the only Dal-ton Hibbs!" His voice echoed through the arena as he dragged out Dalton's name like we were attending a WWE wrestling match.

The crowd stood on its feet. "Dal-ton! Dal-ton! Dal-ton!" they cheered.

Mateo cupped his hand over my ear. "Are you ready?"

A glance at the chute told me I wasn't. Dalton was easing one leg over the top of none other than Twisted Mister. I had to yell in order for Mateo to hear me. "I thought you stopped that?"

"No, I tried to stop that. The stock contractor says the bull was checked out after your incident and the bull was ready to ride. Their saying it's a case of a naive fan getting too close."

My back stiffened. The insult was far from the truth. "You don't believe that, do you?"

"No, but the chute boss and the stock contractor both agreed the bull was good to go."

I looked over at Dalton, who was rubbing his gloved hand up and down the bull rope as he heated up the rosin he'd applied to make it sticky. I couldn't help but think it didn't matter how hot he got that rope—he wasn't going to be able to stay on Twisted Mister and he was going to get hurt a lot worse than Sly.

"What about Dalton's safety?"

Mateo shrugged. "He was apprised of the situation and was more than happy to ride him."

"But you have the evidence of Twisted Mister being drugged!"

"I have evidence that someone at some point drugged something."

"But—"

"Charlie, I can't force the evidence to fit. The lab will run it for prints and test the chemicals and the animal's DNA. The CBR will take a sample of blood from the bull, but it will have to be sent off to the lab. These bulls are worth a lot of money; if someone is harming them, the stock contractors will be the first to want to prosecute the suspects. They are also the last people who want rumors about their bulls being doped." He pointed to two animal control officers watching from the other side of the arena. "Animal Control has already responded and one of them is videotaping the bulls. From there, the CBR will have to ask all the stock contractors for DNA samples, or Animal Control will have to get a warrant for each bull present at the rodeo…if the judge believes there's enough for a search warrant."

"I saw them walk out with *that* bag." I pointed to the bag in his hand, still encased in a rubber glove.

"You saw them walk out with a red bag."

His qualifier got under my skin and irritated my common sense. "I saw, and experienced, the violence of that bull."

"Was it any different than what Missile Tow did to Sly?"

I had no counter-argument. I'd gotten off easy during my encounter.

Dalton moved forward on the bull and signaled for the chute to open. Twisted Mister was out of pen in a flash. Head down, back legs fully extended, the bull spun in circles and gave Dalton the wildest ride I'd ever seen. The entire eight seconds I didn't breathe. Even when it was over, my lungs wouldn't inflate, because Dalton was still on the bull and Twisted Mister changed directions as Dalton threw himself off in the opposite direction.

The clowns moved in and earned their real title of bullfighter as Twisted Mister charged all three before finally disappearing through the exit chute. The crowd roared. They were stomping and whooping and completely in love with the cowboy who'd come back from the dead.

Chapter Twenty-One

I made Mateo stick around until after Travis qualified with the highest score of the night on Anger Management. I was surprised how vicious the desert sand-colored bull turned out to be. His whirlwind twirls may not have been as fast as Twisted Mister's, but his ride was rough and violent. When the bell finally signaled that his eight seconds of danger were over, Travis dismounted with ease and showed off his agility by dodging the bull's horns, not once but twice before he hopped up on the side rails and Anger Management was corralled into the exit.

The appreciation for Travis's skill was evident in the crowd's reaction, but it was obvious that Dalton, with his blond hair, blue eyes, and devil-may-care grin was the crowd favorite. Throughout the entire event, I discovered watching was a whole different ballgame when you actually knew the riders. I wasn't sure I cared for the additional worry, nor was I sure that I wouldn't have a heart attack if I had to watch it day in and day out. And when Travis blew a kiss in my direction, Mateo gave me a look.

I pretended I didn't see either as we headed for the exit.

We made a quick run to Country Mart and I updated Mateo on what I'd learned about the publicity stunts Erik and Taylor were known to organize. He listened intently and asked a few questions, then once again made it clear that I was not to meddle in *his* case. I gave him my standard evasive promise and he eyed me suspiciously.

At the store, watching how the other customers reacted to us, I quickly learned how the rest of the county felt toward Mateo—they loved the man. The men admired him, and the women ogled him. I was beginning to believe that being Mateo Espinosa was a good gig for a guy.

I ended up purchasing one donut and several different covers when I found out I could accessorize the pillow. Instead of being stuck with the standard Pepto-Bismol pink plastic pillow, I was able to choose fun and exciting designs with bright bold colors and patterns, so I didn't have to look like I was suffering from the worst case of hemorrhoids. I chose a feminine pink cover, of course, as well as one with a blue ocean wave and another with a green forest.

Mateo carried my package for me and before we got to the car, he blew up the donut, tugged the pink cover over it, and placed it in the passenger seat. I was in hog heaven, or at least as close to hog heaven as I ever wanted to get, when I finally sat down. At The Barn, he helped me up the stairs to my apartment and said he would stop in and talk to my dad. I'd literally forgotten about my dad in all the hubbub and hoped he didn't get upset over me not telling him about what had happened. Then I laughed at myself. My daddy didn't get upset over anything.

I gave him a quick call and declined his dinner invitation, telling him I had a date with Travis before I went and soaked in the tub for over an hour. Again, I fell in love my new donut. Exhausted and shriveled like a prune, I went to the living room in my towel and somehow fell asleep on the couch.

Scarlet called to check on me and I told her I was fine. I also lied and said my injuries were nothing a few days' rest couldn't cure. She hung up relieved and giggling. I didn't have to guess why she was so happy. She'd been distracted by something, or someone, the entire conversation, and as she rung off, a masculine growl echoed through the phone.

It was hard for me to reconcile the public Dalton with the private Dalton; I didn't know which one was real or which was fake. I hoped Scarlet could recognize if he was worth keeping, or if he needed to be set at the curb the next morning.

I chose my outfit because it was easy to put on: an elastic navy skirt with a button down white sleeveless blouse and navy and white striped flats. I'd removed the bandages on my chest and buttoned the blouse up high to cover the abrasions. There was nothing I could do about my arm; that bandage had to stay. I fixed my hair and applied minimal makeup before I heard a knock on my door.

As I went out into the living room, I saw Travis through the window. His attention was directed toward his feet, where he was addressing someone. I had a very good idea who that someone might be. I opened the door and Travis looked up slowly, taking in my toes all the way to the top of my head.

He whistled, and it may have been the first whistle I've ever found attractive.

"Princess, I don't believe I have ever been in the company of two more beautiful women in my life."

Princess sat up and twitched her nose in his direction, a slow smile spreading across her face. I had to give him credit; bad boy Travis knew how to pour on the charm. Even my armadillo was transfixed.

"Travis, you are everything they say you are."

The wrinkles on his forehead proved he wasn't sure if that was a compliment or an insult, and I decided to keep him guessing.

"I just need to grab my third wheel." I held up my bright pink donut.

A boyish grin spread across his face. "By all means, the more the merrier."

"Would you mind if we just walked down to the diner? I'm not really up to another car ride today."

"I have yet to experience the local cuisine. It would be my pleasure."

"Are you always this formal?"

"Only when in the presence of royalty."

"I'll have to remember that."

We made our way to the diner, where the dinner crowd was larger than usual with all the fans and locals enjoying the festive nature the rodeo brought to town. I saw Peter Kroft and his cameraman waiting for a table like everyone else, and was thankful there was no camera in sight. Several people approached Travis for his autograph and after asking for my permission, he obliged the fans. He surprised me a few minutes later when he turned to a man sitting on a bench outside.

"Excuse me, sir, my girl had a close encounter with Twisted Mister today. Would you mind giving her your seat while we wait for a table?"

The man immediately relinquished his seat, and Travis helped me get comfortable on my bright pink donut. When Scarlet and Dalton strolled up a few minutes later, the crush of people got worse. I wasn't sure who was more surprised, me or Scarlet when she saw me sitting on the bench. With the media hounding her the way they had been, I never expected her to venture out in a crowd. I hoped it was a sign the media had changed their focus after Dalton was resurrected.

Scarlet excused herself from her date and came to stand next to me as Dalton became surrounded with autograph seekers.

"Why aren't you at home resting?"

"Why are you out in front of the cameras?"

"The fridge in my trailer doesn't hold enough food to feed that man. We thought it'd be safer to eat here than anywhere else."

We sat back and watched Travis and Dalton enjoy their fame. They really did look like two boys who'd reached for their dreams and were surprised that they'd actually caught them. They also looked like they could be friends—behind the scenes. "What would you think of sharing a table?" I asked.

Scarlet grinned. "I'm in." Scarlet, never one to mince words, lasted about three minutes before she asked, "What in tarnation are you doing with Travis? What about Cade?"

"Why does everyone keep asking me about Cade? The man hasn't asked me out. Am I supposed to sit at home waiting for him to call?"

I wasn't fooling Scarlet. She heard the irritation in my voice and knew that I really had been sitting at home waiting for him to call. But I was done with that. Besides, accepting Travis's invitation to dinner meant getting more information that would keep the media off Scarlet's back. And as much as she wanted to believe they'd lost their focus, I'd just watched my favorite cameraman get his camera out of their van. Aiden was on the prowl.

Then Liza Twaine and Aubrey pulled up in Aubrey's Volkswagen and I knew things were about to get busy. I started thinking we should cancel dinner when a hostess called out, "Sinclair and Hibbs, party of four."

Scarlet popped up, but I waited for Travis. I was not above accepting a man's help when I'd felt like I'd gone through ten rounds with a bull.

"How do you do this every day?" I asked.

Travis grabbed my donut, not the least bit embarrassed to carry it for me. That alone made him rise a notch higher on my approval meter.

"I wouldn't know anything else. I've been riding for as long as I can remember. But I do tend to avoid getting trapped in a pen with a bull."

There was nothing to say to that, without sounding really bad, so I kept my mouth shut. The four of us got a seat at a prime table. I suspected it was planned by the manager of the diner and Taylor, who was seated at the bar with Cade.

Drat the man. He didn't even notice our arrival.

We sat down in the horseshoe booth with Scarlet and me sitting in the middle with the two guys on the outside; it made it easier when people wanted selfies and autographs. We ordered our food and made small talk while we waited. I was surprised to see Dalton and Travis getting along, and once again wondered if they actually did like each other. Then Dalton intertwined his fingers with Scarlet's and it seemed like everyone in the restaurant noticed. Everything was so comfy and cozy, and I began to worry it wouldn't last.

It was only when Travis brought up the topic of the two graves that the mood became somber.

"I knew it wasn't you in that grave," he insisted to Dalton.

"It would have been nice if you'd convinced my family and Scarlet."

"I really thought that Erik would have contacted your parents to let them know the truth. Scarlet, I can only apologize for not knowing that you two were serious. I'm sorry."

Scarlet took a drink of her sweet tea and avoided eye-contact with Travis. I suddenly felt that hammer coming down on a night that was too good to be true.

"It's okay," was all she said.

"How can I make it up to you?"

"There's nothing to make up."

"Scarlet, please—"

"I said, it's okay. Drop it." The edge in her voice held so much emotion I knew this wasn't just about her thinking Dalton had died. There was guilt in it as well, and for the life of me I couldn't figure out why.

"Are you okay?" I asked.

"I'm fine, Princess."

That was all I needed to hear. Scarlet did not call me Princess unless her mind was totally preoccupied. I ran the whole scenario through my head. The graves. The phone. The buckles. Dalton's return. Wyatt's continued missing status and the talk that the bodies were probably animals. People didn't know about the clothing or the belt buckles—

Dalton didn't know about the buckles. Fuzz buckets.

I looked at Scarlet as the guys talked about the standings and when she finally met my gaze, the guilt was there plain as day. As far as Dalton knew, his brother had no ties to that grave at Enchanted Rock.

Oh, Scarlet. That was one thing she should have never held back from him. If he found out about the belt buckles, he was never going to forgive her. He was sitting here celebrating, believing the only reason everyone thought it was the two Hibbs brothers buried in the ground was because they had both gone missing. Yet there was more evidence. Wyatt's remains were being identified by the coroner as we sat waiting for our Rocker Burgers.

Scarlet squeezed my knee under the table and I knew she was pleading with me to keep my mouth shut. I would, but I didn't think it was right.

The waitress brought our food, and Dalton and Travis couldn't say enough good things about the thick juicy patties smothered with cheese and bacon and fried skinny onion rings.

It was only when Cade stood up across the diner that I knew for a fact our dinner was not going to end well. Unfolding his tall body with an ease that most men his size didn't have, Cade glanced in our direction. His body was anything but relaxed, as he met Mateo at the front door with two deputies.

And that too-good-to-be-real feeling was definitely correct. Mateo glanced our direction and our eyes met over the top of Dalton's head. A small, almost imperceptible head shake told me he didn't want me to say a word. That one little shake said so much and made the burger in my stomach feel way too big for the space. He made his way across the diner with Cade at his side, his deputies going down the opposite aisle. Dalton was the first to see the two deputies approaching. The smile on his face grew, the closer they got.

But his smile wasn't returned. In fact, the deputies looked ready to draw on Dalton if he made a wrong move. Dalton, finally sensing the danger, put down his burger and wiped his mouth with his napkin before setting the cloth square down on the table. Mateo was right behind him, face tight, voice deep and dangerous.

"Keep your hands on the table, Dalton." The crowd at the door began to lean forward. People at nearby tables stopped eating and what had been a constant din of chatter throughout the restaurant, seemed to disappear completely.

Dalton kept his hands palm down on the table, his gaze never leaving the deputies staring him down.

"I need you to stand up, nice and slow, and put your hands on top of your head," Mateo ordered.

Cell phones were being brought out; videos were being recorded. My favorite camera crews, Aiden and Aubrey, made their way in through the front door. The lights on their cameras glaring throughout the restaurant. Our table was more than the center of attention; it was the only thing that existed for everyone in the restaurant.

It was Travis who broke the silence first. "What's this all about, Sheriff?"

"This is between Dalton and me. No one else."

"He's got a right to know why you're detaining him."

Mateo ignored Travis. "Dalton, I'm asking you as a gentleman to stand up and put your hands on your head. Let's not make a scene."

"You're creating the scene—"

"Travis." Dalton cut his rival off. "It's okay. I'll find out what's going on and everything will be fine. Take care of Scarlet for me, okay?"

"I don't need anyone to take care of me," Scarlet said at the same time as Travis responded, "Sure." Yet I could tell one word from Dalton and Travis would be out of his seat. It didn't make me feel very comfortable.

Scarlet grabbed Dalton's hand. "I'm coming with you."

But Dalton just smiled and winked. "I don't think that's going to be possible right now, darling." He pulled his hand loose, slowly rose to his feet, and placed his hands on top of his head. Mateo moved closer as the deputies closed the distance from behind Travis. One laid a hand on Travis's shoulder, reminding him to stay seated.

Mateo handcuffed Dalton one hand at a time, and I thought Travis was going to come unglued. "What the h—"

"Dalton Hibbs, you're under arrest for the murder of Erik Piper."

Dalton's face dropped. All the color drained out of it as if it suddenly chose to pool in his toes. Aiden and Aubrey scrambled for better views. A sea of mouths fell open throughout the diner. I expected tears from Scarlet, but she just sat there in stunned silence.

It was the God-awful noise coming from the bar that turned out to be a saving grace. Everyone turned to look at the source.

Taylor Goode was sobbing in the arms of my ex, and he didn't look the least bit uncomfortable. Mateo was carting my best friend's boyfriend off to jail on a murder charge, leaving Scarlet sitting next to me like a lump on a log. And my first date in months was madder than a hornet in a beehive.

I knew this night was too good to be true.

Chapter Twenty-Two

Somehow Travis collected his anger and convinced Scarlet she wouldn't be able to see Dalton until the next day. A murder charge was not going to go away in a few hours, and the best thing to do would be to wait for Dalton to call her. Most of the reporters left with Dalton and Mateo, yet when the three of us left, it felt like we were on our own walk of shame. And if I felt that way, I knew Scarlet felt it ten-fold.

We walked Scarlet home and made sure the media wasn't lurking in the area before Travis walked me to my apartment. He helped me up the steps and unlocked my door like a true gentleman. I wasn't sure anyone had ever done that for me before. I was relieved when he gave me a kiss on the cheek and didn't try to turn it into something it wasn't, but irritated that I hadn't gotten a grain of information out of him the entire night. Not that I could have with Scarlet and Dalton present, but still, it would have been nice to get something.

I fed Princess and let her out. Then made my way to the bathroom to brush my teeth and wash my face. I had just finished when Princess scratched to come inside. Most armadillos would spend the night eating grubs and digging up flowerbeds. Princess preferred a bath, her cat food, and her bed. Or my pillow.

I've gone through a few pillows since I've been home.

When I opened the door, Cade followed Princess inside.

Drat the man.

"What are you doing here?"

"I think a better question would be what are you doing with Travis Sinclair?"

"Excuse me?"

"At first I thought it was a date, but I know better."

"Excuse me?"

"You're digging into stuff you've got no business looking into." Cade doesn't get mad in public. He doesn't get mad around me. But I could tell by the way he rubbed his neck that he was so wound up he could hardly stand it.

"I think you better go, Cade. Taylor Goode might need you."

We stood staring at each other for a few moments. but I was the first to break. I reached past him and grabbed the tubs for Princess to take a bath. My bandaged arm worked just fine, even if it hurt like the dickens; it was nothing I couldn't handle. It was the squatting down that like to kill me.

I took the tubs into the kitchen to fill them and wondered how I was going to manage to get them filled and over to the door and on her mat. Princess took a bath in one tub, then ran to the other tub to rinse. The mat kept her from dragging water all over the floor, but even on a good day I always cleaned up after her.

Cade followed me and took the tubs from me without saying a word. He filled them, put soap in one, and brought the two tubs over to the door for Princess.

"Thank you."

"How do you plan on doing that every night?" he asked.

"I'll move the mat to the kitchen and fill them with the sprayer. Then I'll ask my dad to empty them in the morning when he comes to work." It was a brilliant plan and I was glad I came up with it so quickly.

"And the days he doesn't work? Or the days Princess needs two baths?"

I lifted my chin, not about to be defeated. "We'll manage."

"Geezus, do you know you are the most frustrating woman to walk this green earth?"

My back immediately bristled. "How can a woman who means nothing to you frustrate you?"

"Means nothing to me?" Cade crowded me, backing me against the sink. "You know better than that."

"Do I? How am I supposed to know better than that?" Cade was looking at me in a way he hadn't looked at me in months. Actually, not since I'd first returned to Hazel Rock and he'd kissed me right here, in my kitchen.

"Because you've always meant something to me."

Suddenly he kissed me. It was hot, and passionate, and holy crap the man could always take my breath away—literally.

I gasped when he pulled me tighter. Pain radiated through my ribs and I wasn't sure if the stars in my eyes were from his lips, or the pain.

Cade released me and the light returned. We were both breathing heavy, but I think it was for different reasons.

"Are you okay?"

I moaned my response. I really wished it was out of something other than pain.

"This is exactly what I'm talking about." Cade ran his hand through his hair. A sign of total exasperation—with me.

"What?" I stupidly asked.

"I know you were snooping around about those murders when someone tried to make sure you were crushed into bull—"

"Don't say it." I stood up straight.

"I was going to say excrement."

"No, you weren't."

"How do you know what I was going to say?"

"The same way you know I was looking into the murders."

He pointed at me like he just got the biggest confession of the year. "So you admit it!"

"I admit that I am not about to sit around and let my best friend get painted into this horrible person by the media."

Cade lost his cool for the first time since I'd returned to Hazel Rock. He was angry, upset, and completely frustrated.

Join the crowd, Mr. Mayor.

"This is why I can't be seen out on a date with you! I'm up for re-election!"

If I could have kicked him out, I would have. "I don't believe we've been on a *date*, so you have nothing to worry about."

He paced back and forth in my living room. Princess decided she'd had enough of her bath and our argument and headed for the bedroom without being dried off. A trail of water followed her all the way to my bed.

Cade was going to owe me a pillow when we were through.

"What do you want to do with your life, Charli?"

His question caught me off guard. "What do you mean, 'do with my life?'"

"Surely you don't want to work for your dad the rest of your life."

That question hurt more than I cared to admit, and the pain came out in my tone. "I run The Book Barn Princess for my father."

"You quit your job—"

"To work the family business."

"Are you wanting to expand? Do you want to have Book Barns throughout the country, in every small town? You could do that." A glint of excitement twinkled in his eyes.

I hadn't thought of expanding. I'd been content with getting to know everyone in Hazel Rock again. Getting away from the big city and just enjoying small-town living. What was wrong with that? Did I have to have grand ambitions?

"I can't have a wife who's always stirring up trouble. I don't just want to be the mayor. I want more."

"A wife." It figures I got stuck on those two words out of everything he was saying.

"Princess, everywhere you go, there's trouble. From the day you moved to this town, you've been trouble."

My back bristled again. "What are you talking about?"

"The eight-year-old new girl in town who saw Jimmy Bob stealing a piece of candy at The Country Mart and tried to make him put it back."

"He was stealing!"

"Yet instead of telling on him, you tried to make him put it back."

He was right of course, but to my eight-year-old self, getting in trouble was a lot worse than being corrected by another little kid. And I couldn't imagine Jimmy thinking any differently. As a kindergarten teacher, I learned otherwise. "I thought that he would give up once he knew he was caught, and then he wouldn't get in trouble."

"Jimmy Bob was twice your size."

"I was almost as tall as he was—"

"You were a little string bean!"

"Excuse me, Cade Calloway."

But he didn't stop there. He kept going. "When you were ten, you picketed the feed store because they were selling kittens."

"They were selling them without the kittens being spade or neutered to people who were letting them roam around town. The kittens were there in the first place because they were strays!"

"And you brought animal rights activists to town over the issue."

"I solved the problem by writing that letter."

"You nearly started a town brawl over kittens!"

"Do you see any stray cats in Hazel Rock? No. Why? Because I brought awareness to a problem."

"My point is—"

"Yes, Cade, please tell me what your point is—"

"I need a partner who knows how to get things done—without the drama."

"A partner? I didn't think we were talking about anything but a date."

"A mayor can't date the wild girl in town."

That comment opened a whole new can of worms that were armed with a lot of pent-up angry estrogen.

"The wild girl? Seriously? In what archaic age are you living in? Oh, wait, I know the age where you can date all the other women in town as long as they're from your economic circle. But not the woman who lives and works in a barn."

"That's not what I said, and you know it. There are ways to get things done that don't end up with you in the doctor's office."

"I heard you loud and clear, JC." Cade used to hate when I called him by his father's name, and apparently, he still did. He picked up one tub and emptied it over the railing of my steps. He followed up by emptying the second tub and stacked the two just inside the door. He turned the lock on the door, glanced in my direction, and walked out, closing the door behind him. He wiggled the handle to make sure it was secure and disappeared out of sight, the sound of his boots stomping down the steps echoed through my heart.

I knew calling him by his daddy's name was below the belt, but so was "the wild girl" comment. I was the least wild girl in this town.

And wasn't that depressing?

Chapter Twenty-Three

The alarm went off and I'd thought I'd died and gone somewhere other than heaven. My body hurt in places it wasn't supposed to, like my pinkies and toes. Princess didn't budge when I literally rolled out of bed and hit the floor.

"Uhng."

I lay there and counted how many places that didn't hurt. There weren't many.

"Who would voluntarily subject themselves to this?"

Princess didn't answer. She didn't understand bull riding or fighting any more than I did.

I finally made it to the shower where the hot spray helped loosen up some of my tight muscles. After I cleaned up, I put food in Princess's bowl. She was still snoring in the other room, so I decided to let her sleep and join us when she finally did get her lazy butt out of bed.

I made my way through the hidden bookcase to the store with my donut in tow. The broad winding staircase to the lower level was much easier to maneuver than the exterior steps to my apartment and I decided to use them until I could move my hips without feeling like someone was kicking me in the backside.

Dad was in the tearoom making sweet tea and taking cheese and herb biscuits out of the very little, very ancient oven. He had sausage gravy cooking in a skillet and I decided I had woken up in heaven after all—I'd just traveled through that other place to get there.

"Morning, Princess."

"Morning, Daddy. This has got to be the best way a woman could start off her day. I'm surrounded by books and the one man I can always count on. It doesn't get any better than that," I said as I placed my cushion on the nearest chair.

He nodded as he put two biscuits on two plates and smothered them with gravy. "Would you like to try some coffee?"

I smiled and shook my head. "Tea."

My daddy had forever tried to get my momma to drink his rich blend of Colombian coffee beans. But from the aroma wafting through The Barn, I suspected he'd made Texas pecan coffee today. Still, I was like my mom. I wanted a sweet glass of tea to start my day. I grabbed a plastic cup, since it was on the counter and a glass would have required me to reach way too far, and filled it with tea. Then I refilled my daddy's coffee mug and brought both over to the table.

We sat down and bowed our heads for grace before digging into my favorite breakfast.

"There was a time when you didn't think you could count on me for anything," he said.

"That time has passed."

"Sometimes the best of men say the wrong things. Things that aren't in their hearts. Things that hurt…" He took a drink of his coffee and watched me from over the top of the cup.

"You've already had breakfast at the diner, haven't you?"

He shook his head. "Nope."

"Coffee?"

He grinned and took another sip. "I used to be able to make you think that I knew things without people telling me."

"I'm not that naive little girl anymore. Did you have *coffee* with a certain mayor?"

He avoided my question with another question. "Did you know the rodeo made a record amount of money for opening day?"

"I figured it would. The place was packed."

"Yes, the crowd was pretty big. Instead of the CBR's usual thousand-dollar donation on opening day, it was ten thousand dollars."

"What? That's impossible. The crowd wasn't *that* much bigger this year."

"That's what Cade said when Ms. Goode gave him the cash deposit last night. He would've had an officer escort her to the bank, instead of meeting her at the diner, if he'd known."

It was daddy's subtle way of telling me Cade wasn't on a date with Taylor last night; it was all business. But what really got my attention was the size of the donation made by the CBR to The Cowboy Ranch.

"But if someone was stealing funds, wouldn't the amount of ticket sales give that away?"

"The tickets are given out on a donation basis. Someone can give five dollars, or they can donate five hundred dollars. It's completely up to the fans."

"Has the ranch ever made that much money during the entire week of the rodeo?"

"Not that I know of, but I wouldn't be the one to ask that question. The Invitational was started by the Calloways."

The only way for me to get more information would be from the mayor himself. Or one of his parents. His mom was a possibility; she always liked me. His dad was a whole 'nuther story.

"How's that donut working for you?"

The fine hairs on my neck stood at attention. That was a loaded question from my dad if I ever heard one. "Fine."

"Better than what that chair would feel like if you'd just let Mateo do his job?"

"Are you trying to ruin my breakfast?"

"I'm trying to make you see another side."

"It's not working."

"The difference between me and Cade is that I know when to throw in the towel."

"That's a good trait to have."

"Your mother taught me."

"His mother didn't teach him."

"Only a wife can teach a man."

"Doesn't look like the mayor is getting married anytime soon." I took a bite of my biscuit and it suddenly didn't want to go down. I quickly took a drink of tea and asked, "He's not planning on getting married, is he?"

Daddy smiled. "No. His head is all caught up in his career…or at least, it was before you came home. You've kind of messed up his plans."

There wasn't anything I could say to that so I took my last bite, stood up, and grabbed both our plates. It hurt more to move both my arms today than it did yesterday, but there was no way I was going to let anyone know that. Yet, somehow my dad did.

"I'll do the dishes; you go get the till ready."

I didn't argue, the alternative would be too painful. I grabbed my donut and took it up to the counter, where I opened the cash register before unlocking the front door. Traffic on Main Street was picking up, everyone heading toward The Cowboy Ranch for the rodeo that was due to start in an hour. I couldn't help but wonder what was going through Dalton's head as he sat in jail and the second round of qualifiers began. Did it matter when you were facing murder charges?

I called Scarlet and got her voicemail. I tried calling the beauty salon. Joellen told me Scarlet had taken the day off, but that she was okay.

What that meant, I had no idea.

We had a steady flow of customers and sold out of the latest releases by Fern Michaels and Joanne Fluke, along with Nancy Bush's latest romantic suspense that I'd been wanting to read. I made a note to order more and the front door swished opened with the buzzer going off as our new customer crossed the threshold. He didn't look as bad as I would have expected, but he was walking bowlegged and his left arm was in a sling. He grinned as he approached the counter.

"I guess you're not competing today?"

Sly Alexander shook his head, a wistful look in his eyes. "I'm afraid I've been sidelined for quite some time."

"Are you okay?"

"My rotator cuff is torn. I'll be heading home to my orthopedic surgeon at the end of the week."

"I'm sorry." It seemed like such a lame thing to say to a man who lived for the rodeo, yet at the same time I couldn't help but think his mom would be happy as all get out that Sly was okay and wouldn't be riding any more this week.

"It's all right. It's not the first time I've been sidelined, although it might be my last."

"It's that bad?"

Sly laughed. "No, I'm that old."

He didn't look that old, maybe a few years older than Cade, but I imagined the most dangerous sport in the world had to be made for a young body.

"What are you going to do?"

"I've already been involved in developing a team, so I plan to take a bigger role in that sooner than I'd originally planned."

"Is that a good thing?"

"It's the best thing. My wife is expecting."

"You're married?" Not that he acted single, he just didn't act married. Or maybe I didn't know what married acted like.

"For the last eighteen months to the most beautiful woman in the world." His happiness was infectious and almost made me believe love was real.

"Does she know about your arm?"

"Are you kidding? She was watching on TV and was calling the guys before I even left the arena. She wouldn't get off the phone until the doctor told her I had to hang up while I went to X-ray. She was not happy, but Taylor calmed her down."

I couldn't help my reaction to Taylor's name. I'm not sure how I reacted but Sly saw it and grinned again. "Not you too? I would think the Princess of Hazel Rock had enough dates to never worry about another woman coming to town."

Dates? Was he serious? I couldn't tell, and didn't want to think about it when I had more pressing questions to talk about, like how much money the rodeo had made in the past.

"Did you hear there was a record donation by the CBR last night?"

"No kidding. Well, that's something to be proud of."

"Yeah, it was ten times the normal take for the opening day."

His eyes rounded. "Is that what Taylor said?"

"No, that's what the mayor said when she gave him the proceeds."

"Wow, maybe there was some truth to what Wyatt used to say."

"What did he say?"

Sly looked around at the empty store, making sure our conversation wasn't heard. "Erik's dead, God rest his soul, but he was a hard man to like. He liked to stir up trouble and stir it up good. When Wyatt and I first started out, we used to room together. We were rivals in everything we did and everything we said. We played hard, and fought harder. We were the stereotypical young and dumb cowboys traveling on the circuit stirring things up. But there was no bad blood between us the way Erik tells it, and it used to really bother Wyatt. The two of them would butt heads more than two bulls in a pasture of cows. And Wyatt always got angry when we came to Hazel Rock, said we were riding for the worthiest cause out there and he thought Erik was stealing the proceeds. When Wyatt disappeared, Erik was the first to speak ill of him."

I wasn't sure if that bode well for Dalton or not, but the fact that Wyatt thought Erik was stealing from the CBR's donations to The Cowboy Ranch went along with the news of the extra-large donation last night. "I guess Erik not being here on opening day, and the rodeo making more money than anyone thought imaginable, might not be a coincidence."

He scratched his jaw. "It is pushing the odds of possibility a little too much for my book."

"Yes, it really is, isn't it?"

My father walked out of the back room and greeted Sly. "I heard you were banged up pretty good. Are you doing okay?"

"I'm good, Mr. Warren. Are you glad to finally have your Princess back? You've been telling me about her for years, and I didn't think I'd ever get to meet her."

My dad's gaze wandered around the store and looked at every nook and cranny, but never met mine. If he had, my emotions may have spilled over. He'd talked about me to the riders; it was a very telling story of how much he loved me and missed me while I was gone.

Dad cleared his throat and wiped his index finger along his bottom lip. "Have you come to pick up the book angels, for your mom?"

"I have, Mr. Warren."

Dad was doing everything he could to keep busy. He grabbed the angels from the shelf behind the register and carefully began wrapping the angels Scarlet had created out of an old hymnal. It wasn't the standard cone-shaped angel with fanned paper wings and a golden ball glued on top for its head. Scarlet had gone all out with two swooping angels descending from the pages of music. Each with long flowing gowns, dainty arms extended as they held their own musical score, and feathered wings created out of some of the interior pages. Their heads were bowed irreverently, while their bodies gracefully curved the open pages. Once again, she had out-done herself and dad was making sure it didn't get damaged with more than enough tissue paper. When he had it in an unrecognizable blob, he placed it in a box and dropped popcorn packing around it. He closed the box before putting it in a bag and handing it to Sly. "Does this mean you're leaving early?"

"Yes, sir. My wife is expecting and she insists our babies are restless without me singing lullabies to them at night."

"You're having twins?" I asked.

"Yes, ma'am. A boy and a girl. Our boy will be named after Wyatt and you inspired our girl's name."

"Me?"

"Well, it was more like your dad's love for you that touched my wife. She was here with me last year and was so taken by the way your father spoke about you. It was obvious how much he loved you and she wanted the same relationship between me and our daughter. We chose a derivative of Princess. Essie and Wyatt are due in two months."

It was just one more telling moment of how wrong I'd been to leave Hazel Rock when I was younger. Just another example to drive home how much I'd hurt my father. While I'd been angry and holding a grudge in Denver, my dad had talked lovingly about me to strangers. And it was another example of how everything was never how it seemed. Otherwise, Sly and his wife would have known exactly how bad a daughter I'd been.

Chapter Twenty-Four

Dad went home around noon to gather up some of the book art he and Scarlet had made while she'd been hiding out at his house. Princess kept me company, sleeping under the register while I sat on my cushion most of the afternoon. I called Scarlet for the fifth time and continued to get her voicemail. Frustrated, I turned to my email and began writing a request for one of my favorite authors to join us for a fall book signing. It was an idea I'd had to celebrate the release of her book, *Waxing Moon, A Midnight Poet Society Mystery*. If I could get Lucy Barton in The Barn, it would be the coup of the decade for me. I wasn't expecting her to accept, but I really hoped she would.

Once the request was sent, I began to fill out order forms on-line for the various books we needed. I was in the middle of a debate with myself over whether we needed more mysteries, romances, or young adult novels when the door swished open and the bell sang.

"Welcome to The Book Barn Princess, how—" I shouldn't have wasted my breath. When I turned toward my new customer, I found out it wasn't a customer at all. It was Aubrey with her camera in tow. The girl was pushing her welcome.

I forced a smile. "What can I do for you, Aubrey?"

"I'm looking for a particular book."

"Really?" The snark escaped my mouth in that one word, but I couldn't help it; she'd earned it lately.

Luckily she was oblivious. "*The Dangerous Eight*. I don't remember if we carried it when I worked here or not."

It's kind of ironic that she quit working at The Barn when I found a dead body in the storeroom, yet now she was being a major pain in the butt and sticking her nose in the middle of a murder investigation.

"Is it about bull riding?" I asked.

"Yeah, it's a reference book about the most dangerous positions, mistakes, and misjudgments a rider can make, along with how to avoid injuries."

The name sounded familiar, but I tended to get all the books going through our store mixed up. I looked it up in the computer to see if it was listed in our new stock program I'd installed a month ago. As it turned out, we'd had three copies until yesterday and in the last of five days we'd sold all seven copies we'd carried. Yet I didn't think I'd seen the book in stock. My father must have been the one to sell them. I made a mental note to order more, and then I looked up the book to see if it was for sale on Amazon. I found it under Erik Piper as the author; it was the bestselling book on bull riding they had to offer. Number one. Not 100,000 or 10,000. Number one. I knew I was missing why this book was important, and by the casual way Aubrey perused through the junk for sale on the counter, I was guessing it had something to do with Dalton.

"What are you up to, Aubrey?"

Teenagers are the worst liars, Aubrey included. They're very expressive with their faces. They practice in the mirror, and with selfies. When their face is a blank slate—no pout, no eyebrow lift, no quirk of their cheeks— then you know something's up. And something was definitely up with the soon to be college student standing in front of me.

"I'm just trying to learn more about the injuries the riders suffer and how they can be avoided. Like Sly yesterday...and you." She tried to hold my gaze but couldn't. Then she made a big mistake. "Scarlet recommended it."

Scarlet. The woman who was in love with a murder suspect. The woman who wouldn't answer her phone. The woman who had her trailer broken into and a backpack with Dalton's stuff, which included a well-worn copy of *The Dangerous Eight*, stolen.

That's where I'd seen the book. In Dalton's backpack when Scarlet had been worried that something had happened to him.

"Scarlet didn't recommend this book. A copy of it was stolen from her trailer," I said.

"Scarlet had a copy of *The Dangerous Eight*?"

"No, Dalton had a copy of *The Dangerous Eight* in Scarlet's trailer."

Everything I was saying seemed to be the wrong thing. That is, it was the right thing from Aubrey's perspective, since she had her phone out texting every last word to someone in her contact list. Undoubtedly, it was Liza Twaine. But I suspected I was giving information that would hurt

Dalton—which meant it was the wrong thing for me to be saying about Scarlet as well.

"Why is the book so important, Aubrey?"

She couldn't be bothered to look up from her phone. She was too busy reading an incoming text.

"Did you actually see that book in Scarlet's trailer?" she finally asked.

I crossed my arms. I'd already held one tightly against my ribs, so it wasn't a huge undertaking. "I'm not answering another question until you tell me why that book is so important."

Aubrey's eyes would have rolled out of her head if she'd been leaning a little to the left or the right when she finally gave in. She scrolled through something on her phone and then handed it to me.

"That's a copy of the search warrant for the cabin Dalton rented at Enchanted Rock. The next image is a copy of the return that the sheriff filed this morning. It lists all the items the police took out of Dalton's cabin."

"Aren't search warrants like a sealed record or something?"

"That's what I thought too. But the judge must order it sealed, otherwise, it's public record, just like a probable cause statement. If you scroll to the next page, that's a copy of the probable cause statement. It lists all the facts of why the police believe Dalton should be charged with murder. I learned all of that this morning. Isn't that cool? This is turning out to be best internship I could have possibly asked for."

I had no doubt she thought it was cool. Scarlet, however, wouldn't. As I scanned through the list of items recovered, I recognized several. A black, military style, single strap cross-body canvas backpack. A black Maglite ST3D016 3 Cell LED flashlight. A well-worn 2010 paper edition of *The Dangerous Eight* by Erik Piper. After that, clothing was listed by style, brand, size, and color. His toiletries were also listed by size and brand. The next item, however, sent chills up my spine. A P320 subcompact 9MM semi-automatic handgun loaded with thirteen 9mm hollow-point live rounds. Again, the serial number was listed.

It was disturbing to see the personal items of someone I knew listed on a public document. Yet it was even more disturbing to learn that he owned a gun and carried it while he traveled—and had it while he was with Scarlet.

The last item made me sick to my stomach. It was added on at the end of the document as if it was an afterthought: a personalized cattle branding iron with a cowboy riding a bull and the number 611.

Fuzz buckets. Dalton Hibbs had been the one to attack me. But why? What had I done to deserve that? What had Erik Piper done to deserve what had happened to him? Or the other person buried next to him?

"They got all of this out of Dalton's cabin?"

"Yup. It shows the address to Crabapple Cabins right up top."

I looked at the document again, and sure enough, Crabapple Cabins # 3 was listed with the street address.

"Am I missing something about the gun?" I asked. A lot of Texans carried guns. We liked our second amendment rights probably more than the folks in Alaska. I think it had something to do with our history of being outnumbered and outgunned at the Alamo.

Aubrey's smile grew again, and I had to admit she was freaking me out a bit with her youthful bright pink braces and her enthusiasm about a murder investigation. She was beginning to remind me of little Darla shaking Nemo.

"Erik Piper was shot in the back of the head—twice. That gun"—she tapped the search warrant on her phone—"holds fifteen rounds."

I looked down at the "thirteen live rounds recovered." "Does Scarlet know?"

"No, and you can't tell her either. This is exclusive information for the five o'clock news."

"Aubrey…"

The young woman in front of me became all business. "No way, Charli. This will cost me my job!"

I pleaded my case. "We're talking about Scarlet. Your mom's boss. Our friend."

"And we're also talking about my entire career that hasn't even begun yet. If I get tagged as a sieve on my very first internship, I'll never get a good job. This is my chance; I can't blow it."

I started to rub my face and forgot about my ribs. The pain reminded me of being thrown over the stall. Of Dalton arriving at the Rodeo shortly afterward. And of Scarlet's reaction to his appearance. Could this day get any worse?

"You didn't answer my question."

"What question?" I'd hoped she'd forgotten.

"Did you see that book in Scarlet's trailer?" She pointed to the book listed on the search warrant return she had on her phone.

"I saw *a* book entitled *The Dangerous Eight* in Scarlet's cabin. But it could have been a different copy."

Aubrey looked at me skeptically, so I added what I'd just learned on my computer search of the book. "It's ranked as number three in rodeo books, and number one for bull riding. We sold seven copies in the last five days. It's a pretty popular book."

I conveniently failed to mention that all the copies we'd sold at The Barn had been brand new. Not well-worn, like the copy that'd been stolen out of Scarlet's trailer, or the one the police recovered from Dalton's cabin.

Chapter Twenty-Five

I closed the bookstore and went to dinner at the diner, with my daddy carrying my donut that had the blue wave cover on it to match my denim skirt and red tank top. I figured the pink had been unlucky, so I needed to change things up. The two of us, and a crowded restaurant, were the best kind of date I could ask for at the moment. The waitress brought our dinner and I was more than happy to sit in the back of the diner in a small booth, capturing absolutely no one's attention. We ate in companionable silence, too hungry to have a conversation.

Scarlet had texted me and told me she was fine, but that she needed some time alone. I could respect that but still didn't care for it one bit. I wasn't sure where she was hiding out from the increasing number of reporters in town. Unfortunately, they weren't here to advertise or cover the rodeo, or the cause behind the event. They were here to air the town's dirty laundry about an up and coming rodeo star being booked on not one, but two counts of murder. The evening news reported Wyatt Hibbs's body had been positively identified through dental records as the first victim in the two burial plots. I wasn't sure what the motive was or evidence found in the case, but it was obvious Dalton had his hands full with the legal system.

Our dessert of peach cobbler and Homestyle Blue Bell vanilla ice cream had just arrived when a very tired Mateo approached our table in his standard non-duty related clothing of a T-shirt, cargo shorts, and hiking boots. He looked like he hadn't slept in a week.

"Am I still welcome at your table?" he asked.

"What would make you think you weren't?"

"Last night you didn't look too happy with me."

"Last night you looked mean."

"That's because you were having dinner with a man who killed two people. I was feeling kind of mean."

I scooted over and Mateo joined us. Jessie and Daisy Mahan looked over and I swore I heard a "humpf" from Jessie. "Are you that popular?" I asked.

"It seems I'm downright unpopular since last night."

"Even with the rodeo circuit?"

Mateo nodded, picked up his fork, and leaned over to take a bite of my cobbler. I looked around at the glares he was receiving, some of them from our very own townspeople like Jessie and Daisy.

"That bad that you can't wait for your own bowl?" my dad asked him.

"That's the first bite of real food I've had in about thirty-six hours. Besides, Charli's watching her girlish figure."

"That's the problem. It is a girlish figure." I pulled my bowl off to the side so he couldn't eat anymore. "We'll buy you dinner."

"Does that make this a date?"

"No."

"I should probably head for home." My dad started to get up, but I grabbed his hand.

"Don't you dare."

Mateo shook his head. "I was just teasing, Bobby Ray. I'm not your daughter's type."

I gave him a look that said he had to be out of his ever-livin' mind and he chucked me under the chin like I was a little girl.

"I came by hoping to ask you two about a book."

My dad settled back in the booth and the waitress came by to take Mateo's order of a cobb salad with no dressing and a glass of water. If it'd been that long since I ate real food, I'd be ordering chicken fried steak with mash potatoes smothered in gravy. The waitress left and Mateo became serious.

"Do you keep track of the books you've sold?" he asked.

I let my dad answer and focused on my cobbler.

"Princess just got us new software last month to keep track of our inventory. Before then, we just logged the sales by the cost of the book."

"So in the past month, you'd know how many copies you've sold of a certain title?"

"Absolutely. She's organized The Barn better than ever."

I would have appreciated the compliment a whole lot more if I didn't know where this conversation was going.

"Do you recall selling any copies of *The Dangerous Eight by* Erik Piper this week?"

"Yup. I ordered it in special for the rodeo just like I do every year. We had three copies in stock, and I ordered seven more, but I sold the last three copies yesterday. Fans were expecting to have Erik sign them at the rodeo."

"Were any of the copies used?"

"Oh, no. We've never been able to keep enough of those in stock."

Mateo turned to me, determined to keep me in the conversation that I wanted no part of. "Did you see a copy of *The Dangerous Eight* in Scarlet's trailer?"

"Yes."

"Was it a new copy?"

"No."

"Was it in Dalton's backpack?"

"Yes."

"The same black backpack that was stolen?"

"Yes."

Mateo turned his body in the seat and gave me all of his attention. It was one of those moments that I really didn't want it. "Why do I get the impression you don't want to talk about this?"

I took my last bite of ice cream and debated licking the bowl. Maybe if I did, Mateo would leave. My dad seemed to know what I was thinking. The corners of his mouth quirked upward.

As a little girl, ice cream became our comfort food at the end of the night. It was the one dessert my mom said she couldn't compete with. After she died, it was the one food that tasted the way she served it and gave us memories of her. Good memories. And I licked the bowl every night, savoring the taste and the memory.

I pushed the bowl away. "I was just enjoying my dessert."

Mateo's salad arrived, and although it looked good, I was debating another serving of peach cobbler and ice cream.

We were silent for a few moments, letting Mateo get some nutrition in his stomach. Yet as hungry as he was, I found him to be a very neat eater. He ate his salad and didn't try to talk with his mouth full. After a few minutes, he took a drink and asked his question one more time.

"Why don't you want to talk about this?"

"Because it directly affects Scarlet's happiness."

"It directly affects the investigation of two homicides."

"I know that. I want to help; I just don't want to hurt Scarlet at the same time."

Mateo took a few bites and thought about that for a few minutes before continuing. "Did you see any writing in the paperback edition of *The Dangerous Eight* from Dalton's backpack?"

"No."

"No, you didn't see any writing, or no the book you saw the writing in wasn't in Dalton's backpack when you saw the writing."

"I don't know what you're rambling about, but no—"

He stopped his bite midway to his mouth and looked over his fork.

"No to both questions."

"Can I ask you a question?"

Mateo set down his fork and put his arm across the back of the booth before he turned back toward me, staring directly into my eyes. He was that kind of guy. Straightforward, everything out on the table. Yet it was also kind of hard for me to think of a man in uniform being so straight with me. That hadn't been my experience growing up in Hazel Rock. I was, however, beginning to believe that I may have judged all, by the ignorance of one. The problem with changing my beliefs was that they were deeply ingrained in my makeup from an early age and altering my beliefs, wasn't going to happen overnight.

"What do you want to ask me?" Mateo said.

"Do you really believe Dalton killed his brother?"

"I believe the facts point to him doing it."

"What facts?"

"The gun that killed Erik also killed Wyatt."

"But I never saw that gun in Dalton's backpack."

"It was in his cabin."

"So what's the big deal about the book?"

"I can't tell you."

"You can't tell me?" I was reverting back to those old beliefs. He was open when it was convenient.

My dad stepped in before I could create a scene, although Daisy was straining to hear across the aisle. Luckily the crowd was too loud. "Charli, you're being unreasonable. Give the man a break."

"But Daddy, this is Scarlet we're talking about. The only person who stood up for me when I returned to Hazel Rock."

"Cade stood up for you. He was a major pain in my butt." Mateo tossed back a drink of his water like it was a shot of whiskey.

"My point is, Scarlet needs me to stand up for her happiness. To make sure the man she loves is guilty, and not just another innocent man going to jail for a crime he didn't commit."

"My job is to follow the facts, Charli." Mateo's voice was low and serious. "I'm going to give you a little tidbit that the media doesn't know…yet. They'll know tomorrow when the paperwork gets filed with the courts, but today, they're oblivious. So, if it comes out before they're filed, I'll know the source and I'll come looking for you. Is that clear?"

"Completely." There was no way, no how I was going back to his jail. Been there, done that, not going to do it again.

"Inside the book, *The Dangerous Eight,* is a hand drawn map to Wyatt's grave. And that's why I wanted to know if you had seen any writing in the copy you saw in Dalton's backpack."

"I didn't open the book. I only moved it out of the way."

Mateo nodded. "Thank you. I appreciate your honesty." He dug in his back pocket and pulled out his wallet. Then he put a twenty-dollar bill on the table and stood up.

"You haven't finished your salad."

"I've lost my appetite. If you'll excuse me." He turned to my dad. "Bobby Ray, I'll see you for breakfast?"

"Of course."

He nodded and then met my gaze. His eyes had lost the teasing sparkle and I was keenly aware that I was responsible for it.

"Charli. Have a good night." Mateo turned and walked away without another word.

Jessie and Daisy glared in my direction. They didn't know what had been said. All they knew was that Mateo had left without eating his dinner and even though they'd been irritated with him a few minutes ago, the fact that he'd left without finishing his dinner was not acceptable. And they knew it was directly related to his conversation with me.

I looked to my dad for support. He shook his head and waved at the waitress for our bill. "I can see where not having me around has hurt your communication skills with the opposite sex."

He was right. I'd never really given any man the time of day after I'd left Hazel Rock. But I wouldn't go so far as to say I didn't know how to communicate with all males. My five- and six-year-old male students loved me.

Chapter Twenty-Six

"Dalton Hibbs posted bond this morning. It's rumored that promoter Taylor Goode of the CBR posted his half-million-dollar bond before the sun could rise over Enchanted Rock. But the question remains, will we see Dalton Hibbs in the next round at The Cowboy Ranch Invitational? Reporting live from the Coleman County Courthouse, this is Liza Twaine for ABN News."

I clicked the power button on the remote and stared down at Princess, sitting on her back legs and begging for a piece of my croissant with blackberry jam. "It's not looking good for Scarlet and Dalton," I told her.

She twitched her nose and winked a beady eye at me.

"So do you think they stand a chance?"

Princess shook her head, put down her paws and waddled away as I put the last bite of my breakfast in my mouth. I wasn't sure if she was saying Scarlet and Dalton didn't stand a chance, or if she was giving up on me. I was talking to an armadillo and not a man who'd liked me enough to spend the night.

Of course, I was probably reading too much into it. She was an armadillo. She wanted my blackberry jam.

I got up and began to get ready for the day, slowly removing the bandages on my right arm before my shower. I cringed as the hair on my arm came off with the Band-Aid, and then again when I got a look at the raw skin. It was just nasty. The doc had told me to take them off in a couple days and today was the day. My shower was easier this time. By easier, I mean I'd learned to deal with my limitations, and yesterday I'd moved my shampoo, conditioner, razor, and soap all down on the bench.

I stepped into a sundress and chose a jeweled purse with matching flip flops for shoes. It was a bold move. Not because of the fashion statement, but because of the style. At the rodeo, you wanted to have your feet covered from what the animals left behind and the number of boots walking around.

Dad drove me to The Ranch and volunteered to pick me up when I was ready to go home, since Sugar was helping out at the store today. I gave him a kiss and thanked him for the ride, but told him I'd find a lift home. There was no way I was going to ask him to pick me up. He'd been putting in long hours all week and if business slowed down enough for him to get a few hours off, he deserved it. The last thing he needed was to be my chauffeur.

I still had my donut with the blue wave tucked under my arm as my constant companion. I decided the night before that pink had nothing to do with my bad luck, nor did the blue. It was just me and that bull's-eye of doom I'd always thought hovered above my head. Somedays I swore it was tattooed on my forehead.

Jessie and Daisy were walking into The Ranch ahead of me and I caught up to them; determined to mend any riff they might have with me. "Good morning, Jessie." I patted him on the shoulder, bearing the pain to be cordial. "Daisy, that's a beautiful dress."

Daisy looked down her nose at me. How she did that when I was five inches taller than her, I wasn't sure. But she did it, and did it well. "That's my husband," she said.

"Yes, ma'am. And he's one lucky man to have you."

Her nose lowered at tad, but not back to its normal level. Jessie tipped his hat and they were gone. Next, I saw Aubrey and Liza Twaine and decided that was one meeting I wasn't going to push. I ducked behind a couple big guys, pacing their gait as they approached the entrance. At the last minute, I cut-off at the back of The Ranch where I was supposed to check in for my shift.

Of course, one of the last people I wanted to see was talking to Taylor. I was glad she had posted Dalton's bond—sort of, but wasn't happy she was in the midst of a very friendly conversation with Cade and her mouth was within close proximity to his ear.

Nosier than I should've been, I snuck up from the side, hiding behind cowboys heading into the barn and other volunteers bringing ice on a four-wheeler out to the arena.

"I don't know what to tell you. I've never had to work this part of the rodeo before."

"But eight thousand? We were slow yesterday," Cade insisted.

Taylor shrugged.

"It's not that we don't appreciate it, we do—" Cade caught my movement out of the corner of his eye and turned toward me. "Prin— Charli. What are you doing here?"

"I thought I'd try my hand at bull riding."

My snarkiness irritated him, but he didn't rub his neck or run his hand through his hair. He decided to wait me out instead.

I hated that tactic. I usually lost. Like now. "I'm here to run the ticket booth."

Taylor wrapped her hand around Cade's bicep and herded him toward the barn. "Go see Daisy. She'll get you set up. She's right inside the side door of the arena."

"Please be careful, Charli," Cade added and walked away with Taylor.

Charli. I never thought Cade calling me Charli, instead of Princess, would hurt. I guess I was wrong.

I entered the arena and knocked on the door to the ticket booth. Daisy answered the door and let me in while Jessie opened one of the windows where a line was beginning to form even though the rodeo didn't start for a couple hours. That's when I realized the line wasn't made up of fans. It consisted of the media, willing to pay for their entrance instead of waiting the hour and a half till their press-pass got them in for free.

That could not be good.

"Why is the press paying to get in?"

"They're all wanting to get the good shot of the crowd's reaction to Dalton Hibbs."

"So he's coming, for sure?"

"It's just rumor and speculation at this point. The mayor asked the sheriff to provide more security."

Dag-nabbit. That meant Scarlet was going to be drawn straight in the middle of it. "Can I make a phone call?"

Daisy shook her head. "What would your generation do if they had to work a solid eight hours without calling or texting someone?"

I gave her a weak smile. "Sorry, it'll just take a minute." I walked past Jessie toward the back of the room.

"That's my husband," Daisy said as she wagged her finger in my direction.

"No worries. I've given up men." Or they'd given up on me. Either way, I was willing to accept my single status.

On the third ring, I'd just about given up on Scarlet ever answering a call of mine again when she came on the line, her voice lower than normal, almost unrecognizable.

"Hello."

"Scarlet?"

"Hi, Charli. I thought maybe you were a reporter."

"From my cell phone?"

"They've called from every kind of phone imaginable. You never know. Listen I'm in a hurry, can you make it quick?"

"Where are you going?" I knew the answer, but I hoped I was wrong.

"Dalton is going to ride today, so I'm trying to make sure I look my best."

"I don't think that's a good idea, Scarlet." I was uncomfortable with her spending so much time with a man charged with two counts of murder.

"It's the best idea, considering the circumstance. Dalton is innocent. If we continue to hide, he looks guilty."

I thought he would look sane, but that was just my opinion. "The media is lining up and paying to get in early and get good seats."

"Are you here to work, or lollygag on the phone?" Daisy asked.

I held my finger up and signaled I'd just be a moment.

"Good, then they'll see how good he really is," said Scarlet.

I'd heard the deep breath she sucked into her lungs before answering. No matter what she said, Scarlet was worried.

"They're going to be looking at you too."

"I'll see you there in a few minutes. Thanks for the heads up."

Scarlet hung up and I stuck my phone back in my purse. I plopped my donut down in the seat by the second window. Daisy had it ready with a cash drawer and a credit card scanner. After a short explanation of how the credit card machine worked, I drew up the blind and reporters started running toward the empty line. Peter Kroft and Aiden were second in line. Peter gave me fifty dollars in cash and then hounded me for information about Scarlet. "Have you seen her? Was Dalton with her? Will she be present for his return today?"

I smiled and replied, "Y'all have a good time now, ya hear?" I printed off one ticket. Then I told Aiden we accepted credit cards if he didn't have the cash. He grumbled something about free press as he handed me five dollars. I wrote the amount on his ticket and told him it was tax deductible and that The Cowboy Ranch appreciated his support. He ignored me and walked away.

Over the next thirty minutes, I collected a couple hundred dollars of donations from reporters alone. The computer program was definitely antiquated. I'd log-in and print out a ticket, but then I could go back and delete that same ticket. They weren't numbered or tracked, and they weren't connected to anything but the laptop in front of me. It would be easy to pilfer a bunch of cash if someone was so inclined.

When there was a break in traffic, I turned to Jessie. "Have you worked the ticket window before?"

"Ever since my hip started giving me fits eight years ago, I've worked whatever sitting down job they had. I've done ticket sales more than a few times."

I pointed at the laptop in front of me. "Has this always been the program they used for ticket sales?"

"For the last eight years, we've been pretty spoiled. Before then, it was all handwritten."

"Really?"

"Yes, ma'am. It was about as easy a milking a bull. I wouldn't recommend it."

I laughed. "I'll take your word for it."

"That's my husband," Daisy said as she stepped into the ticket booth.

"Yes, ma'am and I won't forget it." I winked at Jessie and turned to my next customer.

Fifteen minutes later, and I'd had enough. My backside hurt. My ribs hurt, and the portable fan Daisy insisted we needed was blowing the hairs on my arm. That wouldn't have been a big deal if I didn't have an abrasion the size of Texas on my arm. All the little nerve endings had come to life in a very bad way.

"Would you mind if I took a little break to stretch out. My tailbone is bruised and it's really stiffening up on me."

"I expected as much," said Daisy, although her nose didn't seem to be held too high in the air, so I figured I'd made a little progress.

I left my donut in the ticket booth and walked toward the restroom. The crowd was growing, but most of the fans were using the main entrance. I noticed a group of people who began running toward something in the parking lot and got a bad feeling in the pit of my stomach—especially when the group grew like a snowball rolling downhill.

Not that we see snowballs in this part of the country, but I'd seen plenty in Denver. This snowball was determined to make it to world record size. I could almost see the hands and feet sticking out of its core—the core being a cowboy dressed in a white felt hat, a blue western style shirt with white piping and mother of pearl buttons, jeans, and a pair of worn cowboy boots. I'd never seen Dalton look so old-school Western. Scarlet was with him, wearing a matching shirt and jeans that looked more like skin than denim. Her hat was very similar to his, but maybe a little darker and a little too big for her head. Her brown hair was braided and fell over one shoulder in a loose, beautiful twist. She'd traded in the cowboy boots for a matching set of high heels. Dalton's fingers were laced through hers, and they had eyes only for each other.

It was kind of sickeningly sweet.

To my right, Travis Sinclair and Dusty Lamb stopped to watch the spectacle at the entrance to the barn. Neither one looked happy. My dad would probably describe their expressions as madder than two roosters in an empty hen house, and I'd have to agree. When two more cowboys joined them, things really began to look like some blood was going to be spilled. And as if on cue, Dalton looked up to check out something other than Scarlet's mouth. Scarlet followed his gaze to the group of riders gathering, and visibly paled. That's saying a lot for a woman with an alabaster complexion.

It was Dusty who broke the growing silence. "Dalton Hibbs, you're no longer welcome here. Especially wearing that."

Dusty was out of line, but no one argued. In fact, a few of the fans were nodding in agreement. The riders just stood their ground with stoic faces in support of Dusty's comment.

Dalton and Scarlet faced-off with them together, still linked, still standing strong against stronger adversity. "This is Wyatt's shirt and Scarlet's wearing mine. Our mother got these shirts for us the day I went pro. Said people needed to know who we were, not only by our character but how we dressed. Wyatt about died when he saw it. I'm thankful my mom didn't see his expression. But from that day on, he wore it to every rodeo he entered. I never wore mine, and I wish that I had. Because my brother showed the world what family meant to him. Today, I'm wearing Wyatt's shirt, in honor of him."

His declaration was met with silence. The crowd became uncertain, and the riders lost some of the ire. Dalton stood up a little taller. "And I'm riding for him."

The two cowboys I didn't know stepped forward, but Dusty and Travis stepped directly in front of them, stopping their progress.

"He can't get away with this!" one of them yelled.

"He's not going to…because he's going to turn and walk away, out of respect for Wyatt," Dusty explained.

Dalton, however, was having none of it. He shook his head and turned toward Scarlet. "Why don't you and Charli go find a seat close to the gate? I want you there when I take the lead from Travis."

"That's not going to happen because you're not going to be riding in the Invitational or any other bull riding event." Travis crossed his arms over his chest. He looked like he was ready for a showdown at sundown. "I don't know if you're guilty or not—"

"I'm not."

"But you being here isn't appropriate. And you know it."

"All I know is that my brother is dead." Dalton struggled to keep the emotion from his voice. "And I'm going to ride in his honor. No one, and I mean *no one*, is going to stop me."

"Fellas!" Taylor came rushing from the back of the Ranch with Cade and Joe Buck on her heels. Joe wasn't wearing his usual friendly smile; he also had his bouncer look that said these bull riders might participate in the most dangerous sport in the world, but he was much more dangerous than any bull. Cade frowned in my direction, as if I'd caused this whole chest-pounding incident, before he turned his attention to the others. He and Joe eyed each cowboy to see which one was going to blow his macho lid first.

My money was on Travis.

But somehow Taylor weaved her magic and got all the guys to meet inside The Ranch and have a calm discussion. Cade insisted the residents of The Cowboy Ranch have a say in how the evening would proceed, and even Dalton agreed to the vote. He wasn't happy, but he also recognized the event was for them, not him.

I dragged Scarlet to the restroom with me, determined to talk some sense into her.

"He's been charged with murder. On two counts."

"He's innocent."

"I know you believe that, but have you seen the evidence against him?"

"It doesn't matter." She wore that stubborn look on her face, like her heart could make the truth bend to her will. I've worn that look a time or two myself. Eventually, she'd have to accept the facts, or find more evidence to prove them wrong. I decided to show her a few things from the law's perspective.

"Have you seen the probable cause statement against Dalton?" Aubrey had shown it to me and it wasn't very encouraging.

"I don't have to. He told me everything."

"Dalton made a statement to the press that he was going to unseat his brother right before Wyatt disappeared."

"Courtney Force says she's going to unseat her father in the NHRA Funny Car National Championship too. It doesn't mean she's willing to kill him to win. It's called having a competitive drive."

"I don't know who Courtney Force is, or even what funny car racing is, but Dalton's statement isn't the only thing hanging over his head," I insisted.

Scarlet didn't care. It was obvious that nothing I said would change her mind. She knew what she knew, and that was it. What she knew, however, shocked me so badly I bypassed cardiac arrest and went straight for brain dead.

"They found a gun in Dalton's cabin," said Scarlet.

"You...You know about that?"

Her patience was endless. "Of course I do. He told me."

Chapter Twenty-Seven

"Is it his gun?" I asked.

"Are you asking out of concern for me, or are you working for Mateo?"

"For you." Although, I wasn't above telling Mateo if I thought she was in imminent danger.

"Dalton has no idea where it came from. He's never seen it before."

"What about his cell phone? They found it in Erik's grave."

"He thought he'd lost it but Erik must have taken it."

"And he didn't try to get a new one? Come on, Scarlet. No one goes without their phone that long."

"He did order a new one, and he had it shipped to his hotel. He figured a couple days off the grid would do him some good."

I wasn't even going to try and wrap my head around that. I went on the next bit of evidence. "That gun was used in both homicides."

"That proves the murders are linked. Not that Dalton pulled the trigger."

"It was found in his cabin minus two bullets. Erik was shot twice."

"Again it proves they're linked. Not that Dalton's guilty."

I chalked that up to love being as blind as a Texas blind salamander. Neither had eyes; only shock waves could make them see. And Scarlet hadn't been shocked hard enough…yet.

I moved on. "Why did he treat you so badly that night at the bar? Why didn't he call you and let you know he was going to disappear? Why did he make everyone believe you were a groupie one night stand when he came back?"

"He doesn't remember anything after our first two dances at The Tool Shed Tavern. He doesn't remember walking off the dance floor. He doesn't remember putting me on the bar. He doesn't remember any of it."

"Yet, you can't deny the man treated you terribly."

"He did. But he doesn't remember it, nor does he know why he did it."

I wanted to knock some sense into her, but that would put me on the same level as Dalton. "That's no excuse. What will he do next time he drinks too much?"

Scarlet folded her arms and began tapping that beautiful sky-blue heel on the bathroom tile. "Are you about done?"

I wasn't even close to being done. "Why didn't he call? He let you worry for days... You thought he'd fallen off a cliff and was lying in the woods, injured."

"He thought I would think he was off with another woman."

An indignant noise escaped my lips. "And that's better?"

"It is to a man who's been told that I was going around town saying I had another notch in my lipstick case."

"What?"

"Erik told him that I'd swept him to the curb like yesterday's trash and was going around bragging about another rider I'd rode hard, like I was a groupie or something."

"Oh."

"Yeah, oh." It was Scarlet's turn to get fired up. "So excuse me if I'm not feeling particularly broken up about the man's death."

"But—"

"That doesn't mean I wished him dead. It means I'm not going to mourn him now that he's gone."

I could understand that, but there was one fact she was forgetting. Dalton attacked me with a branding iron and left his mark on my barn. "What about my hair and the brand he left on The Barn?"

"I asked him about that. He didn't know anything about it. So let me ask you a question, Charli." I could tell she was starting to get angry with me and my constant pushing.

"Shoot."

"Do you really believe a bull rider with the size of Dalton's arms couldn't overpower you and leave a brand on your forehead if he tried? You're a beanpole."

I was kind of tired of being compared to a bean. It was insulting as a woman. I had curves; they just weren't hairpin curves. Then again, maybe my curves defined a hair pin more appropriately. "I don't know."

"It wasn't him."

"I never saw the guy's face. I honestly don't know. All I know for sure is that the branding iron that left its mark on my barn was found in his cabin." And that wasn't all, but I was guessing Scarlet hadn't seen the morning news. "Did you read about the book Dalton had in his backpack?"

She shook her head, still not open to much of anything I was saying.

"Inside Dalton's copy of *The Dangerous Eight* was a map to Wyatt's grave."

That one tidbit changed everything. Scarlet hadn't known about it. I could see the wavering of doubt in her eyes—until she shut it down. Slammed that door without a glance back at the resounding consequences. Then she went another direction. "I've been doing research on potential suspects."

"What are you talking about?"

"All the people who were here when Wyatt disappeared."

"The entire population of Hazel Rock?" At least I was excluded from her list.

"No, don't be silly." She rubbed her chin. "Although they could be included..." Thank God she shook that idea right out of her head. "There are a few people here, but mostly those on the rodeo circuit."

It was my turn to look skeptical. She continued anyway.

"Look at Jessie." Scarlet said.

"Jessie Mahan?" Scarlet was beginning to grasp at imaginary pieces of straw in a hay basket.

"You've seen that evil eye of his."

"I've seen his *blind* eye. His cornea transplant went bad and he lost his sight."

"Exactly! He got hit in the eye while he was helping Wyatt in the chute on Wyatt's very last ride. The bull bucked and Wyatt's hand reared back and struck him in the eye. Jessie was mad."

I couldn't see Jessie being mad at anyone. The guy was as tame as a bunny. "Daisy wouldn't have let Jessie out of her sight long enough for him to get away with murder."

Scarlet's face lit up. "That's it! They're in this together."

The only argument I could muster was an eye roll.

"Okay fine. I'll scratch Jessie and Daisy off the list."

"Thank you."

"What about Sly Alexander? He and Wyatt were always at each other's throats. They battled back and forth for the championship. They fought like—"

"Like, brothers. Sly is naming his baby boy after Wyatt."

"That's to assuage his guilt," she insisted.

I decided to use her heart against her hare-brained idea. "Does Dalton think Sly could have killed Wyatt?"

"Well no, but—"

"Let it go, Scarlet." My voice echoed off the tile walls as if I was repeating myself over and over.

"What about Erik and Taylor?"

"Erik is dead and Taylor kind of has her hands a little full picking up the pieces of the invitational."

Scarlet moved on. "Travis has always spoken poorly of Wyatt—"

Aubrey walked into the restroom before Scarlet could argue further. The young woman stopped when she saw us. Part of me felt sorry for her. She'd been pursuing Scarlet as a story for so long she wasn't sure what to say to her on a personal level. The other part of me thought she needed to experience the backlash of putting a story before a relationship. Aubrey looked at Scarlet and waited for the anvil to drop on her head.

Scarlet, however, took the high road. "How's your internship going?"

"Fantastic! I couldn't have asked for a better assignment." She beamed from ear-to-ear and I could tell she was truly happy. I could also see that she could be a real pain in the patootie.

"I'm glad." Scarlet looked in the mirror, adjusted her hat, and swiped at a smudge in her make-up that wasn't there.

The young girl, with her curls bound in a ponytail and freckles spattering her nose and cheeks, looked about twelve as she peered at Scarlet's reflection. "Can I ask you a few questions, Scarlet?"

Scarlet eyed Aubrey in the mirror, then slowly turned. In that look, I saw Aubrey dying a slow and painful death if she asked the wrong questions. Scarlet had her limits, and I'd already pushed most of them. "I can't promise I'll answer any."

Aubrey quickly put her camera down on the counter and pulled her phone out of the back pocket of her jean shorts and turned on the voice recorder. "This is Aubrey Buchanan reporting for ABN News. I'm here at the Cowboy Ranch Invitational speaking to Scarlet Jenkins in the...er... the women's restroom."

I rolled my eyes and hoped someone would delete that bit of information.

Aubrey continued.

"Ms. Jenkins, I couldn't help but overhear that you've been researching other possible suspects—"

"Aubrey Buchanan! Were you eavesdropping on us?" I asked.

Aubrey covered the mic on her phone. "I'm a reporter now, that's what we do," she said and then continued before I could object further. "I've also been looking into other possible suspects with the idea in mind that the killer would be lurking in the shadows. You know how they say the killer always returns to the crime scene?"

My shoulders dropped with impatience. I was beginning to know what Mateo felt like when I meddled. "Sometimes he doesn't," I muttered.

Aubrey's cute brow scowled in my direction. "Sometimes he does."

"What if the killer's a she?" I asked just for the sake of argument.

"That's what I'm saying," added Scarlet.

"You're jumping at possibilities without proof," I insisted.

"But what if I have proof?" Aubrey was holding her phone up to her mouth like it was a microphone.

Her comment stopped Scarlet and me cold. Like we were playing a game, and Aubrey'd just said, *Simon says don't breathe.*

We broke all the rules of Simon Says and reached for Aubrey at the same time. We pulled her back into the farthest part of the restroom, our backs against the last stall door.

"What do you mean you have proof?" I asked.

Aubrey was pretty pleased with herself, but cautious as well. She peered over her shoulder toward the door and held her phone up in the middle of our mini huddle before continuing in a hushed voice. "I found several interviews online that were given after Wyatt didn't show up for his last night of competition eight years ago. Sly and Jessie spoke out against Wyatt. Said his disappearing act was in poor taste and a disservice to the fans and the riders at The Cowboy Ranch." I knew about both statements, that was nothing new. "But Travis did one the day after Wyatt disappeared. He said, and I quote, 'Wyatt Hibbs is going to find himself in an early grave.'" She leaned back on her heels, completely satisfied with herself.

Scarlet was brimming with hope.

I wasn't so enthusiastic. "Why did he say that?"

"What do you mean?"

"In what context did Travis say that?" I asked.

Scarlet jumped on the bandwagon faster than a roadrunner dodging a bullet. "Does it matter? For all intents and purposes, Wyatt was already in a grave when he said it. I'm not a fan of a coincidence that big."

Aubrey nodded, but I stuck with my question. "In what context did Travis use that phrase?"

Aubrey kicked her feet around a little bit before answering. "He was talking about the way Wyatt stayed in the pen too long with a rogue bull."

"A rogue bull?"

"Yeah there was this bull, Lucifer, that was totally out of control in the pen."

Scarlet jumped in. "That's the bull that he was riding when Jessie got hurt."

Aubrey nodded, getting caught up in the excitement all over again. "Wyatt had to get off him, wait a few minutes, and then get back on. Only Lucifer did it again. On the third try, Wyatt got on. It was his last ride and his highest scoring, but the other riders were critical of him and the CBR. Saying Wyatt should have told the judges the bull wasn't fit and the CBR should have pulled the bull."

"What happened to the bull?"

"It acted up again on its next outing and the CBR disqualified it."

I was beginning to think I knew that bull. "Do you know who the stock contractor was that owned the bull?"

Aubrey started flipping through her notes on her phone, then stopped when she found the screen she was looking for. "Pierce Brown of Starlight Corral. Why? Does the name mean something to you?"

It meant a whole lot to me. His bull had bruised my ribs and my tailbone. The nasty abrasion on my arm was due to someone subjecting that bull to hormones he shouldn't have had, and I thoroughly expected the tests on Twisted Mister to revealed that he had a heavy dose of testosterone in his blood.

"Nope. Nothing," I told Aubrey. The last thing I wanted to do was to put an eighteen-year-old girl in danger, but I was going to tell Mateo everything she'd just shared with me. Whether it was related to the murders, I wasn't sure. It just stunk to high heaven and back.

Scarlet turned back to me. "I gotta get going. Think about what I said. Think about Travis and what he's capable of."

That was the problem. I had been thinking about Travis. Wondering if my date knew more about the bulls and drugs than what he was revealing. Wondering if he only asked me out to get information about what I knew. Wondering why he hadn't even attempted to text me or call me after our date. For a man who claimed it was no accident that we always ran into each other, he'd been pretty scarce since he walked me to my door and kissed me on the cheek. Even today, standing right in front of him, I hadn't registered on his radar at all. It'd been like I didn't exist. And maybe that should concern me more than it had.

Chapter Twenty-Eight

Daisy came looking for me about the time I left the restroom. Not only was she protective of her husband, she was a drill sergeant when it came to work. I went back to the booth and took my place on my donut for the next couple hours.

At eight o'clock it was getting close to Dalton's turn to ride. I glanced at my phone, and looked over at Daisy, hoping for a signal that the gates were closed. I wanted to be there to see the end of the event. Not to watch Dalton, but to watch everyone's reaction around him. Aubrey's comment about the killer returning to the scene of the crime made me wonder if a killer would also be interested in how he—or she—ruined someone else's life. Was that a point of joy to a murderer? Did he think, *Ha! Sucker!* or *That guy's so stupid, I could set him up all day long and no one would know*, or would his thoughts be more superior minded: *I could get away with killing anyone; they're all inferior to me*, or was he out there fretting that someone, somewhere might catch on?

My money was on all four. The killer I had in mind was someone who would experience conflicting emotions. One-minute superiority, the next inferiority. One-minute brave beyond his or her abilities, and the next a complete coward. In this case, it just made sense to me—and I wanted to see if I could recognize that person in the crowd. Weed him out from all the rest of the spectators who were caught up in the drama of the moment. A part of me also wanted to win, but my motives were much different than the killer's. Scarlet's future hung in the balance, and I wasn't willing to sit idly by and let a coward win.

"That's it. We've sold to capacity. No more stragglers coming in at the last minute to watch," Daisy announced.

"So we can leave?" I was off my donut faster than I thought possible. At least faster than Jessie's rise out of his chair.

Daisy waggled her finger at me for the umpteenth time. "*You* can leave. That's my husband, he has to stay."

"Thank you, Daisy. Bye Jessie!"

I made my way toward the pens, hoping to at least find a place to stand and watch the people milling around in back and in the audience. Camera crews were stacked on top of each other, but it appeared Liza Twaine and Aubrey had the best spot in the area, since Liza's station was broadcasting the event live. I finagled my way through just in time to see Dusty Lamb signal to the gatemen to open the gate. He was riding a bull named Air Raid that got so much height when he kicked you'd think he was ready to take flight. I was shocked to see the bull kick and then raise his head, his entire body off the ground as Dusty battled to stay on him. Each kick a true testament to Dusty's ability not to go head over heels across the bull's head as Air Raid lowered his nose, and kicked at what looked like a ninety-degree angle. The buzzer barely sounded before the bull added a nasty twist and Dusty lost his balance. His feet lifted behind him. He released his grip and was sent over the bull's front shoulder.

The clowns swarmed and Dusty rolled out of the way to his feet. In a matter of seconds, he was on the rails and Air Raid was through the exit chute. Dusty took his hat off and waved to the crowd with a confident grin.

I could hear Liza giving color commentary about Dusty and was surprised by how much she actually knew about bull riding. She finished her bit about his triumphant comeback from a near career ending injury and said the fans could expect big things to come out of the junior rider in the event.

Then Aubrey relaxed her camera and Liza listened intently on her ear piece. She argued with someone as the next two riders were thrown off short of the eight-second bell. Her voice gradually got louder and louder. Aubrey looked around and started filming what had to be fluff pieces of clowns dancing, gatemen talking to pretty girls in the crowd, and bulls wandering in the pens behind the chutes.

I moved closer to hear what problems were stirring behind the scenes.

"You can't do that!" Liza screeched into her headset.

Aubrey rubbed her earpiece and winced with the noise.

"He's why everyone is here!"

Something else was said on the other end and Liza's face inflamed. "I don't give a flying fig what the sponsors want or don't want. If you don't show his ride, the CBR, our station, and my reputation will suffer!"

I looked at Aubrey for confirmation. Were they really considering not showing Dalton's ride on television? Aubrey gave me a subtle nod and went about filming the leader board and the roping cowboy at the other end of the arena.

Liza's perfectly cold composure was gone. She was steaming with anger. "He's making his way over here for an interview before his ride. Are you telling me I can't do it or I'll be fired?"

It was unheard of in the Championship Bull Riding circuit to not show the top few leader's runs. The lead position was where everyone wanted to be. Yet the sponsors were demanding the station not show the potential winner's ride.

Rumors were making their way through the crowd. The gatemen and clowns were looking toward the cameras, which were suddenly turned in every direction but that of Dalton Hibbs walking across the arena. Some fans jeered, some patted him on the back in support. There was a wide range of emotions being played out.

I pulled out my phone and tried calling Scarlet, but my call went to voicemail. I scanned the crowd near the chutes, but couldn't find her anywhere. If Dalton came over here and found out his interview had been canceled, there was no telling what that would do to the man. I certainly didn't want to find out.

Peter Kroft and Aiden waltzed down the aisle like they owned the place.

"It seems you're having problems with your sponsors," Peter said to Liza but made sure his voice carried through the crowd. "Denying the fans the number one rider is unheard of. Isn't a man innocent until proven guilty?"

Liza was like a hungry sow with an empty trough, snorting and huffing with no real substance behind the noise. The people around her, however, were beginning to see what was going on. They grumbled and complained hearing Peter's declaration of innocent until proven guilty over anything else. They paid good money to see Dalton ride, and they thought the fans at home should be able to experience the event as well.

"So are you going to give up your position to free media, or are you going to try and block our special report?"

Liza managed to spit out two words: "Special report?"

Peter's white teeth glistened in the light. "KBC is broadcasting a live shot of Dalton Hibbs' ride. And since you won't be interviewing him, we thought it only prudent to allow Dalton the opportunity to say something to our viewers that isn't censored by sponsors."

Liza stomped her heeled foot and was about to let into Peter when the camera turned. "This is Peter Kroft reporting from The Cowboy Ranch Invitational of Championship Bull Riding in Hazel Rock, Texas. Yesterday the leader in the all-around scoring for the CBR Tour, Dalton Hibbs, was charged in the Coleman County Courthouse with two counts of murder in the first degree. Charges to be taken seriously, yet charges that have not been found to be true in a court of law. Charges that could be dropped at any minute or adjudicated. We don't know.

"What we do know is that in this great country, anyone accused is presumed innocent until proven guilty. That the press is free and not corrupted by special interest groups or political pressure. Yet the reason for this broadcast is just that. ABN has banned its reporters from interviewing Dalton Hibbs and has chosen not to show his ride that could clinch The Cowboy Ranch Invitational...."

I didn't hear anything after that. Liza Twaine was stomping her way up the stairs with the fans in the stands heckling her the entire way. I stopped Aubrey before she got caught up in the scene Liza was making with the hecklers.

"What's going on?" I asked.

"We were told that the network would be showing a piece that honored Wyatt and Erik instead of Liza's interview with Dalton."

"Wow. Has that ever been done before?"

"You're asking me? This whole scene is new to me. I'm just glad I've got a front row seat. It will make a great exposé for my freshman media class at East Texas University."

"Are you sure you want to follow Liza with that camera and show the crowd you work for the same station? It's not like these people know you."

At about that moment Liza flipped someone in the crowd the bird and got beaned in the head with a paper cone of blue cotton candy.

Aubrey giggled. "Don't tell her I laughed. Even though I've learned a ton from her, she's a bit difficult to work for."

"So the interview with Dalton is canceled?" I asked.

"Apparently so. I heard that Cade wasn't happy. Dalton's actually hired him as his defense attorney."

Oh, boy. Cade had represented me in the past, although the case never went anywhere because I was immediately cleared of any wrongdoing. But Dalton had been charged and that pitted mayor against sheriff. That could not end well.

"Taylor threw a conniption, and the execs were sweating the backlash of the public, and from what I hear, Peter Kroft is going to take our interview with Dalton." Aubrey was eyeing the crowd with more than a little bit of trepidation. "I'm not sure I want to walk through that gauntlet."

I slowly removed my sweater, struggling with not one, but both arms before putting it over her camera. "Act like you're not associated with Liza. Most of these fans haven't noticed who you are, they're focused on her." It was the best move, all things considering.

"Thank you! I'll be sure to get it back to you."

"Only if it doesn't get egged."

Aubrey gave me a quick and painful hug, then headed up the stairs.

There was a break in the riding. I wasn't sure what caused it, but the clowns started entertaining the crowd with various dances to different kinds of music. The fan favorite seemed to be when they started crawling around on the arena floor like a famous eighties pop singer as her music played through the loudspeakers. I knew what was on that floor beside the six hundred tons of dirt they brought in for the event. All you had to do is look at the backside of the bulls in the pens and see what those clowns were rolling in. Nasty doesn't begin to describe that smell.

A cowboy offered me his seat as he put his kid on his lap and vacated his prime real estate. I accepted his gallantry with ease as I waited to see if Peter would interview Dalton in Liza's old spot.

A cheer from the crowd a few minutes later signaled Dalton's arrival. There were still some boos mixed in, and I honestly wasn't sure where I stood on the issue of him riding. What did make my heart pitter-patter was the man dressed in a cowboy hat, western jeans, and cowboy boots who sauntered down the aisle behind him. To many, Cade looked like an attractive bodyguard who knew how to wear a pair of jeans. To those of us who knew him, he looked like our mayor and now Dalton's defense attorney who'd make sure anything that was said wouldn't hurt Dalton in court.

What interested me the most was the location of the interview. Most of the riders were interviewed outside their staging room as they headed to and from the chutes. Yet Dalton's was in the middle of the crowd where they could turn on him quicker than a scalded haint could run.

Chapter Twenty-Nine

"This is Peter Kroft, for CNCB News, reporting live from The Cowboy Ranch in Hazel Rock, Texas, with a special report."

The crowd cheered. The interview was also streaming live through the arena, and although not everyone had a front row seat to the interview between Peter and Dalton like I did, they could hear everything that was said over the intercom while Cade stood on the sidelines right next to Dalton, making sure nothing was said that would hurt his client's case. The man hadn't even acknowledged my presence despite being two feet away from me.

Peter's cameraman, Aiden, was sitting on the step behind me, zeroing in on the three of them standing at the railing that served as a barrier between the arena and the fans. It would make a great story to watch on the news later that night.

"I'm standing with the champion, Dalton Hibbs, who was charged with two counts of murder yesterday in the deaths of Erik Piper, promoter of The Cowboy Ranch Invitational and author of *The Dangerous Eight*, a number one best-selling book about bull riding." Peter turned toward the cowboy standing in the middle of the two men, making the interview seem more intimate.

I watched as Cade whispered something in Dalton's ear and the cowboy nodded.

"You were also charged with the murder of your brother, Wyatt, who disappeared eight years ago. Would you like to tell our viewers about that?"

"All I'm going to say about the charges is that I'm innocent—"

"What about the evidence against you?"

"I'm not here to debate the evidence—"

"Didn't they find the murder weapon in your cabin? What kind of gun was it?"

Cade interrupted before Dalton could speak. "Mr. Kroft, out of respect for the victims' families, including Dalton"—Cade put his hand on Dalton's shoulder in a consolatory manner—"we ask that you not bring up the details of the case and that we stay on point. Specifically, that we discuss the cause that has brought all of the fans to the arena today— The Cowboy Ranch."

Dalton took over before Peter could protest. "I would like to tell the fans and the viewers one thing." The silence grew with the anticipation. "Erik Piper didn't write *The Dangerous Eight*, my brother did. And I aim to make it right."

Cade's jaw flexed.

"You're saying that Erik Piper stole your brother's work?" Peter asked.

"I'm saying that Wyatt Hibbs wrote *The Dangerous Eight* and that's all I'm saying. But I would like to take a moment and tell you about Wyatt."

Cade's feet shuffled. He was not pleased with Dalton going off script. I couldn't say that I blamed him. That bombshell about the book had the crowd stirring and the gossip flying.

"Wyatt loved bull riding. He loved the animals." Dalton's voice cracked and he hesitated. His eyes began to glisten as he began to work his bottom lip. It was as if at that very moment, Dalton realized his brother was never coming back.

Aiden shuffled on the step behind me, and I knew he was angling for that money shot—the one that captured a strong man breaking.

Dalton cleared his throat and swallowed visibly. He smiled—at his inability to talk, at his memory of his brother—and a tear slowly rolled down his cheek. It was as if it was the first tear he'd ever shed. His lips curled inward, and his emotions threatened to get the best of him as he worked his bottom lip with his teeth and swiped away that lone sign of love between siblings.

Peter stood and waited. Holding the mic in front of Dalton, letting the crowd hear him sniff. And if I wasn't mistaken, he'd moved it just a fraction closer, to let his audience experience the raw emotion of a grieving man.

"Wyatt loved the animals," Dalton repeated. "He would spend hours in the pens back home, brushing them, making sure they were comfortable, healthy, and he'd talk to every single one of them like they were individuals. Even when he was on the circuit, he'd go down to the pens and talk to the bulls. No one respected the animals the way Wyatt did."

Dalton looked up into the crowd as another stray tear fell from his eye. This time, he didn't try to hide it. Didn't swipe it away or stop the others from forming. I could hear sniffles around me. The crowd was completely drawn into his emotion. Including me.

"He taught me everything I know about bull riding. Taught me about respecting women, and doing the right thing—the honorable thing and I want to do the honorable thing right here and now." Dalton took off his hat and held it across his chest. "I owe an apology to Scarlet. I treated her horribly the other night and embarrassed her in front of her friends and people she didn't know. There's no excuse for my behavior. None, whatsoever. She's an intelligent, beautiful woman and I'm lucky to have her on my arm any day. So, Scarlet, darling, wherever you are, I hope you'll let me make it up to you."

The crowd cheered, the noise traveling through the arena in waves as they stood up and applauded the man accused of murder. Dalton put his hat back on his head and smiled the killer smile of his that we'd all grown to love so much. And I understood why Scarlet had faith in him— believed beyond any shadow of a doubt, that he was innocent.

Dalton put his hands in the air and motioned for spectators to have a seat and quiet down so he could continue. Rallied by the support of the fans, Dalton's voice was stronger. "The Cowboy Ranch was something Wyatt felt strongly about. He wanted to help the riders before him who rode the rough way for the rest of us and made bull riding what it is today. These men deserve our respect and our support. Wyatt didn't care if his ribs were bruised, his shoulder dislocated, or his fingers broken. There was no way he was going to miss The Cowboy Ranch Invitational…until someone made sure he'd never ride again. Wyatt loved the challenge, loved the competition, not just between him and the bulls, but between the riders. He loved the camaraderie. That's why I want to ride in his honor tonight. That's why I sought the approval of the residents of The Ranch and they gave it to me unanimously. Now, I'm asking you—the fans—do I have your permission to ride in Wyatt's honor? To wear his riding outfit and let him go out with all the glory he should have had eight years ago?"

The crowd went wild before he even finished. Hats were flying and fists were pumping as "yahoos and yee-haws" traveled through the bleachers. Cade couldn't have been happier. He was wearing a big smile on his face as he held Dalton's hand up in the air like he'd already rode and won The Invitational.

And I guess in a way, he had, because the fans were behind him 100 percent.

Peter shook Dalton's hand and Dalton turned and waved his hat in the air to the crowd. They ate it up; even I couldn't help but clap. Then Dalton turned and hopped over the railing to the sawdust arena floor below. Several of the bullfighters shook his hand and smacked him on the back as he made his way over to the chutes. That camaraderie Dalton had been talking about, was alive and well.

* * *

I thanked the man next to me for the seat and was gone before Cade finished talking to Peter—no doubt giving a defense attorney's spiel about the innocence of his client—which I actually was starting to believe in this case. I'd tried to watch the crowd throughout the speech, but I had to admit, I was drawn into Dalton's tribute as much as anyone else. No one had looked overly suspicious, other than me, and I thought I'd try looking in a few other areas where the key players congregated. I made my way to the walkway around the arena and was heading toward the pens when I saw Mateo walking with Scarlet.

Scarlet's brows were drawn and her eyes were focused straight ahead. She was a cowgirl on a mission or a path of destruction, and Mateo looked a little bit worried about how that operation would end. I stepped in her path, and she almost plowed right through me. Recognition finally hit her and she pulled up short just in time.

"Charli, you're going to get hurt stopping in front of people like that."

"You look like you needed an intervention."

"Thank you. I couldn't agree more," Mateo said, but I kept my eyes on Scarlet. "Now if you two will excuse me, I have an arrest to make."

"I want to be there," Scarlet argued but I could tell by his abrupt departure that Mateo wanted no part of her interference so I stayed in front of her, blocking her path.

"Since when are you one to sit back and let things happen?"

"Since I can't move my left arm, and my right arm hurts like I fell in a bed of prickly pear cactus."

"Well, I need to be there when Mateo arrests Liza Twaine."

"Liza Twaine?"

"Yup. That woman is the one who broke into my trailer."

"Liza Twaine?" I knew I sounded like a broken record.

"It wasn't Dalton. I told you it wasn't, and this is just one more piece to the puzzle that proves his innocence."

"How does Mateo know it was Liza?"

"Her fingerprints. He got a hit this afternoon on the prints he took from inside my trailer. Liza had a DUI back in 2010 in Harris County. Mateo came over and asked me if I'd ever had Liza in my trailer. When I told him no, he asked me if I was sure." Scarlet's head bobbed back and forth in disbelief. "As if I'd ever forget that woman and her batty eyes walking inside my trailer."

"Why would Liza want to break into your trailer?"

"I don't know, but she's the one who stole the backpack and the book that Dalton swore he didn't take. Which means she set him up for the murder as well."

It was an interesting change of events and it definitely made the case against Dalton weaker by the moment. Scarlet started to walk around me, but again I stopped her forward progress.

"Don't you think it would be better for you to go tell Cade and Dalton what's going on? As his defense attorney, Cade's going to want to be present when they interview Liza."

Scarlet's lower lip jutted out. She wanted to see Liza Twaine put in cuffs, but her first priority was Dalton. "O.M.W. You're right. I just wanted to see those fancy bracelets clink on her wrist something fierce."

"I'll go watch and I'll tell Aubrey to get it all on tape. How's that?"

Scarlet beamed, her face lit up almost as much as it usually did. I hoped that light was there to stay. She hugged me quick and hard, and I resisted wincing as she pulled away. Somehow I had to stop people from hugging me until my ribs healed. Maybe I should bypass showers for a while—that would keep people at a distance.

Scarlet nearly skipped down the steps to join Cade and Dalton and I headed toward the pens where Mateo had gone in search of Liza. I arrived as he pulled Liza out of the riders' break room with her hands behind her back in cuffs. Aubrey looked shell-shocked as Liza told Mateo she knew her rights and the network's attorneys were going to eat him for lunch and his deputies for dessert.

I caught Aubrey's eye and motioned for her to get the event on film. I was shocked by her quick action. She didn't hesitate, capturing Liza's struggle and filthy mouth while Mateo politely asked her to come along peacefully. She didn't listen. She created a scene all the way out to the gate where they were greeted by Aiden with his camera rolling and Peter Kroft with a live mic in his hand.

"Any comment about being arrested on burglary charges, Liza?" Peter asked.

Liza glared as he stuck his microphone in her face. I actually enjoyed his timing for a change.

Scarlet and Dalton stood by the ticket booth with Cade. Cade was looking very much like an attorney giving his client instructions before he left to follow Mateo and Liza.

After Mateo had departed along with Liza and Cade, Scarlet kissed Dalton.

"For luck," I heard her say.

"I don't need luck when I got a good woman by my side." Dalton kissed her again and Scarlet's right foot rose in a dainty sexy lift. Aubrey captured it all. And again, I was thinking the cameras could be a good thing.

"Did he already ride?" I asked Scarlet.

"No, there was a television delay. Apparently, the sponsors of ABN News now want the ride recorded, but on delay."

Aubrey turned to us, her freckles standing out on her cheeks as she pushed against the earpiece in her left ear and the color drained from her face.

"You want me to give commentary during his ride?" she asked.

Scarlet and I looked at each other and grinned.

"Yes, sir. I know the rodeo very well," Aubrey said. "I'm on my way." She didn't even look as she turned her camera back on and followed Dalton down the corridor. Getting an exclusive view of the champ's walk to destiny. Hopefully.

Scarlet and I headed toward the area that Taylor had actually roped off for Scarlet at Dalton's request. Sly was sitting in one of the four box seats and stood up to let us pass by. Then he held my seat down while I put my donut in the chair and turned around to slowly lower myself.

"A lot of pressure on Dalton right now," Sly said as the crowd hushed.

Scarlet began wringing her hands. "You have no idea."

"Probably not to the same extent, but I know what it's like to ride after you've lost a loved one. Every bone in your body wants to honor them and do 'em proud. For Dalton, there's even more to it than that." He patted Scarlet's leg and turned his attention to the chute.

Scarlet looked at me and I gave her an encouraging smile. Taylor arrived and sat on the other side of Sly just in time to see Dalton's ride. Beyond, "Hello" and, "Thank you, for the seats," we didn't have time to say anything as Dalton climbed over the side of the chute. Everyone watched. The arena filled with the kind of silence normally found on a golf course, not a professional bull riding arena, as Dalton wrapped his hand, pounded the rope, and moved up into position on the bull's back. He signaled to the gatemen and the gate swung open. Time stood still as the blond bull actually backed out of the chute. I glanced at the scoreboard to catch the bull's name. "Angel" was lit up in red, and I wondered if that was fate speaking for Dalton.

Angel dipped his head and kicked with such force his back came up and smacked the brim of Dalton's hat. The hat fell into the dirt and the crowd cheered as Dalton stayed on. The bulls head swished from right to left, as his body twisted from left to right. Again, Angel bucked, trying to best his rider, and Dalton's white chaps flew in the air. For a moment, I thought his legs had released from their grip, but the ride went on. The crowd stood. The cheers increased. The camera flashes grew in intensity and frequency. The clock ticked as Dalton hung on, his form perfect and his blond hair bouncing freely with his white hat gone. It was almost as if he'd lost his halo. People saw the man—flawed, yet extremely talented on the back of an Angel.

The buzzer sounded and the clowns moved directly in front of the bull, distracting him as Dalton jumped off on an upward kick and landed on his feet. Angel took the bait, and went for the clown in front of the exit chute and disappeared from the arena. The crowd roared. Dalton's fists slammed the open air before he dropped to his knees and pointed toward the heavens.

I whooped for the pure joy of seeing an incredible ride, then regretted the emotion immediately, as my ribs sang a different tune. I looked at Scarlet, who had tears in her eyes and tracking down her cheeks. Sly was grinning and Taylor's eyes were filled to the brim as she stared at the scoreboard.

Up in lights, side by side, were images of Wyatt riding Lucifer and Dalton riding Angel. Both riders wearing the same outfit; the only difference was that one was still with us, and the other was gone. Wyatt's record score of 96.5, however, had just been broken by his little brother with a 96.75.

History had been made.

Chapter Thirty

I slept better that night than I had in the past several nights. I was thankful that the pain was slowly but surely dissipating even if it kept me from sprawling out across my bed like I normally did. When I woke up, the sun was shining and Princess was awake and rearing to go, which was unusual, but not unheard of. We each ate breakfast and had a bath. I got dressed and we headed over toward the secret passageway and made our way down to the bookstore. Just inside the tearoom, I found a very large object covered with numerous dark trash bags. The thing stood almost as tall as me with pointy peaks and rounded bumps that looked like nothing in particular. A large sign was taped to the front that read, "Do Not Peek." In parenthesis down below in smaller print, my dad had written, "That means you, Princess."

I stuck my tongue out at the bag but got a giddy feeling like Christmas morning. "I think he means you," I told the rodent at my feet.

Princess snorted. I'm not positive, but I'm pretty sure she meant, *In my dreams.*

Dad wasn't scheduled to come into work until around noon, but luckily he'd made plenty of sweet tea the night before. I called the bakery and ordered some cookies for the Monday morning kids' book art class. This week I was going to have them find a hidden sentence on a page and draw something to represent their own personal story over the rest of the print. I'd made an example of using the line "A perfect family day" with the individual words circled and the image of my father teaching me how to skip a rock down by the river.

I'd drawn the picture after going through some old photo albums my mom had put together, and found one of my dad and I down at the river. I remembered that day vividly with a picnic on the bank, my mom nestled on the shore on top of a blanket. The cancer had been ravaging her body, yet she'd been determined to enjoy her time with us like any other family. As soon as I saw the photo, I felt compelled to make it into something special to give to my father for his birthday at the end of the month. At the edge of the page, I drew my mom's hands with the camera, leaving out her frail body so that he could remember her the way he always spoke of her—whole, and full of life.

Princess waddled up to the front door and made the buzzer sound even though the door was still locked. It was her favorite pastime; something about the noise gave her joy and I never questioned it. Maybe it reminded her of her own family, back in their burrow when she was young. Whatever it was, it never seemed appropriate to disturb the ritual.

Our morning was steady with visitors getting ready to leave town. Some were staying for the closing ceremony that night, while others were heading home to get ready for the work week to begin. Since most of the shops had opened early for the special weekend, many had decided to stop in and do a little shopping on their way home. It was welcome business and we hoped they'd come back the following year.

When the buzzer went off, I was expecting to see a couple of middle aged women with their husbands in tow. Instead, a handsome cowboy sauntered up to the counter with a grin on his face.

"Fancy meeting you here, Princess," he said with all the charm I knew he had.

"Why, Travis. I do declare. You must have more brains than a pink armadillo if you could figure out how to find me."

Princess snorted from under the counter and waddled away. I think she disagreed.

Travis leaned over the counter and crowded my space. His elbow on the counter with his jaw resting in the palm of his hand, he asked, "I probably should have come by sooner, huh?"

"That would have been the gentlemanly thing to do, after taking a woman out to dinner," I chastised as I leaned over and rested my elbow on the counter and met his eyes at the same level.

"I messed up." He stated the obvious.

"You did."

"And I'm going to have to pay for it, aren't I?"

A flirtatious smile spread across my face. I couldn't help it. "You are."

"Can I see you again?"

"You're seeing me right now, aren't you?"

"I mean when I come back to Texas. I have to leave before the ceremony tonight, but I'd like to take you to dinner when I return. Would you go out with me again?"

His eyes weren't as dreamy as Mateo's, but I could easily get caught up in them if I allowed myself to. "That would depend," I said.

"On what?"

"On when you're coming back, and whether or not I'm available."

Travis grinned and snuck a quick kiss on my lips. "I'm not sure when I'll be back, but when you see me again, I'll be bearing flowers."

"That's the least you can do," I called to the smiling cowboy who walked out my front door. Only time would tell if he'd return.

Dad showed up a little early to help shut The Barn down and take me to the rodeo to see the closing ceremonies. And to check to see if I'd peeked at his surprise. He'd even put a thin piece of fishing line across the bag. When I expressed mock outrage, though I really had been tempted, he got that twinkle of teasing in his eye and started talking about the ceremony. He'd insisted it was a sight to see and I couldn't miss it. As I finished one final sale and wished the customers safe travels home, Taylor walked in the front door. She was wearing her usual get-up of a fancy dress and even fancier heels to match. I looked down at my jean shorts and *Buy the Book* T-shirt and shrugged. At least my aqua colored flip-flops matched the lettering on my shirt.

"Good morning, Bobby Ray. Charli. Are you ready for closing ceremonies?"

"He insists it's a must see," I said.

Taylor winked at my dad. "Oh, it is. You really can't miss it."

I looked back and forth between the two and began to worry. Not that my dad didn't deserve happiness, but Taylor was maybe five years older than me and the thought of my father dating someone that young gave me the willies. Luckily, Dad saw where my mind had traveled and laughed in my face.

"You're all the trouble I need, Princess."

Mateo entered the store and was greeted by the real Princess of The Barn. She squeaked and wiggled and hopped around like a puppy welcoming its owner home.

He reached down and scratched her ears. "What's that all about, little one?"

"Did you have waffles for breakfast?"

Mateo looked at my dad like he'd been spying on him. "Yes."

Dad nodded. "I knew it. She can smell waffles a mile away. She doesn't care for pancakes, but waffles are a whole 'nuther story."

Princess looked at my dad, then Mateo. I could have sworn she shook her head in disgust before waddling off.

"Good morning, Sheriff." Taylor smiled but I couldn't help but notice how her hand stayed glued to her side as she gave Princess a sidelong look. It wasn't the first time someone didn't want to have any armadillo cooties.

"Ms. Goode, nice to see you again."

"Likewise." She turned back to my dad. "Bobby Ray, did you have time to finish that project for the closing ceremony?" Taylor asked.

"I did. I've got it at the side door waiting for you."

"Excellent."

"Do you need any help, Daddy?" I asked.

"Oh no, I'm not giving you a chance to peek," he said. Taylor and Dad headed back toward the tearoom, talking the whole way.

"What's that all about?" Mateo asked.

"Daddy made something for the ceremony today, but won't let me see it."

"And you didn't peek?" His left eyebrow rose, skeptically. "I find that hard to believe."

"I think you better remember who kept Scarlet from following you yesterday when you arrested Liza Twaine."

"Yeah, that's what I stopped by to talk to you about."

That uncomfortable feeling started creeping up my neck. "Oh?"

"I had to let her go."

"What?"

"She admitted she broke into Scarlet's trailer, but she was looking for clues to track down Dalton. She knew we weren't going to let the media near the grave site and since you and Scarlet were there, she thought it was the perfect time to have a look-see in Scarlet's trailer."

"But she committed a burglary—"

"It was criminal trespass."

His response was too quick and way too nonchalant for the trauma that break-in caused—the sense of violation Scarlet felt. Trespass was a charge for someone walking on your lawn, not for someone who rifled through everything you owned. "She broke into Scarlet's home."

"And she didn't take anything. It's a class B misdemeanor."

"So she's out?"

"Posted her bond last night. But you should know the charges will probably be dropped." Mateo looked over his shoulder, not wanting Taylor or my daddy to hear. "She gave us some evidence in the homicide case."

"What evidence?"

"Evidence. And that's all I'm going to say."

"And you're telling me this now because…"

"Because I thought you could keep an eye on Scarlet today and make sure that she doesn't tick off my witness."

"You mean Liza."

"Yes, Liza. I'm going to get my hair cut now, and I'll tell her what I've told you, but I don't trust Scarlet to keep her mouth shut."

"Since when has Scarlet not kept her mouth shut?"

"Since the day she was born?"

"You're funny."

"Some people think so."

There was a thud at the back of the store that stopped our conversation.

"Did I hurt it?" Taylor asked.

"No. It's okay. Let me get Mateo to help. Mateo!" my dad called.

"Coming, Bobby Ray." Mateo looked me in the eye. "Remember, I'm counting on you to keep Scarlet out of trouble."

I sighed heavily and capitulated without a fight. "Fine."

Mateo disappeared toward the back of the store as two more customers came in. When I saw one of the women was carrying an armadillo purse, I scooted Princess behind the counter. I wasn't sure how she'd react to one of her kind being a handbag.

A warm breeze wafted through the store as I heard my dad and Mateo grunting instructions back and forth. "Turn this way." "Angle it that way." "Go back." And finally, a loud metal clunk right before Mateo yelled, "Owww! *Dios Mio.*"

I knew that sound, a little too well.

I ran back to find Mateo holding his head. Dad was holding my mom's sign and Taylor was digging in her purse for a tissue to stop the blood that was seeping through the strands of hair on the back of Mateo's head. The over-sized package was sitting in the courtyard.

"I thought I told you to hang that thing properly?" Mateo asked my dad irritably.

"I did, but apparently, you're not treating Princess appropriately. Otherwise, her mother would have never dropped it on your head."

Mateo looked up at the intact bracket and back down at the sign that appeared to be in top condition.

"If you hadn't been so secretive and taken it through the front door, nothing would've happened." Both men scowled in my direction. I held up my hands, "I'm just saying…"

"Let's get it loaded into Taylor's truck before the entire side of the building falls on my head," Mateo grumbled.

I took the sign from my dad, who was grinning like a pet raccoon, but hid it when Mateo looked in his direction. They took the package to the front of the store with Taylor scurrying along behind them holding a tissue to Mateo's head. The loading into the back of Taylor's big black SUV occurred with no further mishaps.

Out of breath, my dad asked, "Taylor, could I ask one more favor?"

"Of course." Taylor smiled, turning on that charm all the men in town seemed to love. "Anything for you, doll."

Daddy blushed and Mateo and I shared a look. He was thinking the same thing I was about Taylor's interest in my father.

"Could you give Princess a ride to the rodeo? She's still unable to drive and I don't want to rush our customers out the door."

"Absolutely, that's not a problem at all." Taylor turned toward me and I wondered if I was looking at my future step-mom. "Are you ready, Princess?"

"Yes, ma'am. Let me grab my purse." I said.

Mateo had to have the last word. "Don't forget your donut."

Chapter Thirty-One

We got in Taylor's vehicle that had been parked in the sun, and the temperature had already risen to above my comfort level. Taylor started the SUV and I welcomed the cool air blowing out the vents. The interior of the vehicle was a whole lot nicer than my daddy's truck. The seats were leather, and the dash was covered with wood trim. The stereo played the latest country hit through so many speakers that I imagined sitting in a field and having a dance party with the windows rolled down. Taylor slipped off her shoes to drive and put her red lace heels in the backseat before we headed out of town.

"Those are gorgeous shoes," I told her, a little bit of envy tinged my voice.

"Thank you. I just got them at a boutique in Oak Grove. I broke the heel on my favorite pair of red stilettos the other day, but it worked out well since I found these."

"How do you manage to wear stilettos around the arenas? The buildings aren't exactly made for shoes you'd find on a fashion runway."

Taylor laughed. "No they're not, but I've found stilettos give me the confidence I need in a man's world."

"It'd be the opposite for me. I'd fall on my face at their feet, at least every other day. It'd be humiliating," I confided.

"It's a matter of what you're used to. I could hike in heels before I could walk in flip-flops."

I started to laugh but lost all enthusiasm as something in that statement nagged my brain.

Fuzz buckets. I looked at Taylor who was staring straight ahead at the road. Her complexion still beautiful even though a few wrinkles had started to crease at her eyes.

She made a quick glance in my direction when my laughter stopped, her eyes scanning my face for the reason. "Is something wrong?"

"You were hiking in your red heels when you broke one," I said.

Taylor's face drained. And my heart began beating so hard I was pretty sure I could fly if I could just get out of Taylor's killer wheels.

"I suppose it's times like this that make a Southern saying really resonate. I mean, what else could I possibly say but, *bless your heart*." She pulled a gun out of her driver's door pocket and held it across her lap, pointing at me with her left hand.

"You could stop the car and let me out and just keep driving. I won't say a word."

"That cute sheriff of yours would have it out of you after one roll in the sheets."

I put my hands up, despite it hurting like the dickens, and leaned against the passenger door. The last thing I wanted was to get shot. I imagined it would hurt a lot more than bruised ribs. "There are no sheets between us."

Taylor laughed. "Princess, that's only a matter of time with a man like that."

"Nope. I swear, no sheets. I've sworn off sheets."

Taylor kept driving like we were on a girl's day out. But we weren't. She passed the exit for The Ranch and hit the highway. If I didn't know I was in trouble before, I did now.

"I said that once upon a time, when a cowboy left me," Taylor said. "He was the next best thing to apple pie. An up-and-comer. Held the record for bull-riding and the night he broke it… He stood me up. Disappeared and never came back for me." A tear slid down her cheek.

"Are you talking about Wyatt?"

She sniffed but kept talking. I slowly reached for my phone in the side pocket of my donut and jabbed some numbers without looking down at the keypad. I cleared my throat to cover the noise of the ring on the opposite end and prayed whoever I had randomly dialed would be able to tell what was going on.

"Wyatt said he was going to marry me before he disappeared. Eight years, eight long years I've been waiting for that man to return so I could exact revenge on his cold heart. Come to find out, he's been dead the whole time. His heart was cold before it disintegrated into nothing."

"So you didn't kill Wyatt?"

"I loved Wyatt—would die for Wyatt." She swiped at her tears and her face hardened. "I did die for Wyatt. I don't know the Taylor he said he loved anymore. She's been gone for too many years."

"Who killed him?"

"That's the funniest part of this whole story." She laughed, but it was more manic than humorous. It was downright freaking scary. "Erik killed him. Just shot him dead for no good reason.

"At least that's what I thought until Cade told me our deposit was way too big on the first day. And then the second day. Then I realized Erik had been stealing the funds all along. The computers don't connect to anything; each one can easily be doctored for an audit. The donations vary from customer to customer, and most are done in cash. Who's going to miss cash with no real record keeping? Since the day I started working with Erik, I'd asked him to use a better system when we did charity events. But he insisted keeping it simple was the best way to deal with small town types."

Small town types? Jiminy Christmas if the guy wasn't dead, I'd kill him myself. "So he killed Wyatt because Wyatt figured out he was stealing the money?" I asked.

"That's only part of it. Erik liked drama. Thought it created a buzz around the circuit for the media to grab hold of. We weren't doing too well the year Wyatt disappeared. The bulls were lack-luster and caused the scores to be low. The riders were demanding better bulls and Erik found a way to deliver."

"What do you mean 'deliver'?"

She turned down highway 965 and I knew exactly where she was going. I wished I didn't.

"He brought in Pierce Brown and the Starlight Corrals as a stock contractor. His bulls are given so much testosterone and other chemicals I don't know how they pass the testing."

"They pass the testing because they dope them *after* they've received their medicals. I saw them doping Twisted Mister." I was really hoping that sharing my information with her would create a bond between us, but the farther we went, the more manic she looked. "Why are we going East on 965?" I asked just in case someone was listening on the other end of my phone. "Are you taking us to Wyatt's grave?"

Taylor paused and slowly turned her head in my direction. The slow movement reminded me of *The Exorcist*. It was the spooky look, right before green vomit spewed from Linda Blair's mouth. "Where's your phone?" Taylor demanded.

I blinked.

"Where's your phone!" She spit as she yelled and I truly expected it to be green. It wasn't, but her complexion was mottled. Her pupils held a nanosecond of sanity before it disappeared completely. I turned my phone off and held it out for her to take. She put her gun back in her door and snatched the phone.

"It was in the pocket on my donut," I explained.

She pulled up the password screen as she swerved toward the shoulder of the highway. That didn't seem to faze her in the least but scared the bejeezus out of me.

"What's your password?"

"Rock."

"That's not very original, considering where you live. I need the numbers," she demanded while holding my phone over the top of the steering wheel.

I thought it was very original. I'd set it before I'd returned home. Hazel Rock was the last thing on anyone's mind in Denver. "7-6-2-5."

She typed in the numbers and my apps appeared. I put my hand on my door handle, thinking I might stand a better chance with pavement at sixty-five miles an hour than with a deranged woman with a gun.

She scrolled through my call history. "Scarlet. Daddy—how sweet— and Scarlet again. You do live a pathetic life, don't you?"

I frowned. That was a low blow. "I wouldn't call it pathetic."

She clicked the phone closed and tossed it into the console. Either I'd somehow dialed Scarlet or I'd never dialed a number at all. Fuzz buckets.

"Why did you dress up like a man and attack me with the branding iron?" I asked. If I was going to die, I wanted to know every last detail.

"Honey, I would not dress up like a man if you paid me to."

"But—"

"Look at my arm." Taylor pulled up the sheer sleeve of her blouse and showed me two burns on her forearm. They were puckered and old, but still looked like they had to have been painful.

Yet try as I might, I still couldn't muster up any sympathy for her.

"What happened?" I asked.

"Erik had this *thing* about pretty women. He liked to mess up what he called 'their perfection.'" Her voice dripped with hatred. And she definitely spiked my curiosity.

"Why?"

Taylor rolled her sleeve back down. "Why does any man like to hurt women?"

I didn't know. My mind got stuck on Erik burning my face. I couldn't fathom being a victim of branding just because a man wanted to damage my looks. It was inhuman, and I was beginning to think Erik Piper got what was coming to him.

"Why did you stay after he did that?"

"I couldn't let go of Wyatt..."

"So how did the branding iron get in the cabin?" I asked.

"Unfortunately only Erik can answer that question. I have no idea."

"What happened to Erik?" I asked as we turned off 965 onto the dirt road.

"I killed him. After Dalton disappeared, I caught Erik planting an old copy of *The Dangerous Eight* along with a gun in my room. He said they belonged to Wyatt and thought I might like to have them. I'd never read Erik's book before; I'd never really been interested in it. But I was touched that Erik would leave me something that belonged to Wyatt, even if he was a mean SOB and all he was giving me was a gun and a book. Then I opened the book and recognized some of the writing. Wyatt had been working on a book before he died, and the pages I read in Erik's book were exactly the same thing that Wyatt had been working on. I flipped through the book and realized Erik's book was released right after Wyatt disappeared. Either it wasn't Wyatt's copy or Wyatt was still alive—and in hiding. I thought maybe he was writing books under an assumed name and Erik was covering for him. The hope was almost overwhelming. I saw the map on the inside of the book and demanded Erik take me to Wyatt. But he refused... And that's when everything changed.

"I picked up the gun and told him I'd shoot him right there on the spot if he didn't take me to Dalton. We followed the map in the book, and Erik made excuses the entire way. He said Wyatt had run off to Mexico with an under-aged girl. That had been one of the many rumors that had been making the rounds when Wyatt first disappeared. But I knew Wyatt wasn't that kind of man." Taylor stared straight ahead, but I was guessing the only thing she saw was Wyatt's face.

"We reached the grave right before sundown," she continued. "Erik had already been there and cleaned off the brush. He exposed Wyatt's belt buckle and when I saw it, my life ceased to have meaning. For years, I hated Wyatt Hibbs for breaking my heart, and as it turns out, I'm the one who gave up on our love. He died cherishing it."

Tears were flowing down her cheeks, and I knew the best thing was for her to embrace that emotion and the loss. Bring her back to the young woman who knew how to love, not the half-crazed shell who'd pulled a gun on me. But she wiped her tears with the back of her hand and any emotion she had in her eyes died. She refused to let her light be relit.

She parked the SUV in the same place I'd parked my daddy's truck days earlier and looked over at me.

"It was another PR stunt. He was setting the scene. He'd drugged Dalton at the bar; that's what made him act the way he did. Dalton's a gentleman just like his brother, he'd never act like that on his own. And then Erik put Dalton up in a cabin just to stir the suspicions a little more. I knew about the drink and learned about the cabin when I made him take me to Wyatt's grave. But I didn't know where Dalton was holed up.

"I even helped Erik at the bar, but I didn't know he took Dalton's phone. I wasn't there. I think he was carrying it around so that it would ping in different areas throughout town or something. I don't know. He was the master at setting up a scam."

She turned off the ignition and pulled out the keys. "Stay in the car until I come around to get you." She eased out of the vehicle backward, facing me the entire time. I thought she might flinch when she hit the gravel in bare feet, but she had no reaction at all. She never took her eyes off me as she rounded the vehicle and approached the passenger side. Her muted instructions came through my closed window. "Open the door."

I opened the door and was about to step out when she told me to get her shoes. Her red lace shoes. It's kind of humbling when you realize your killer is a better-dressed person than you are.

I handed her the shoes and she put them on one at a time. I knew I had to keep her talking, look for the opportunity to take advantage of her weakness or die trying. My stomach rolled and acted like it was about to heave my last meal in her direction.

I asked her another question that had gone unanswered. "Who threw me into Twisted Mister's pen?"

"I honestly don't know. I can only guess that you ended up ticking off Pierce, and he had one of his hands toss you over."

"Is Pierce Brown drugging his bulls?"

The smile that spread across her face reminded me of those Halloween masks that turned a happy expression into horror. "Is Texas called the Lone Star state?" She asked.

I didn't have an answer as she waved me out of the truck, but I had another question when the door closed with a thud.

"Why Dalton? Why'd you set him up for both murders? You know how much he and Wyatt loved each other."

"Wyatt's body had been buried for eight years and no one found it. I never expected you and Scarlet to find the graves. I was going to dump the gun and the book in the ocean, but once the graves were exposed,

I had to do something fast. That's when Dalton called me and told me he'd lost his phone and had ordered a new one. He gave me the address to the cabin just in case there was an emergency with his parents. I knew he'd left his backpack in Scarlet's trailer and I hurried over to her trailer to get it. Dalton became my only option. That's when I saw the reporter breaking into the trailer. When she came out empty handed, it was my opportunity to get in and grab his backpack and then take all three items up to his cabin when he was due to check out."

She looked at me as if her story made complete sense. She had no other option, or so she said. "It was the only way." She waved her gun toward the path and I began walking back toward the gravesites I'd sworn to never visit again. I could think of a whole bunch of different ways to handle the situation, and none of them involved setting up Dalton... or killing me.

We pushed through the brush and passed the spot where her heel had been. It and most of the trash were gone, and I only hoped the police lab found her DNA on it somehow and linked it back to Taylor. It would be too late for me, but at least she wouldn't be getting away with murder.

By the time we reached the grave sites, my heart was in my throat. Sweat was dripping down my back and down the sides of my face. My shirt was soaked clean through. I swallowed down the bile threatening to spew from my stomach with a large gulp.

"Turn around," she ordered. Taylor was done playing games. Done talking. My only consolation was that she didn't look much better than I must. Her beautiful dress was wet and stuck to different parts of her curves, making it bunch in all the wrong places, and her hair was frizzing.

But the most frightening thing I saw was the teenage girl who'd followed us down the path. I didn't know how she'd gotten there, or when she'd appeared, but it could not be good for her to be in this position. The very last thing I wanted was for Aubrey to die with her camera up to her eye.

"Taylor, you don't have to do this." I tried to reason, but Taylor wanted no part of it. Her eyes had dulled as if acceptance of the deed she was about to commit seeped in.

"If I don't want to go to jail, I do. I'm sorry." She raised the gun.

Aubrey yelled, "Stop!"

Shock caused a spark of life to return to Taylor's eyes as she swung the gun around toward the young girl standing behind her.

"No!" I charged Taylor and smashed down on her forearm with everything I had, striking the arm that held the gun the way Mateo had taught me. The weapon discharged with a loud explosion to close to my ears before it flew out of her hand and skittered across the ground. She swung at me with her left, but I blocked it with my right and grabbed her. We spun and twisted, tripping across the rocky dirt, each of us trying to get the upper hand when suddenly, Taylor fell backward—taking me with her. She landed on her back, knocking the air from her lungs with a less than feminine grunt and me on top of her.

My ribs screamed, but I knew I couldn't just lie there. My opportunity had arisen, and it was time to take advantage of the chance I was given. I reared back with my right arm and punched her in the face. Pain vibrated through my hand, up my arm, and through my body. I looked at her, huffing and puffing for everything I was worth, and realized I'd knocked her out cold—with just one punch.

It was only then that I realized where we were. We were six feet under—in Wyatt's grave.

I pushed myself to my feet and saw a camera recording my face. "Get me out of here!" I yelled and two strong arms lifted me up from behind.

"It's okay, Charli. I'm here."

I turned and looked up into Mateo's milk chocolate eyes. Nothing ever looked so delicious.

Chapter Thirty-Two

Sometimes nosy teenagers are a blessing. Like when you're being driven to a remote area by a crazed maniac and a teenager sees you pass The Cowboy Ranch. Aubrey knew something was up and if she hadn't followed, Mateo would have arrived after I'd been shot and fallen backward in a pre-dug grave.

Not only had she saved my life, but she'd recorded everything, which cleared me of having to wait to give my statement. I was able to get a ride home in a police car immediately so I could take a shower. There were some things I could not tolerate. Lying in a grave was one of them.

Daddy, along with Scarlet, Joellen, and Mary, were at The Barn when I arrived. Apparently, my call had gotten through to Scarlet after all and Taylor just hadn't noticed the time stamp of the call. She and Mateo had listened until Mateo grabbed her phone and hopped in his patrol car. Mary had also received a call from Aubrey, and Mary put her daughter on a three-way call with Mateo when the girl refused to stop following us.

Mary had been pacing and cussing up a storm for the past hour about her flighty girl who was going to end up dead on the side of the road if she wasn't careful. I kind of agreed, but then again, I wouldn't be standing in The Barn refusing hugs if it hadn't been for Aubrey.

Scarlet helped me get my clothes off and threw them in the washer for me as I stood under the hottest stream of water I could tolerate. When I was dried and dressed in a jean skirt and a T-shirt that read, *Book 'em, Dano*, I walked out with my hair in a towel. Scarlet had me sit at the bar in the kitchen, with a pillow underneath me on the stool, since I'd forgotten my donut in Taylor's truck. She cleaned out the wound on my right arm and a few new scratches I'd received from Taylor. Then she went about fixing my curls and applied my makeup.

I might have questioned all the special treatment, but I was still in a daze from my morning excursion through crazy land. It was a good excuse to never date again; I like my sanity.

"Are you ready?"

"Ready for what?" I asked.

"For the closing ceremonies."

I immediately began to whine. "Oh, Scarlet, I don't want to go to that. Really, you can go on without me."

But Scarlet was having none of it. She needed me there and somehow she even got my daddy to guilt me into going to represent the store like I'd planned. I allowed Scarlet to put my cowgirl boots on my feet and then I was herded out to her car. We drove to The Ranch with Scarlet filling me in on everything that had happened while I was in the shower. I mostly nodded my head; it was all I had to give.

Scarlet drove her teeny two-seater BMW down the sidewalk at The Ranch and parked next to the door.

"Are you kidding me? Someone's going to give you a ticket," I told her.

"It'll be worth it."

I wasn't sure I agreed, but it was her ticket. I was just along for the ride.

I grabbed the throw pillow I'd been reduced to using and we went into the arena. Jessie and Daisy were standing at the ticket window. Jessie was smooching on Daisy's neck and looked up as we approached. Scarlet winked and I elbowed her, regretting the move almost as soon as I did it.

"That's her husband," I told Scarlet.

Daisy grinned. "Darned tootin'."

We walked on through the gate and down to the seats Taylor had roped off for Scarlet. It was kind of ironic how well she'd taken care of Scarlet while hanging Dalton out to dry for her crimes. Sly wasn't in his seat, as he'd taken an early flight home to be with his wife and babies. I couldn't wait to meet them next year.

Dalton was down in the arena with a bunch of the other riders standing around, shooting the breeze. He'd already received his belt buckle and his trophy along with a large cardboard check that'd apparently already been donated to The Ranch in his brother's name. Most of the crowd had made their way out of the arena, except for the locals and a few stragglers seeking autographs. We'd barely gotten semi-comfortable in our seats when the lights dimmed and the crowd hushed. I could make out a small stage being moved out into the middle of the arena and then something was placed on top of it.

Cade's voice came over the intercom. I couldn't see him in the arena, but he was here—somewhere. "Ladies and Gentleman, we want to thank you for joining us at the twenty-second annual Cowboy Ranch Invitational. The residents at The Ranch and all the cowboys and cowgirls who receive treatment here, appreciate all your support. You have truly made a difference in their lives. Thank you to our sponsors and stock contractors who donated their time and bulls to make this event possible. Thank you to our hundreds of volunteers, as we could not pull off this event without you. We appreciate the hospitality of the local businesses and the donations they made to the cause.

"But there's one volunteer we want to give a special thank you. She's been gone from Hazel Rock for over a decade...."

I looked at Scarlet. She was grinning from ear-to-ear. "Oh Scarlet, please tell me he's not doing this."

Scarlet winked and a spotlight hit me in the face. I squinted against the lights and put my hand up to block it from completely blinding me. Scarlet pulled my hand down.

"I'd like you to meet Charli Rae Warren. To the locals she's known as Princess, to people who come and shop in our town, she's known as The Book Barn Princess."

Jessie yelled from behind me. "I thought that was the armadillo's name!"

A laugh filled the arena and my face heated.

"Well, we are blessed with two barn princesses here in Hazel Rock, and probably quite a few more in the crowd. But Charli came back to us a couple months ago and when she heard that the Invitational was still going strong, she organized the local businesses in our town to donate one day of sales to the cause. Ten businesses signed up and created more revenue than we ever dreamed possible. So, we just want to welcome our princess back home properly. Charli, if you could come down center stage."

"Scarlet, I'm gonna kill you," I whispered as she helped me stand up. I walked over to gate where they'd put steps leading down into the arena. A rodeo clown met me and helped me down onto the soft dirt floor, and we walked over to the stage as a spotlight followed our progress.

As we approached I saw the most beautiful throne sitting in the middle of the stage that I had ever seen, and I knew exactly who'd made it. The six-foot tall chair back was framed in hand-carved dark antique walnut in the shape of a six-prong crown. The arms were also hand-carved animal paws that curved around toward the matching legs. The plush fabric on the back and on the seat, had been removed and replace with something even more gorgeous—pink and white book bindings. And dangling off to one side of the arm was my pink donut.

I looked around for my father but couldn't find him anywhere. The clown put my donut in place, and I sat on the throne as some of my favorite country songs began to play.

"Our hats are off to you, Princess!"

Three clowns began to dance to the music. Their faces were painted, and their hair was dyed. Their clothes were baggy and their shoes were tied. Not one had on a pair of cowboy boots. The crowd was clapping and whooping with the beat of the music.

The first one I recognized was Cade. Taller than the rest he came up and plopped his hat on my head and kissed my hand. The man had the moves of a Casanova; the women in the crowd whooped it up like they were watching one of those male strip shows.

When another clown jumped up and tossed Cade's hat to the wind, Cade danced off and there was my daddy in front of me dancing to "Wild One" by Faith Hill. It brought back memories of dancing on his boot tips when I was a little girl, and I wanted to dance with him so badly I could hardly stand it. Then he bowed out and the next clown came up.

The last one had more sass and salsa, but his hair threw me off—a thick, straight line was shaved on the left side of his head. I didn't know anyone with that bold of a haircut. I stared at his face as he moved to a rock beat that I thought I'd remembered hearing from a certain marked vehicle. It was only when I got a look at his rich chocolate eyes that I recognized Mateo.

And I laughed until I thought my tears were from the pain in my ribs, and not my emotions getting the best of me.

Mateo joined my other two clowns, clapping and dancing and acting goofier than I'd ever seen the three of them act in public before. They began pulling spectators from the crowd and soon the entire arena was full of people dancing and having a good time. Granted, I wanted to be with them, but I had to admit that it was refreshing to be the one to sit back and be entertained.

Scarlet came by with Dalton on her arm, and I could tell it was the beginning of something great—if they could survive his traveling schedule. Dalton yelled, "Thank you, Princess!" And that was that. There was no way anyone in Hazel Rock, Texas was ever going to call me Charli again.

A little later I sat on the back patio at The Barn and Daddy brought out two bowls of sliced peaches and Blue Bell vanilla ice cream and a third bowl just for Princess—the armadillo who trailed after him. I took my bowl and set Princess's down on the ground between our chairs, her dessert of blue berries and blackberries would have been tempting if I didn't have something better. Princess began snuffling with her snout and clanking her hard shell against the stoneware bowl as we listened to the frogs and the crickets while enjoying summertime in Hazel Rock.

"What's going to happen to Pierce Brown and the Starlight Corral?"

"Mateo already has one suspect in custody. The vet tech turned himself in this evening and gave up the name of the guy who tossed you over the rail. Animal Control took the tech's statement about drugging the animals and will be serving a search warrant on Starlight Corral in the morning. I imagine the bulls will be confiscated. The Championship Bull Rider's Association has also been notified to take away his permits. Pierce has got his hands full with the legal troubles."

"Good. Those bulls don't deserve that. I imagine we won't see much of Mateo anytime soon."

Dad smiled. "Nope, that boy will be putting in some hours on this cluster."

"What happened to his hair?" I asked.

My dad nearly choked on a peach as he chuckled. "When you dialed Scarlet's phone, she put it on speaker so she could finish cutting his hair. But Mateo recognized you were in trouble before Scarlet did and as she was bringing the razor back, he jumped out of that chair."

"Holy crap! That was an accident?"

"All he cared about was getting to you in time." My dad had a certain sparkle in his eye.

I let that sink in for a bit before I answered. "I'm sure Mateo is the type of man who would do that if anyone was in trouble."

Daddy shook his head with a smile. "Maybe so, Princess. I'm just glad you're home safe."

"Me too, Daddy. Me too."

Then I thought of my mom dropping that sign on his head. "Why do you think Mom dropped Eve's Gate on Mateo's head?" I asked.

"Your mom had terrible aim, Princess. I think she was trying to hit Taylor."

We both started to laugh, then looked at each other…and licked our ice cream bowl clean as we thought about my mom.

Three career paths resonated for **Kym Roberts** during her early childhood: detective, investigative reporter, and...nun. Being a nun, however, dropped by the wayside when she became aware of boys—they were the spice of life she couldn't deny. In high school her path was forged when she took her first job at a dry cleaner and met every cop in town, especially the lone female police officer in patrol. From that point on there was no stopping Kym's pursuit of a career in law enforcement. Kym followed her dream and became a detective who fulfilled her desire to be an investigative reporter, with one extra perk—a badge. Promoted to sergeant, Kym spent the majority of her career in SVU. She retired from the job reluctantly when her husband dragged her kicking and screaming to another state, but writing continued to call her name, at least in her head.

Visit her on the web at kymroberts.com.

If you enjoyed A REFERENCE TO MURDER, be sure not to miss the first book in Kym Roberts's Book Barn Mystery series!

When kindergarten teacher Charli Rae Warren hightailed it out of Hazel Rock, Texas, as a teen, she vowed to leave her hometown in the dust. A decade later, she's braving the frontier of big hair and bigger gossip once again . . . But this time, she's saddled with murder!

Charli agrees to sell off the family bookstore, housed in a barn, and settle her estranged dad's debt—if only so she can ride into the sunset and cut ties with Hazel Rock forever. But the trip is extended when Charli finds her Realtor dead in the store, strangled by a bedazzled belt. And with Daddy suspiciously MIA, father and daughter are topping the most wanted list . . .

Forging an unlikely alliance with the town beauty queen, the old beau who tore her family apart, and one ugly armadillo, Charli's intent on protecting what's left of her past . . . and wrangling the lone killer who's fixin' to destroy her future . . .